11/12

ROOTLESS

CHRIS HOWARD

SCHOLASTIC PRESS | NEW YORK

Library of Congress Cataloging-in-Publication Data

Howard, Chris.
Rootless / by Chris Howard. — 1st ed.
p. cm.
Summary: In a world devastated by war and disease, a young tree builder searches for the last trees on earth.
ISBN 978-0-545-38789-7 — ISBN 0-545-38789-2 [1. Environmental degradation — Fiction. 2. Trees — Fiction. 3. Voyages and travels — Fiction. 4. Science fiction.] I. Title.
PZ7.H82832Ro 2012
[E] — dc23

2011041109

10 9 8 7 6 5 4 3 2 1 12 13 14 15 16

Printed in the U.S.A. 23

First edition, November 2012

The text is set in Alisal.

Book design by Phil Falco

For my father

PART ONE

CHAPTER ONE

They figured me too young for a tree builder. I could see it in their eyes. Bunch of rich freaks, staring at me like I needed to impress them. But I did need to. That was the problem. The wagon was about out of juice and my belly was so hard I couldn't even stand to scratch it. I built the best trees in the Steel Cities, but you'd never know it from the drought I'd hit.

"You thinking evergreen?" I said, looking at Frost, him being the man wanting trees.

"We'd like to see the seasons, Mister Banyan." Frost was a big bucket of a guy with too many chins, and the hair he'd bleached white to look older left his face looking twenty years too young.

"That's the real trick, ain't it?" I said, shaking my head. Make a big deal of every request, Pop had drilled it into me. The client pays more and ends up twice as happy.

"Just get all the scrap you need," said Frost. Man practically smelled of cash. His wife all lit up with sparkles in her hair and studs on her face. Hell, even their watcher looked polished – his dreads clean and fluffy, his long beard woven with fabric. Not a mark on him, either. The sign of a bodyguard you do not want to mess with.

I took a look around the dirt lot. Acre at least. Blank and ugly, full of dust and sky. But not for long. Not if I built a forest to get lost inside. Shade from the sun and a break from the wind. Show the world you could still own something special.

A decent slope gave some perspective to play with, and I'd give them the seasons, all right. Plastic leaves wired up to turn color and shrivel on metal branches. I'd give them spring blooms and fall colors.

"Good news, Mister Frost." I made a smile, extended my hand to him. "Seasons are my specialty."

Frost returned the smile but ignored the handshake. He just stood there with his arms resting on his belly, and his mouth all twitchy at some internal joke. Then he stomped over to his wife and put his arm around her pointy shoulders and I felt bad for her just having to be so close to the guy. She was a stunner, no question. Gray eyes and dark skin.

"The question is," Frost began, his body trembling as he pawed his wife's polyester top, "can you build this?"

Then Frost tore open the front of her shirt and the woman was practically naked, right there in front of me.

I'd never seen a thing like it.

She was more pretty than I knew what to do with, no doubt about that. But it was the tree that took my breath away.

It was tattooed on her skin in a thousand different shades. The roots spread down her right hip and a thin white trunk curved across her belly, branches reaching all the way up. A fragile tree. Flexible. With golden leaves falling as the tree swayed in some imaginary breeze.

I felt sweat trickle down the groove of my back. But Frost's wife looked ice cold, her silvery eyes staring straight through me until I finally turned my head away.

Frost laughed and stepped away from the woman, leaving her there, her shirt ragged and open.

"Can you build it, boy?" It was the watcher who spoke. Voice as big as he was. Unblinking eyes the same color as his skin.

I stared at the dirt, shaken. Frost reckoned himself a tough guy, doing that to his woman. And a man like that don't deserve nothing pretty.

"Can you build it?" the watcher said again.

I had a bad feeling about this one. But a worse feeling was the empty howl in my guts. I needed the job and I needed it bad. And what was I going to do? Quit?

"Yeah," I muttered, all the swagger drained out of me. "I can build it. But I'll need a place to pitch my wagon. And I need an advance on some corn."

"You can stay here. In your forest." Frost laughed as he gestured to the dirt. I looked out at the sparse shapes of the city — the filthy steel domes and bunkers, the crumbling concrete remains. The wind was picking up and it came screeching around the buildings, whipping the dust into a shotgun spray. I pulled my goggles down, buried my nose in a rag, but the rich freaks were caught off guard and they choked on their pampered lungs.

"Make yourself at home," Frost muttered, after he'd quit coughing and the wind had died back. He shrugged at the watcher. "Crow will get you the corn, but it'll be deducted from your fee."

"Which is what?"

"Whatever I think you're worth. Old world Benjamins, if you're lucky." He stuck out his hand then – one finger missing past the knuckle, his skin puffy and moist. "Work hard, Mister B," Frost said, shaking my hand. "And keep away from the house."

I turned and stared at the steel building that blocked the lot from the street. Pretty new, by the look of things. The monstrous metal pillars gave it a spiky appearance, like a giant piece of barbed wire. I spotted a window on the top floor with two faces in it. Looked like small versions of Frost and his wife – the wiry brown girl was about my age. The boy was younger. He was picking at his nose, digging around in there like he'd lost something up it, but the girl was just staring straight at me, her forehead pressed at the dusty glass.

"Don't worry," I said, turning back to Frost. "You won't even know I'm here."

I'd got the wagon parked as far from the house as possible, squeezed up against the old brick wall that lined the far edge of the property. The house on the other side had a pool and I could hear people splashing around, laughs and jokes sparking in the night. Sounded like a grand old time. Hell, it even sounded good to someone as scared of the water as I was. I'd steer clear of the pool is all. Just hang to the side. Be nice to have someone to talk to.

I had the hatch lifted and was sprawled in the back of the wagon, surrounded by my tools and supplies. The pliers and hammers, sheets of metal and rolls of wire. I had my head propped on a box of LEDs, a sack of screwdrivers beneath my feet. On one side of the compartment hung the blowtorch and nail gun, my gloves and an extra pair of goggles, and on the other side, I had stashed my advance. Enough popcorn for one more week. Three meals a day.

The microwave pinged and I pulled the popcorn out. Superfood, GenTech calls it. Engineered for everything a body needs. And maybe that's true if you eat enough of it. But most folk look yellow and bent over and all stretched out and thin. And even someone rich has to fake looking older – no matter how full your belly, most everyone ends up with crusted lungs, sooner or later.

I cracked the purple bag open. Mac'n'Cheese, by the smell of it. I guess they used to get cheese out of cows, back before every critter had been swallowed and spat. But now we just got whatever GenTech figured cheese should taste like. Still, the corn was sweaty and stinking in my hand, and as glorious a dinner as I'd any right to expect.

I picked up Pop's old sombrero. The hat was woven out of corn husk, punched full of holes, and stained with my old man's sweat. Stick my face inside, I could still catch the smoky scent of him. And pulling the hat on, I imagined telling Frost he could shove his job where the sun don't shine. Because my old man would have split, no matter how desperate. Soon as Frost started treating his lady like dirt.

Pop used to say we'd build a forest of our own, once we saved enough to quit drifting. He said we'd build a house in the treetops, hidden away from the suffering and spite.

Weren't going to happen now, though. It had been almost a year since Pop had been taken, and missing him still stung like a broken tooth. Sure, I'd gotten used to building without him, taking care of the wagon, eating alone. But the silent times crept up and turned things hollow.

I took off the hat, lounged back and studied the house, watching the lights flicker on and off. And when I was done eating, I didn't feel like sleeping and I didn't feel like figuring how I was going to build the tree mapped out on Frost's wife. So instead I reached in the box of LEDs and rummaged around. Pulled out my headlamp. And my book.

I never did take to reading, but Pop had been able. My mother taught him before she starved. Before she passed on. So maybe the book reminded me of the mother I wasn't able to remember, as much as the father I couldn't forget.

But the book also reminded me of the stories Pop used to read me. The stories of the old world. Tales of folk that marched along rivers that ran cold and clean, fish to be caught and things to be hunted, grass growing tall and valleys full of flowers and trees in the mountains that pushed at the sky.

Trees full of seeds and blossom. Branches weighed with nuts and berries and other things just waiting to be picked off and chewed.

The book was stained the same rusty color as my wagon, and I flipped through the pages, put my face to them, and breathed them in as if I could breath the stories in, too. But it was then I heard a scrabbling sound come digging around outside.

Close. Real close.

I slipped the book beneath a sack of nails, making sure it was well hid. Then I scooted out the back of the wagon and threw myself into the dark.

"Who is it?" I hissed.

But right away I saw him. The fat kid from the window, squatted down by my rear wheel like he was pissing on the tire.

"You're the tree builder," the kid said with a chubby grin. He jerked up as I shone the headlamp at him. "You live in my house."

"I don't go near the house. Strict orders."

"Too bad." The kid snickered. "We got lights. And a television."

"It works?"

"Like a dream."

I leaned against the wagon. Played some old movies, is what the kid meant. Still, if there were trees in those movies, you'd get to see them alive and well. The branches swirling and dancing, leaves puffing in the wind.

"So it's too bad you're not allowed in the house." The fat kid snickered again.

"Maybe we start being friends and your old man will have me over."

"Doubt it," the kid said, sticking his head in the back of the wagon, snuffling around at my stuff.

"Don't be shy, now," I told him. I watched the house, wondered if just talking to Frost's kid might get me in trouble.

"You liked it?" The kid was tinkering with the nail gun.

"Put that down," I said. "It ain't a toy."

"But did you like it?"

"What?"

"Her tree." The kid pulled his head out of the wagon and stood there, leering up at me in the darkness. I shut the headlamp off.

"I've never seen it myself," he said.

"Well, shit. You ain't supposed to see your momma naked, son."

"Don't call me son. You're not much older than I am. And she's not my momma, neither."

"What is she then?"

"My dad won her. In Vega. Her daughter, too."

"Your sister?"

"If that's what you want to call her."

"She got a tree on her and all?"

"Why?" The kid got all leery again. "You want to see her naked?"

"Beat it," I said. I was sick of him. Little punk rooting around in my shit.

"Maybe you want to read some more."

I didn't say anything for a bit. Just stared at him.

"You spying on me?"

"What are you reading?"

"Ain't reading nothing."

All of a sudden I could hear a noise coming out of the house, a door slamming shut. Footsteps in the dark. The kid must have heard it too, because he went bouncing off into the night as Crow appeared out of the darkness. The watcher had a pair of headphones on and big plastic sunglasses pushed up in his dreads.

"What you doing, little man?" Crow plucked the headphones from his ears.

"Nothing at all."

"You building?"

"Can't build in the dark, tough guy."

Crow smiled. His teeth huge and white. Then he drifted off and I was alone again, wishing I could have gone looking for someone else to build for. But Frost had given me corn and put juice in my wagon, and now that bastard owned me till the work was all done.

I put the book in a new hiding place, buried it behind the popcorn.

Because there aren't many of them left, books like that. People burned most of them to keep warm during the Darkness. And after the Darkness, there were no new books because there was no more paper.

The locusts had come.

And there were no more trees.

CHAPTER TWO

The guy at the scrap farm cut me a good price on the metal, on account of he'd known my dad. "Best tree builder in the Steel Cities," the man said, squinting at me with his glass eye.

"He'd have appreciated you saying it."

"I warned him. Told him the same thing I tell everyone — ain't no good reason to head out west." The man sucked at his shriveled cheeks, chewed his lip. "No good reason at all."

"He reckoned we'd find work."

"You even made it to Vega?"

"Almost."

We'd glimpsed the Electric City in the distance, and next day me and Pop would have reached it, too. But in the middle of the night, Pop woke me with his hand across my mouth, told me he'd heard voices. He told me to stay put. Told me to just wait in the wagon and not to come out.

"There was a dust storm," I said. "And folk lurking outside."

"And your dad got taken."

I nodded.

The man rubbed a finger on his glass eye and stared out across the rows of junk metal and plastic, his face all puckered and sorry. "I heard there are slavers. I heard they snatch folk up. Cut deals with the Salvage Guild."

"Could be," I said. Was a time I'd thought stories about the taken were just told to frighten you from wandering out of sight. Must have been a dozen tales about what happens to those who go missing. Them that vanish and never come back. I'd bought into this one about slavers, though. Ended up checking every salvage crew in the Steel Cities, north to south, but I never found Pop's face nor spoke to a crew boss who'd seen him.

"Others say it's freaks out of Vega," said old One Eye, and my stomach twisted. I'd heard this one, too. The one about a meat trade. Corn's all that grows and people are all that's left, so I guess someone might be sick enough to mix up the menu.

"Be honest with you," I said, trying to keep my cool. "My old man being turned into someone's dinner ain't nothing I can think about."

I remembered how I'd sat in the back of the wagon, sweating and shaking and scared. There'd been nothing left to see when the red dust quit spinning. And there was no place left to look now. Nearly a year had gone by.

"All that matters is they never come back." I leaned and spat. "I reckon getting taken just means you wind up dead."

The man studied me with his good eye. "Pull that wagon around, son," he said, turning away. "We'll get her loaded up."

It took me six trips to haul the metal, and I had to wait out two storms along the way – hazard winds churning dirt in a frenzy, dust clouds shutting down the sky. I wound up low on juice hauling the last load. The wagon started to crawl and whir reluctantly.

The scrap farm was outside the city, deep in the shantytown sprawl that hangs around the south like a bad smell. The wagon got too slow passing the tents and teepees, the heat frying the plastic shacks and sizzling on the crappy tin roofs. Before long, a filthy mob of little ones were swarming and pressed on my windows, singing snatches of old songs and screaming at me with swollen gums, their faces all covered in sores. Got so I was scared of running over the smallest ones, and I fired up some corn till the bag popped and the microwave pinged. Then I threw the bag across the street and soon as it burst open, those kids were pecking and scooping at the dirt.

So that was one less meal I could count on. But what else was I supposed to do?

I hadn't rounded but two more bends when I spotted the GenTech tanker. You could hardly miss it — bright-ass purple truck all chock-full of corn. There were agents on either side of it, dust dirtying their purple duds, fancy goggles protecting their eyes. Masks shielding their lungs. They had their guns out, their spiky clubs raised. And out the back of the tanker, they were selling rations, making a killing on the prices like always. Even lowest-grade corn's something most count by the kernel. Brew it into fuel or stuff it in your belly, either way, the stuff don't come cheap. Not when only GenTech can grow it and it's the only damn thing left growing.

Sure, you can try planting those kernels yourself, and they'll grow just fine if you find enough water. But each kernel on each new plant will be coded with GenTech in little purple letters. And then, when the agents find you, they'll kill you.

Simple as that.

Shantytown was thinning out already. The winter exodus had started — strugglers braving the long road west to Vega in the hope of some better life. At least it was winter, though. Got to be a special kind of desperate if you head west in the warm months. Vega sits on the far side of GenTech's fields, and those fields are where the locusts hatch all summer long.

Cornstalks are the only thing left a locust can burrow inside, see. And they keep close to the one place left they can nest. But locusts can't feast on corn kernels. GenTech made it so you got to cook the corn before you can chew it. They twisted the corn so it could survive about any damn thing at all. But they did such a good job that nature bred something equally wicked — if there's a way to kill locusts, then it's a way that ain't never been found.

And that's why you steer clear of the cornfields in the summer months. Only folk out there are poachers tucked in their tunnels or the field hands that GenTech don't pay worth a damn. Because once they hatch, locusts swarm after the one thing left they can still call dinner. And that'd be people.

That'd be human flesh.

My last dollar bought me a half hour of hose time at the drinking station, and I sat on the hood of my wagon, listening as dirty water dribbled into the tank.

A ragged posse was gathering down the block, huddled around an old Rasta who was whipping his tongue. The Rasta was bent over so hard his beard was sweeping at the dirt, his hands clutching an old hockey stick he'd dressed as a staff and wrapped in his colors — red, gold and green. He kept rambling on about Zion and the King who'd lead us across the ocean. Raise enough funds and they were going to build a boat, the man said. Boat big enough to get past the Surge.

And that's when the Rasta lost most of his crowd. Because there was no getting past the Surge. No way. And there was no king going to lead you someplace where there were wild things growing. Pop had told me. Anything worth believing, you better be able to see it with your own eyes.

I studied the dusty street, the plastic walls and dried patches of piss. And I guess it was being left with just shantytowns and Steel Cities that got folk started with the tree building. Because even for the rich freaks, life's ugly. But build a tree, and you got something worth looking at. Something worth believing in.

"Busy working, no?" a voice rumbled behind me.

I spun around and saw Crow stepping out of a tent on the corner. He had his shades on, headphones dangling around his neck. Dude towered above me. Must have been seven feet tall.

"Six loads," I said, pointing at the metal stacked out the back of the wagon. "Gonna need more juice when I get home."

"Home?" Crow laughed. An old, slow sound. He stared up at the blood red sun and it bounced like a fever off his glasses.

"I'll brew you the juice, little man," he said, starting off down the street. "But you a nomad. No mistaking."

When I got the last load back, Frost was standing in the middle of the lot and frowning at the stacks of scrap.

"You get enough?" he mumbled, and I could tell from the stench of him, the sour shape of his cracked lips, he'd either hit the bottle when he woke up or he'd been working at it all night.

"With this load we're good," I said, pulling out some rusty sheets of metal and a case of old headlights. Frost just plopped his fat ass on the dirt and sat watching me.

"I painted you a marker," he said. "Middle of the lot." The liquor had made his voice sloppy and I could tell he'd clawed his way out of some gutter before he got himself rich. If your family didn't hoard well in the Darkness, there's only a few ways to get wealthy in the Steel Cities. Work for GenTech Corporation or the Salvage Guild. Scavenge well for yourself and barter better. Or else you're a murderer and a thief.

"So what's it for?" I said, spotting the big red X Frost had sprayed on the ground.

"Never you mind." Frost prodded a finger at me and I noticed the burn marks on his thumb, the skin all broken and red. So he was a smoker as well as a drinker. A crystal junkie. And that meant that whatever gutter he'd crawled out of, Frost was now stuck in one that goes all the way down.

He staggered up and started toward the house. Probably going to suck some crystal and sleep off his hangover, duck out of the heat that was rising from the ground now, hard as it beat off the sun. The hazard winds were picking up, too. Dust storm coming.

"Keep it clear, Mister B," Frost yelled as he wobbled away. "Keep it clear."

I'd no idea why Frost would want a gap in the middle of his forest, but I paid it no mind. Once I'd got the wagon full of juice, I could charge up the tools. And when the skies cleared, I'd start cleaning the metal and making it shine.

Pop said trees didn't just use to look pretty and grow food for eating. They didn't just give shade and break up the wind. They cleaned the water and held the soil together, and they made the air feel good for those breathing. Just stories now, though. Even my grandfather hadn't seen a real one. People date the Darkness more than a hundred years back.

So they're just stories and statues. And that's what I'd be building. A forest of metal and plastic, velvet and lights. Trees I'd seen my father build and that his father built before him. Trees I'd seen in photographs or scratched in pencil. And trees I'd made up all on my own, named after words I loved. Names like Ponderosa Pear. Or Angel Leaf.

I'd create a whole stand and then build the tree tattooed on Frost's wife. A tree I'd not seen built before, nor seen drawn or once heard described. But a tree I'd no doubt had once stood breathing. You couldn't make up something that looked so right.

CHAPTER THREE

Next day I had the understory pretty much nailed. I'd learned to leave tall stuff till last. Build the canopy right away and they end up wanting to skimp on the details – guy like Frost couldn't care less about the details, I guarantee. So I'd laid a load of old tire I'd cut up nice and jagged, and it gave a good squishy feeling underfoot. Out of that, I'd rigged plastic mesh to look like grasses, planted up some metal shrubs I'd been piecing together.

Up north, I'd come across a fleet of carts folk used to wheel around markets the size of a village. I'd de-wheeled every one of those carts, and now I hung the wheels on bent piping so they spun if the breeze caught right. Might not look much in the daytime, but you get some LEDs blinking and those wheels turn real pretty. Those are the kind of details you get if you build from the ground up. Your forest comes alive at night.

I had that understory looking good and was laid out on the rubber, gluing strips of wire, when the girl from the window came right up, snapping pictures of me. She had an old world camera that clicked and buzzed and spat you out a copy of whatever you were looking at. A real fancy bit of salvage.

I could barely see the girl, sun was so bright. She stood above me, a skinny shadow, and the weight of the sky hammered down above her, frying me up and making the rubber melt sticky on my clothes. I wiped the sweat and dust off my face and I strained my head up, shielding my eyes.

She just stood there, one foot lifted and tucked behind the other, flapping her pictures around and watching for the colors to appear.

"Never said you could take my picture," I told her.

"Never asked," she said. "These are my trees. I can take pictures of them all day long."

"Your trees?" I said, going ahead and sitting up. "Well, I got news for you. These ain't trees, they're flowers." I nodded at a spiky mound. "Bushes, some of 'em. But not a damn tree in sight."

She glanced at her pictures, blew on one of them. "Then you'd better get back to work. You're supposed to be building trees."

"Hell," I said, staring up at her. "Between you and the watcher, anyone would think this is a rush job. Only one seems in no hurry is the guy that's footing the bill."

"Frost?" the girl said, her voice losing its swing. "You've no idea."

"He gonna get mad, you talking to me?"

"Of course." She fixed me with the same kind of look her mom had used when I'd been staring at that tattoo. "If he gets back and catches me out here."

"How long you got?"

The girl shrugged.

"Long enough to show me your pictures?"

She slumped down next to me, covering her mouth as the dust curled around us. Then she tucked the photos into her hip pocket. Out of sight.

"What's your name?" I asked her.

"Zee."

"Mine's Banyan." I reached out my hand like we might shake or something. But Zee just glared back at the house.

"Ever seen the ocean, tree builder?"

"The ocean?" I said. "Yeah. I seen it."

"Know how far it is from here?"

I thought about it. Journey gets steep in places. "Two hours in the wagon. Three coming back."

"Take me to see it," Zee said, as though this were the kind of request I got most days. "Take me there and I'll show you my pictures. All of them."

I laughed, but her face stayed stony. I started to say something but she shot up, began walking back toward the house.

No thanks, pal. That's what I was going to tell her. No way in hell. Risk my neck to go look at the Surge? Some rough roads out there and the coast's a whole lot rougher. And Frost wouldn't approve a damn bit. She was crazy. And I'd be crazy to go.

But then I saw the photograph she'd left on the dusty rubber beside me, just sitting there in the little dent her body had scooped out.

One photograph. A single picture.

I snatched it up and stared at the image.

Trees.

Whole stand of them.

Trees that bent in the wind, rolling beneath a pure blue sky. My heart beat hard in my chest, my head spun. The trees were twenty feet tall at least. White bark and yellow leaves. Like Frost's tree. The tattoo tree. Only these trees were living. These trees were alive.

I'd seen photographs before, of course. Trees in photographs. Smudged images, cracked with time. But the picture in my hand was recent. Had to be. Because there, slumped on the forest floor, bound with metal chains against a tree trunk, was a man dressed in rags. A man with hair like mine.

A man with a face that was all my father's.

I staggered up on stiff legs and peered at the house, studying the windows for sign of the girl. Her mother. Hell, I'd have taken the fat kid at that point. All I wanted was to scream at someone till there were no words in me. But the house just stood there, every window blank.

I'd been sweating all day and now I was thirsty, my whole body buzzing in the heat. I stumbled across the sticky rubber and grabbed water from the wagon. The sun was dropping and with it the wind started to settle and the dust eased up. All I wanted was to look at the picture again. See the trees and my old man's face. I sank down so my back was against the front of the wagon, the metal hot on my skin.

Across the lot, my understory looked crooked and clipped, nothing like the forest in the picture. I stared at the photograph. Leaves shaped like petals, branches outstretched like wooden fingers. And I stared at Pop. Arms bound behind his back. A faraway look in his eye.

It was him, all right.

I felt a churning in my belly. Whole load of feelings I'd thought I was too tough to feel. My old man had been taken. Snatched away from me in a dust storm. For months I'd looked for him, and for almost a year I had feared him dead. But now here he was, frozen in a photograph. Strapped to the things he'd spent a lifetime trying to forge.

Pop always told me there was nothing left. No forests but what we built. No flowers or moss or vine. Don't go believing in fairy tales, he'd tell me. Don't go kidding yourself.

But I tried to think if somehow he could have known different and kept it secret. What if the picture was older than I was? My whole life I'd been running to keep up with that man, and he and I had never seen a sky like that one – the air clear of dust, everything sparkling it was so damn clean. But Pop looked old in the picture. Streaks of white in his hair, silver making his stubble glint. So the picture had been snapped since Pop had been taken. This was my dad after he'd been stolen away.

I searched the photograph for a weapon or a stranger. I studied Pop's body for wounds. But there was nothing else. Just the beautiful trees and my father chained against one like a man who'd been caught in a trap.

My head ached like I'd tried shoving too much inside it. I turned the picture over. The GenTech logo in purple ink, faint and scratchy. And that just got me more confused, because what the hell did they have to do with anything? And how did the skinny chick have the damn picture anyway? I thought about her, stuck in her house with her chubby little friend. Frost scratching for crystal and groping the momma's tattoo.

I stood up. Stared at the house as its lights blinked on in the dirty twilight. Had the girl taken the photo herself? She was the one with the picture box, after all. So had she been there with the leaves and branches? Had she seen my father chained up and bound?

I stuffed the picture in my back pocket.

And then I started toward the house.

CHAPTER FOUR

Before I had the chance to hammer at the steel door, it came flying open at me. I was on the back porch already and the fat kid could see I was all kinds of pissed.

"What are you doing?" he squeaked, and I was about ready to thump him for no reason except for how mad I was. I stared past him into the house.

"Where's your sister?" I whispered.

"She ain't my sister, tree boy." The kid cracked himself up and I pushed him aside, ready to just sneak in the back door and see what happened. But then Zee came rushing out, cutting me off. Her eyes stretched wide with fear.

"Not here," she said. "He's back." Her voice was hushed as she wrestled me across the porch. But when we reached the top of the steps, I quit shuffling. Stood my ground.

"Sal," she hissed at the fat kid. "Go inside." The kid's mouth hung and quivered like he was about to start crying. "Please," Zee added, softening her tone. "You got to keep your daddy in there."

"You're going to run away again," he said, glaring at her. "Without me."

"But we look out for each other now. Remember?"

The kid ducked away, still bugging out by the look of things, but he closed the door and left us alone.

Zee stared at the house. She watched the windows. "You can't be here," she whispered. "Frost won't like it."

"I don't give a damn," I shot back, though it wasn't really true. The sun had sunk like a stone and with it my resolve had faded.

Stay away from the house, Frost had told me. The rich get spooked if you go spying on their shit.

Still, I pulled the picture from my back pocket and held it up. "Where the hell did you get this?"

"We can't talk here." She shook her head at me, her hands trembling on my chest.

"I ain't leaving till you tell me what this is."

A door slammed in the house behind us, and Zee jumped at the sound.

"It's trees," she spat, her head bent around at the house again, her hands trying to shove me off the porch. "Real trees. I thought you'd like them."

"Like them? You know who this is?" My voice had gotten louder now. I jabbed at the photograph.

She stared at me, confused. "Some guy in trouble."

"Some guy, huh?" I shoved her hands off my chest, leaned in close. There was another thud in the house, then the sound of someone shouting. "Where'd you get this?" I said.

"Zee?" the voice moaned inside the house. Frost's voice.

She pleaded at me with her eyes, begging for me to do the right thing. "It came with the camera," she whispered, frantic now. Steps inside the house. Frost yelling. Closer. "From Crow," Zee said. Then the steel door began opening behind her. I could hear it, see the light splitting out from inside.

"The ocean." Zee fixed me with a look. "Take me and I'll show you every picture I've got."

I went to speak, but my feet were yanked from under me. I was dragged down off the porch.

"What the hell are you doing?" Frost yelled as he stomped out of the house. I heard Zee scream as he came toward her. But the old bastard hadn't seen me in the darkness.

"I told you," Frost bellowed. "You don't go outside the house." There was a struggle and Zee screamed again. I felt awful for it. I should have shouted something. Done something. But I was too busy now. Too busy being dragged off toward my wagon with Crow's hands around my neck.

Crow thumped me once in the gut then left me on the rubber floor of the forest. I didn't dare get up. I just waited as the watcher spun the wheels on my flowers, stepping carefully about the understory and flicking a switch to set the LEDs blinking. One of the wheels was squeaky as it spun and Crow shook his head. "Needs oil," he said, as if he was talking to himself. "But you do good work."

Crow had his dreads wound inside a hat that looked about a hundred years old, and I spotted the scar burned on the back of his neck — a red lion. The mark of a Soljah. Me and Pop had built for those Rastas, up in Niagara. It's as good a spot as any and prettier than most. And I had no idea how you'd go from being a warrior in Waterfall City to being a watcher for a bastard like Frost.

"You heard of Zion, little man?" Crow said, and he spun at the wheels again.

I just nodded, but he wasn't looking at me so I went ahead and tried speaking. "Yeah," I muttered. "Of course."

"You reckon the trees there are made of metal? The flowers got squeaky wheels?" Crow squatted next to me.

"Doubt it," I said, wondering if he'd hit me again.

"Me too." The watcher smiled. "So you believe what they say? Build a boat big enough and you'll see Zion?"

"A boat?" I hadn't figured Crow for the religious type, and it pissed me off for some reason, him questioning me like that. Either he could beat me or turn me in, or he could just go right on to hell. "I seen the Surge," I said. "Ain't no boat big enough."

"No boat big enough. But that don't mean the place don't exist."

I tried sitting up and my ribs ached.

"So where'd you get the picture?"

Crow laughed that deep rumble of his. "Miss Zee likes you, I think. She likes you."

"The photograph. Where'd you get it?"

"What she show you? Trees?" Crow smiled when I stayed silent. "Course she did. Look familiar?" He drew a shape across his torso. "Like the tattoo, no? Spooky. Right?"

I didn't know what to say. The son of a bitch was just toying with me and there wasn't a thing I could do about it.

"Look," he said, standing tall. "You're cool, little man. Crazy cool. But mess with Frost or Miss Zee or any of mine, I gotta break you. Understand? Just keep to building. Or I'll break your ass in two."

I understood, all right. But for good measure, Crow kicked me so hard in the balls that I howled my guts out and smashed at the dirt. Then he just left me there, sniveling on the ground as the LEDs twinkled. And in the house, I could hear Zee wailing as that mean junky bastard went grunting and shouting and slapping his fists.

CHAPTER FIVE

Frost railed on for another half hour and then the house fell silent. I watched until the lights blinked out of the windows. And by then I'd decided what I was going to do.

Just didn't see any other option. Sure, I was scared of Crow. And Frost. Scared of being caught and beat. Scared of being thrown out. No job meant no money and not enough juice to go finding more work. But I had a picture in my pocket of my father – wrapped in chains but still breathing, and somehow surrounded by what looked like a stand of real trees. That image burned through every thought in my head. It was damn near all I could see. I knew there'd be no calm without answers. And Zee was the only one who might give them to me.

I went round and round, thinking about Pop, thinking about the photograph. And then thinking about that skinny lass who'd dumped all this on my lap.

Now don't be a damn idiot, I tried to tell myself as I stared at the house. But I figured if I could sneak Zee out while the others were sleeping, I just might get her to the ocean and back before sunup. And if she showed me the rest of the photographs, I'd start getting some answers. Find out where that camera had been.

I put the wagon in neutral and rolled it silently to the street then halfway down the block, parking it against an iron fence. I stood in the dirt road and studied the steel buildings all bulky in the blackness. Rich-freak homes grown out of the rubble of whatever had gone before.

I hugged the side of Frost's house when I scooted alongside it. And when I got around back, I hopped onto the porch and waited in the dark.

Nothing. No sound. No action anywhere.

Wasn't till I started creeping up to the door that the damn thing opened and Crow stepped out on the porch.

I ducked back, pressed down flat in the darkness as the watcher strolled to the steps. He had his headphones on and I could hear the music leaking from his ears. He stopped and stood there, just a few feet from me, humming along to some tune.

I didn't breathe or move or do anything. I just waited. Frozen. Until finally Crow drifted down the steps and disappeared into the lot.

I wondered if he might look for me in the forest. I wondered if he'd notice the wagon was gone. But then I crouched up and darted across the porch and I slipped right on into the house.

The hot metal walls amped every sound as I groped my way through the gloom. I cut down the hall in one direction and found a room that was full of pots and pans and boxes of corn. Fresh corn, still on the cob.

I spun back the other way, searching for stairs, figuring Zee would be sleeping on the top story. That's where I'd first seen her anyway, staring at me out the window. But I was starting to realize I'd no idea where the girl would actually be.

A silvery light was spilling into the hall at the far end and I made my way toward it. The silver glow was leaching from under a plastic door, and the door creaked as I pushed it wide. I peered into the room.

My heart thought twice about beating.

It was Frost. Not six feet from me. But he was passed out. Asleep. His face was planted on a desk full of binders and books and I'd never seen that much paper. On one side of the desk was an empty pipe and on the other was a pouch full of crystal, and I wondered if Frost ever went a whole day clean.

The silver light was oozing out of an old television set, and for a moment I watched the gray chips swirling on the screen. But then I saw the maps.

They were huge and crinkled, plastered on the wall. And there was a ton of them. Marked up in ink and labeled. Big chunks of green pointing at each other across patches of blue. Someone had drawn a crude picture of the tattoo tree and taped it in the middle of the wall. I inched closer, straining for a better look. But I heard a door squeaking shut and I froze.

Footsteps. A voice singing.

Crow. Back inside the house.

I left Frost drooling in his pile of paper and I backed up into the hall. I stopped. Listened. I tried to focus myself. Breathe. But it was like my brain wasn't working. My thoughts were all stuck in the same gear.

I tried the next door. The last door. And there, spiraling up into the shadows, was a tower of metal stairs. I yanked my shoes off and laced them together, and then I slung them around my neck as I ran upward, soft and quick.

The top floor was even hotter and I was sweating now, wiping my hands on my shirt. I found a room with a tub, another with an unmade bed. Three more rooms. All empty. Bare steel walls shiny in the dark. But then I found a room that wasn't empty.

Jackpot.

Zee was curled up and her momma was stretched out beside her. Neither of them had much on, it being so hot and all, and right away I could see Frost had bruised Zee up pretty good. But there was something else wrong with her. I watched as her chest rose and with each breath she made I could hear the gurgling sound of things growing tight inside.

I could hardly believe it.

She was cooped up in this house. Out of the dust. But that wheezing sound, there's no mistaking it. Only crusted lungs make a noise like that.

I spotted the momma's tattoo sticking out, like a flame of color. I crept closer and studied the roots and branches bending across the woman's belly. And as I looked, I noticed something about the leaves I'd not seen before. Each leaf had a number on it. A long number, printed in tiny black ink.

Zee blinked herself awake and stared at me, a big grin on her face as her eyes grew wide. She grabbed a bag off the floor and crept over to join me, and she was beaming at me the whole time like I wasn't in the worst place on earth I could be.

We tiptoed down the stairs and crept along the hall, listening to Frost snore and sputter. Crow was down the far end, still singing, rattling at the pots and pans. But then we were out the door, on the porch, bolting around the house and out on the street.

Zee was still grinning as she sprinted toward the wagon, though I could hear her broke lungs all straining and squeezed. I still had my shoes around my neck and they were bouncing and jiggling, whacking me in the face. And I kept thinking about Crow checking each room in the house and him finding Zee missing.

And how, if that happened, there'd be no going back.

CHAPTER SIX

The roads were mostly vacant as I steered through the night, heading east toward the ocean. We left all semblance of the city and the shantytown sprawl, and soon the only lights we saw were the odd scruffy settlement or lonely passerby.

Closer you get to the coast, the more nothing there is. Been that way forever. Folk stopped building too close to the Surge a long time back, afraid of everything they had breaking off and slicing into the water. That was the risk in heading out that way, seeing as you never knew when the land might crumble, the cliffs disappear.

"You always sleep in that room with your momma?" I said, spooked to the bone that Crow was going to find Zee missing.

"Not always," Zee said. "But it helps her sleep." She'd been snapping pictures with her camera, but they were smudged and dark and she shoved them in the bag at her feet.

I watched the old stone road as it droned beneath the wagon. "And how often you think Crow comes and checks on you?" I said, not being able to quit thinking about it.

"Now and then."

I tried to picture Crow passed out and snoring. Done for the night. I mean, you got to think positive. That's what Pop would have said.

I fired up the CD player on the dash and gave it the half dozen thumps it took to play the disc jammed inside. The music made me feel a bit better. I clicked to this track near the end, a song about dead flowers and some girl called Susie. My dad used to drum the steering wheel and we'd holler the chorus at each other.

"And I won't forget to put roses on your grave."

Better build heavy roses, Pop used to joke. Otherwise folk would steal them.

I stared at the bag at Zee's feet — the bag full of pictures. And I thought about that photograph in my back pocket. The photograph of my old man bound up in chains.

I cranked down on the accelerator.

It wasn't two hours and I knew we were almost there. I could tell by the way the spray reached up and blocked out the stars. I turned down the music and started to get worried the cliffs had worked their way inland. But when I pulled up, I could see the same stretch of fence, the old lot full of cars like corpses, the trash that gripped at the earth. Pop had taken me out here once. Back when I'd asked about Zion.

"Here we are," I said. "My half of the deal."

Feeble metal signs hung on the fence, warning you from getting too close. But when I cut the engine, Zee hopped out of the wagon wearing a wild-ass grin. I had to run out after her, tackle her down in the dirt before she got too near the edge.

"What are you doing?" She blinked at me with angry eyes, her body coiled tight.

"You got to be careful," I said, getting to my feet and helping her up. "Let me see how stable it looks."

I brushed her off and she wheezed and cussed and hid her face like she was ashamed of something. Like she hated me seeing her all choked up and weak. I had her wait as I stepped to the edge, surrounded by that great rush of noise, moaning and howling like the baddest wind you ever known.

I've heard it said people used to come to the coast for fun. The beach, people called it. They'd play around in the water and the ocean was just tame as could be. Breaks rolling in just a few feet tall.

Few feet tall?

I stared down at the waves clawing at the cliffs. Higher than any building in Vega. Spinning around like liquid twisters, a thousand stories high. Huge walls of water, pounding and breaking and making my ears hurt. The spray rose up and stuck in my nose, and out there past the breakers I could see the whole world rising and falling, carving in on itself like someone had just pulled the plug.

Something about the moon, people said. Something happened to the moon and brought it closer. I guess it didn't used to fill up such a big chunk of sky. But it wound up close at the end of the Darkness. There was twenty years of night and when the sun came back, that moon was so close it made the ocean go crazy as hell.

I almost drowned once. Tying chains for a river willow and I slipped off the bank, and no matter how hard I thrashed I kept sinking. Everything muted. Ready to burst. Pop pulled me out of the yellow slime, but I never could face the water after that. Never could learn how to swim. I mean, the Surge would fill you with dread if you could somehow breathe underwater. But for me it was even worse. Even high up as I was, it made my heart hammer at my bones.

I gestured to Zee, had her step closer. Some days you'd not get to the fence, the spray was so bad.

But today was Zee's lucky day.

She peered down through the wires, and her eyes grew as wide as the waves were tall. The spray beaded up on her skin, and her mouth hung as she stared down at that frothy stampede, the rise and fall of that giant swell.

"I don't believe it," she shouted above the noise of the water. "It's all like this?"

"They say the west coast's even worse."

Her face was wet from the spray hitting her, but I was pretty sure she was crying, too. Her face wasn't all crumpled or anything, but her lips were pinched real tight. I reached out and took her hand.

"Come on," I said, and I tugged her back to the wagon.

Zee didn't want to leave right away and I was in no rush to find out what was happening back at Frost's place, so I turned on the light inside the wagon and we sat in the front seats, our clothes all damp and salty.

"You'd never get across," Zee said, her eyes still staring at the blank space where the stars should've been. I followed her gaze.

"Nope."

"So how do we get out?"

"Out?"

"Somewhere better." She said it so quiet I could barely hear her, like the words had hardly worked their way loose. "The Promised Land."

"Right. Zion. Across the water."

I felt bad for mocking her. She slumped in her seat and balled her eyes up and then she let the tears come loose. She was real quiet about it. But somehow that made it even worse.

"The rest of the pictures," I said, not knowing what else to do. And besides, a deal's a deal.

"Fine." Zee tried to clear her throat. She held her bag open and I grabbed it, rummaging through a stack of photos of the sky and Frost's metal house, Zee's mother and Sal. Even pictures of me, wiring up the understory.

But that was it.

I stared at her.

"Screw it," she said. "It's not my fault."

"Screw it? Screw you. You got me out here for nothing."

"It's all I've got. It was Crow's camera."

"But the trees?"

"Came with the camera. Crow fixed it and that picture spat out. You are going to give it back?"

"What the hell do you think?"

She twisted around in her seat and hacked on a cough. "You have anything to read?"

"Why?"

"Because I'm upset, and when I'm upset I like to read."

"Must be nice," I said. I figured she wasn't worth getting angry with, but at the same time I was fuming. Crazy girl had me all the way out here for nothing. And who could I ask now about that picture, about my old man who'd been taken and the trees that weren't supposed to exist?

I threw a bag of popcorn at Zee and fired up the wagon, turning it around to begin the long climb from the coast.

"'GenTech's been putting Superfood on the table for more than a hundred years.'" Zee read it off the bag like the words were going to make her quit crying and coughing, like it was a story that would calm her right down. "'Through good times and bad, we've found a way to feed people. Corn. It's what's for dinner.'"

"Yeah," I said. "Breakfast and lunch, too."

"I read books," she said, wiping the tears off her face. "From when there were laws and governments. And there used to be a thousand companies making the food."

I'd heard that. But it makes no sense — everyone could have just grown food for themselves.

Zee was quiet for a bit, shaking the bag of corn and gazing out the window.

"So where else have you been?" she said finally.

"I've been around."

"Vega?"

"Almost."

"Far south?"

"Never seen the Wall, if that's what you mean."

"What about north?"

"Built trees in Niagara."

"And past that?"

"Ain't nothing past that," I said. "Nothing but the wastelands. Lava and steam."

"The Rift."

“That’s what they call it.” I stared across at her. “I’m telling you to drop it. Nothing grew back after the Darkness. Nothing but corn. You ever seen a locust?”

Zee shook her head.

“Better hope you don’t never do,” I said, like I’d seen one. “They’ll rip your skin off faster than you can piss your pants.”

“Then Zion’s far off. Or hidden, somewhere safe.”

“Grow up,” I said, wishing to hell she’d quit chirping on about it.

“So how do you explain the picture? The trees and that sky so clear?”

“Ain’t no explaining it,” I said. “That’s why I gotta find out how Crow got the camera.”

“He got it from people he used to work with.”

“A watcher job?”

“No. He used to work for them. For GenTech.” She said it like it was the most normal thing in the world. But how do you go from being a Soljah to a GenTech agent, and then wind up as a Steel Cities watcher?

It didn’t make sense. No one hates GenTech more than the Soljahs.

“Crow worked for GenTech?” I stared at Zee. “You sure?”

She held up a stack of photographs and showed me the back of each one. The GenTech logo in purple ink.

“Don’t mean nothing,” I said.

“You’re right,” she said. “It doesn’t. Not now I’ve seen the Surge. They’re crazy. The pair of them.”

“Who?”

“Crow. And Frost. They’re as bad as each other. Build a boat big enough. Frost and his stupid coordinates.”

"Coordinates?" I said. My foot had eased off the accelerator and I pulled off the road as the wagon ground to a halt. I stared at her. "What coordinates?"

"That's why they're working together, hunting their prize. Crow's been searching for years. That's what he did for GenTech, I guess. Chasing rumors and clues."

"Clues to what?"

"The trees," Zee said, staring at me through the darkness. "The last trees on earth."

CHAPTER SEVEN

What if it existed? The idea jammed inside me. What if it was real? A place where wild things grew. Not just a photograph. Not just a trick or a dream. Trees. Real trees. Real enough that people were looking for them. That GenTech was looking for them. And somehow my father had wound up in their midst?

I suddenly thought about Frost's house, my understory of squeaky wheels. And if there were trees out there with roots getting deeper and limbs reaching high, then what good had it been building forests out of crappy bits of tin?

I climbed out of the car and a rotten salt wind blew off the Surge and stung the dust around me. I felt sick. Swallowed whole. And I wished to hell I could just sleep. Shut myself down, shut myself up. But all I could see behind my eyelids was my old man's face.

I kicked the back wheel of the wagon. It just didn't make any damn sense. None of it did. And though Pop was coiled up in chains in that picture, it made me almost bitter that the folk doing the taking hadn't snatched me up, too. I'd been just left here in the dirt with the junk and the hungry. I kicked the wheel again. Then I slammed a fist at the wagon and damn near broke my hand.

"Stop," Zee cried, staring at me across the roof of the car. "We got to figure out what to do."

"Do? I'm gonna drop you off, that's what I'm gonna do."

"Then what?"

I stared back at the Surge. Then I looked west where the land crumbled like bits of cornbread. And I imagined soil bound with roots and wood for the burning and shade from the sun and a rest from the wind. And I pictured Pop, the metal chains wound around him, strapping him to the tree. Why? What was he doing there? It didn't matter. If it were me in trouble, I knew my dad would come running.

"How long you had that camera?" I said.

"Crow tracked it down a few months back."

"And who was it he got it from? I mean what was their name?"

"I don't know. Want to ask him?"

"I will if I have to."

Zee went to say something but the words got knocked out of her. She fell as the wagon slumped and the ground rumbled and the world split wide open.

"No," I whispered, staring back at the ocean.

Zee's holler rose up like a siren but I didn't need another warning. I yanked open the door and jumped behind the wheel, cranking the engine as the ground let out a sigh and compressed again beneath us.

The road sank about fifteen feet.

"Get in," I yelled, reaching across and tugging Zee into the car, slamming down the accelerator.

I stared into the mirror, watched dirt rise like smoke across the night. Another boom and the wagon slipped, but I floored it, willing it to keep going. Zee was kneeling up on her seat now, spun around to stare behind us, watching as the cliffs disappeared in the distance, gasping each time a new chunk of earth got gobbled by the furious Surge.

For years the cliffs had stayed where they were. But now they were hollow. Broken. And the world was collapsing.

Zee kept squealing till her lungs got choked. Then she was coughing. And when she weren't coughing she was begging me to go faster. As if I weren't thumping at the engine, fast as it would go.

Hard to see now. Dust filling the darkness. I could feel the road stodgy beneath the wheels. Dirt any deeper and we'd have been swimming in it.

Swimming.

I thought about that watery death, clawing its way closer. And I knew swimming wouldn't help you, but not having the option still made it so much worse. I could almost feel the water in my lungs already, my chest tightening, just as it had all those years before. My limbs useless. Everything squeezing shut.

I stared straight ahead, tried to blink the fear out of me. But then Zee cried my name like I'd pinched her.

"What?"

"I think it's stopping," she called. I strained my ears to listen above the sound of the wagon. Was that it? Silence?

I stomped at the accelerator. Far from convinced.

But another few minutes and the dust began clearing, and what was left of the road had stayed where it was. I wound my window down, stuck my face out in the night.

The Surge felt far away. In the distance.

But then the ground began ripping apart right in front of us. A huge gash, breaking open the road and getting wider. As if the world had grown so weary it was tearing itself to pieces, slicing its brittle remains into shreds.

CHAPTER EIGHT

For a moment the wagon was airborne, the whole night grimy and blind as we arced through it. Then our front wheels hit dirt again and the car plowed to a halt.

Behind us the cliffs exploded into the water, and the spray shot upward until all we could see was dust and ocean and every little thing dissolving into sky. But we were still there. Hanging on. Our front end was buried in sand but the bulk of the wagon hung out over the ocean. Just dangling there. A thousand feet high.

Zee was huddled on the dashboard, her eyes shiny, blinking at me. And I realized she was waiting on me to do something. Anything.

Could have just crawled out the windows. Run west right then. But there's nowhere in the world you can get on foot, so I clicked at the ignition.

The engine stayed dead.

I glanced down at the Surge and thought it had calmed a little, as if the earth had soothed the water, diluted the waves. But back out past the breakers, I'd never seen it so big, the arc of the whirlpools stretched so wide. And beyond them, at the wobbling far corner of the world, I could see red streaks as the sun refused to quit. Here it came again, that scorching ball of heat.

I coaxed the engine back on the sixteenth try, like getting a fire going on wet plastic. The wagon eased forward, digging into the sand, but the back end was too heavy and we sank again. Stalled.

I stared back at all my shit. The tools and supplies.

"Hold on," I whispered, shoving Zee tighter on the dashboard. And then the wagon bent and rocked as I wriggled toward the hatch at the far end.

It was so dark. Dusty. And I was sweating, slippery and afraid. Everything quiet now but for the sound of the water twisting and foaming below us, the wagon creaking, the rear end dipping lower with every inch I slid.

The hatch was sticky, weighted with sand and rocks, and I had to pry at it, jamming it free. But then the wagon squeaked and shifted. And it started to pitch real low.

I was staring straight down at the bulging waves and Zee was screaming. Everything was moving. Boxes sliding past me, piling up against me.

I got the hatch wide with my whole body shaking and I shoved out the scrap and the nails. LEDs. Sheets of steel. I watched it all plummet through the first rays of dawn, disappear into the water raging white.

I had one hand clasped inside the wagon and my eyes stuck on the Surge. But the wagon steadied a little, eased up. I threw my tools to the front end, shuffling after them until I was horizontal. Flat instead of tall.

The dirt was holding. For now.

"Stay there," I said, keeping Zee shoved at the windshield. I slipped into the front seat and spat dirt from my teeth as I cranked the engine and rolled us forward, the front wheels clawing their way deeper into the sand until we were right up in it, back end and all.

"Come on," I whispered, easing the engine a little stronger. A chunk of dirt shifted beneath us, just enough to get us going, and damned if the wagon didn't buzz right on up, topping off, not exactly racing along or anything, but as that sun rose red behind us, we were crawling our way west.

Zee scooted off the dash and wound herself against me, nuzzling her face in my neck and half crying, half laughing like a shanty loon. I'd never come close to being touched like that. I mean, a girl. Pressed against me. I could hear the broken sound of her lungs, and for a moment I wanted to wrap my arms around her. Tell her she was safe.

But the moment passed.

I shoved Zee aside and swerved the wagon. Because there, right in front of us, a lone figure stood in what was left of the road.

CHAPTER NINE

Our wheels spun to a halt and the dust rose in dirty pink sheets. I waited for the air to clear and stared back at where the road should've been. And I was about to crack my door open, when the man started from out of the dust like he was himself a part of it.

He had long, twisting dreads, painted gray by the sand. And buried beneath that swarm of hair was a face old as I'd ever seen, with a beard hanging heavy and long.

"Holy shit," I whispered as the Rasta floated closer through the dirt clouds. It was the same old fool from shantytown, the same hockey stick held like a staff before him.

"Who is he?" Zee said, her hand on my arm.

We watched the man reach the front of the wagon and peer in at us, smiling with a set of big brown teeth. He started mouthing something and finally I got sick of just sitting there and I opened my door to climb out.

"What the hell you doing out here?" I yelled at the old coot.

"I and I be seeing the sunrise." His voice was thin, like he'd worn it out. "Sun come up all the way from Zion this morning, bringing me news of the Promised Land."

"You walk out here?" I stared at the man's bare feet, so old they'd practically grown into a pair of shoes all their own.

The old guy nodded, smiling. "I sure be happy to see you, sire."

"Why? You wanting a lift?"

The Rasta let out a burst of laughter. Just one quick roar. "You come here from the ocean, man. I see you. Spat like Jonas from the whale."

I stared back at the sun crawling up the horizon, the spray of the Surge turning misty in the distance. "Listen, pal," I started to tell him, but he cut me off, throwing his staff up at the sky and his voice all of a sudden booming so loud I jumped back at the sound of it.

"Jah has returned home, my lovelies. The roots that feed this giant tree. Sent 'cross depths of the ocean. Over hills and valleys of water." The Rasta was almost singing the words, and he kept on with them as he ran to me and collapsed on the ground, dropping his staff at my feet. "Like the King before you, may you lead me back to that Promised Land."

Zee was out of the car now, running around the wagon and kneeling down to the pile of twisted hair and rags, reaching her hand to steady the old man's shoulder as he swayed around in the dirt.

"You've been there," Zee said, half asking it but mostly saying it like it was fact. "The Promised Land."

"Seen it with my own eyes." The man stopped rocking and stared up at Zee with his brown teeth gaping as his face broke out in a smile. "And Jah touched me with his own hand."

The Rasta sat back in the sand and reached to the rags across his belly, he fumbled around and finally pulled up his shirt. And there, stretched across his skinny ribs, the black skin had been transformed into something else. Like a sickness or something.

I stared at the man's strange skin, bubbled and rough and hard. Zee had recoiled and was up on her feet, backing away.

"What the hell is that?" I said, kneeling down, trying to get a closer look. But I already had a pretty good idea of what it was, though it was not something I'd ever seen before. And I knew it wasn't something that should be growing thick on human skin.

"Little slice of the Tree of Life, sire." The Rasta grinned at me and tapped at his belly. A solid sound. Not like bones or flesh, but nor was it the sound of plastic, stone, or tin.

"It's wood," I said, staring in his huge eyes, and those eyes just smiled right back at me, as if they might tell a hundred stories between each blink. "It's bark."

"And Jah will free us when we all get back there, sire. When we build a boat that's big enough."

"Holy shit," I whispered. Then I stared at Zee. "You seeing this?"

She was just shaking her head, freaking out. Hell, it was a freaky sight. Closest thing to a real tree I'd ever seen, though. Bark. Real bark. Somehow embedded in the old man's skin. I reached out and touched the knotted chunks and it was wood, all right. Just like in the old stories. Wood you could chop with an axe. Polish up or burn.

"Where the hell you been, old timer?" I said to him. "How'd this happen to you?"

"I'm a child of Zion," he said. "Eaten of the Tree of Life and then turned from the righteous path. But you will lead me back there, for I am fearful no more."

I pulled the picture from my back pocket and wiped it clear of dust. Then I held the photo to the old man and his eyes grew glassy.

"Jah, man," he wailed, happiness splitting his voice in two.

"This," I said, pointing. "This is my father."

"Sure it be, sire," the Rasta whispered. "If he still be alive."

"Alive?"

"But it be winter. Usually spring before there's killing."

"What killing?"

"Murderers." Tears beaded up on the old man's cheeks. "In the spring. Murderers, the lot of them."

"Your father?" Zee snatched the picture and shook it at me. "This guy's your dad?"

"Yeah," I said. I stood, wobbled to the wagon and leaned against it, steadying myself as everything spun inside. "It's Pop."

"The King" was all the Rasta would say. "The King."

CHAPTER TEN

We drove in silence. Each one of us in a world alone. I'd fired up some corn for the old dude and he ate sprawled in the back of the wagon, wearing my dad's old sombrero and drifting off to sleep.

I'd got nothing more out of him. He'd just babble on about the King and the Promised Land, and look solemn when I mentioned Pop.

Every now and then, I'd feel Zee stare across at me. She'd go to speak but then drop it. Hell, I don't know, maybe she could hear my brain overheating, see the smoke coming out of my ears.

I glanced back at the poor freak in the back of the wagon, his head resting on my nail gun, his stomach made of wood. Something had happened to him. A mutation, maybe. But not like any I'd seen.

"Do you believe now?" Zee said finally.

"Believe in what?"

"Zion. The Promised Land."

"I reckon there's trees out there. Someplace the locusts can't get 'em. But where?"

"I don't know," Zee said. "But I'll go anywhere. Trade anything. Whatever it takes."

I frowned, thinking. Up there in the distance I could see the edge of shantytown, the broken shacks blistered in the sun. And beyond those ragged streets was Frost's house. The whole place would be in alarm by now. Their girl missing. The tree builder nowhere to be seen.

"You should have told me it was your father," Zee said.

"Yeah? Why's that?"

"Changes things, don't you think?"

I rolled my eyes at her. But she was right. It changed everything. Pop was a half of myself that had always been there. And I'd become stretched and faded with that other half gone.

"You reckon that place is Zion," I said. "But the way my dad's chained up in that picture sure don't make it look like paradise."

"It doesn't matter."

"It matters to me."

"But if people have been there," Zee said. "If they've found it, then we can get there, too."

"Or Frost can," I said, thinking about that room of his, full of maps and books. "Man must have a plan."

"Crow's got him convinced Zion's out there." She pointed behind us. "Across the water. But they're waiting on something before they set off."

"What they waiting on?"

"Beats me. It's only because Frost thinks I'm stupid I know anything at all."

"And what do they aim to do if they get there?"

"You kidding? People will pay a whole lot for a little slice of Zion."

"Is that what you want? Find the Promised Land so you can sell it off?"

"I just want to breathe clean air." She jabbed a thumb at her wheezy chest. "Find a place to be free."

"With that bastard Frost?"

"Not if I find a way to get rid of him."

"Maybe you should just keep running."

"With nowhere to go and nothing to eat?"

"Then maybe you're as free as you're ever gonna get."

"What?" Zee sneered. "You think you're free? Roaming around in your rusty wagon and scraping for something to eat. You're not free. No one is. Not as long as GenTech's the only ones who can grow anything."

"There could be fruit trees," I said. "They could be fruit trees in that picture."

"And who knows what else might be growing?"

"Well, wherever there is, you'd have to stay put. Locusts keep to the cornfields, but they might make an exception, you give them a new place to nest."

"Find Zion and I'd never leave. Never."

"Not if they chain you to the damn trees." I thought about Pop. And then I stared across at Zee. "I need you to tell me about the coordinates."

She smiled, but not at me. It was like she'd gotten something she wanted, and she sank back into her seat. "I'm not telling you anything else, tree builder. But if you want my help, then you can do what I say."

"What the hell's that mean?"

"It means we're a team. We work together as long as it makes sense. One of us needs to do our own thing, the team's over. Right then."

"Sure," I said. "Works fine for me."

"Then step on it. Crow will be in shantytown this morning."

I slammed on the brakes, though the shacks were still a good ways in the distance. "Crow?"

"Yeah. Today's when he drops my mother off with the Tripnotyst." She stifled a cough. "Her weekly appointment."

"You want to talk to Crow?"

"No." Zee shook her head. "I want to get my mother back."

"We can come back for her later," I said, thinking about my dad and the old Rasta's warning. "Race this crowded, we need all the head start we can get."

"We're not leaving her behind, tree builder. Frost's got her shattered and strung out on crystal, but she's still my mother." Zee glared at me. "And we're gonna need her if we're gonna find us those trees."

CHAPTER ELEVEN

The tattoo. That's what Zee said we needed. But that's about all she would say about it.

I left the wagon stashed at the scrap farm and the guy there told me he'd keep his eye on it. I didn't tell him I had a freaky old Rasta buried in the back of the car. Didn't tell him I was planning to go kidnap me someone else, neither.

Zee was dressed in one of Pop's old shirts, my extra goggles hiding a good part of her face and an old rag wound around the rest of it. I padded an extra bit of cloth against her nose and mouth, doing what I could for her busted lungs.

I'd never walked that stretch of shantytown before, and it wasn't so much that it looked different than it did through the car window, but I swear it smelled twice as bad. The wind had started up and the sand blew hot and stinky. Still, I was grateful for the camouflage.

"So what the hell's a Tripnotyst?" I said, my mouth all full of grit.

"Supposed to help you remember things." Zee's voice was muffled by the rags, and almost drowned completely by the wind.

"Like what?"

"I don't know." She shrugged her skinny shoulders. "I remember everything. Most stuff I'd rather forget."

"Then what's your momma forgotten?"

"If we knew that, she wouldn't be going to the Tripnotyst. But Frost reckons her tattoo's from the same place as that photograph."

It was the tent I'd seen Crow emerge from just a couple days before, back when I was killing time and waiting for my water tank to fill.

We loitered out of sight, hidden behind a stall selling salvaged plastic toys shaped like animals. Folk trading for memories of a time before the Darkness and the locusts and the barren new world.

"You think he's in there?" I asked Zee. But before she could reply, we watched the tent flap roll up, and Crow came strolling out with his shades pulled on and his headphones plugged in.

We ducked behind the stall and peered around the side of it, studying Crow as he rolled on by. I tried to guess where he was going, what thoughts were buzzing inside those big old dreadlocks.

"Now's your chance," Zee whispered, shoving me forward. "Get my mom out of there. Tell her you're with me."

"What about the Tripnotyst?"

"Tell him whatever you have to."

"And what are you gonna do?"

"I'll keep watch, idiot. Make sure Crow doesn't come back."

I waited till the watcher was out of sight and then I sprinted to the tent door. I glanced back and saw Zee huddled between the water tanks at the drinking station. And then, before I could think anymore about what I was doing, I yanked off my goggles, eased up the tent flap, and plunged into the dark.

• • •

Inside that tent was as black as any place I'd ever been. The plastic flap fell behind me and suddenly the street seemed a mile away. I blinked, searching for light. Then I just stumbled forward with my hands stretched out ahead of me.

There was a gurgle of static, a buzz of electricity. And was that music? I strained to listen. No. Just the drone of machines.

I felt wires underfoot and dropped down and groped at them, crawling along with the cables until I hit something solid. Walls and edges. Some kind of container, about twice my size. I stood up and felt around at it. I stuck my ear to the wall of the metal box, and through the hum I heard voices.

Then something else.

I spun around. Faced back the way I'd crawled in. I heard the sound again. A tiny scrape. And suddenly, just a few feet from me, a lighter caught and flamed, puncturing a hole in the darkness.

The flame spat and flickered, coloring the tent with an orange glow, and I watched the flame kiss the end of a pipe, smoke and cinders hissing as the pipe was puffed and chewed. Before the lighter cut off, I had enough time to try and read the eyes staring at me.

But those eyes were impossible to read.

"Welcome back, Mister Banyan," said Frost, chomping at the pipe like it was breakfast. Then he snuffed out the lighter and all I could see was the crystal making patterns in the darkness as Frost made his way toward me.

CHAPTER TWELVE

Frost was a whole lot faster than I'd expected. He was juiced on his pipe and moved like a blur. His fingers clawed the dark as I bounced and ducked. Spun. Rolled away. He was too fast and too damn big and he sealed all my exits as he tumbled down upon me.

I was trapped. Pinned to the ground with my face in the dirt, my back feeling like it might snap in two. Frost just sort of waddled atop me and sat there. He shoved the crystal pipe at me, the flame crazy in my eyes.

"Did you need more supplies, Mister B?" Frost said. "Or did you get your grubby little hands on something else?"

I struggled but it was useless. My muscles barely twitched when they should've been beating his fat ass into tomorrow. He was sweaty and reeked and I wanted to gouge his eyes out, shove his ugly teeth down his throat.

I cried out. Tried to drain the fury from inside me.

"Quit your whining." Frost whacked me on the head.

I screamed again, loud as I could. He sat off me and rolled me over, pinned my chest with his flabby knees. He was sucking at his filthy pipe, and the crystals were bright enough I could see him draw a knife with his right hand just as he pulled my shirt open with his left.

It all happened at once. The thin blade pressing at my belly and the tent peeling apart behind me. Sunlight illuminating the ugly look in the fat man's eyes.

"Stop," a voice screamed from the doorway. Zee's voice.

Frost stared away from me and squinted at the gash of daylight. I felt the knife still pressed at my belly, breaking the skin now. Breaking my freaking skin.

"You can't," Zee said, and she let the tent flap fall thick behind her. "Let him go," she hissed through the void. "The trees," she said. "The trees."

Frost kicked me in the head as he got to his feet. He thumped over to the corner and fired up a neon strip that hung from the ceiling. The tent pulsed with a cruel white light, and the walls bulged inward as the wind howled outside. Frost pointed his knife at Zee.

"Talk," he said.

She ran up and pushed me over, everything happening too fast for me to glimpse her face, catch her eyes. I just felt her hands upon me, groping at me, digging in my pockets. She coughed as she stoked up the dusty floor.

"Here," she said, trying not choke. And as she backed off me, I rolled on my side and watched Frost staring at the photograph, his eyes all stoned and wide.

"It's his father," Zee whispered.

"How'd you get this?" Frost jabbed the picture with his knife, his face scrunched and twitchy.

"His father," Zee said. "Think about it."

Frost thumped at the steel box. There was a clank, then a clicking sound, and then damned if the box didn't start to open right there in front of us.

Frost probed his thumb at the bowl of his pipe, working up the crystal. Then he shoved the picture in his pocket and turned to the skinny broad with the gypsy earrings who was climbing out of the steel box like it'd just given birth to her.

I had a clear shot at the door and bolted for it. But Frost was too fast and seized the back of my neck with his pudgy claws. He dragged me across the dirt with my legs kicking, shoved me toward the steel container.

The gypsy woman was jabbering and waving her arms around, and her wrists shook with shiny bangles, her hands aflutter in the neon light. Frost just ignored her. He lifted me up like I weighed nothing and he threw me down inside the box, right on top of the woman I'd come looking for.

I was sprawled out on top of Zee's momma but she didn't move a muscle. My face was buried in her belly, pressed up against the tattoo tree, and I could breathe in the smell of her skin. I squirmed up, but Frost forced me down, keeping me inside that steel coffin and yelling at the gypsy woman to get back inside it with me.

"Your wife's still in deep," the gypsy said.

"Then leave her sleeping. But hook up the young punk here and tell me what you see." Frost pushed the gypsy in on top of us so we were squashed tight.

"What direction?" the gypsy called, and Frost held up the door for a moment.

"His father," Frost whispered, staring down at me. "Everything he's got."

CHAPTER THIRTEEN

There was barely room to breathe, let alone move. The inside of the container was bathed in a blue glow and I was jammed against Zee's mother, wriggling my way upright.

I squatted against the ceiling and that was as tall as I was going to get. The gypsy sat across from me, cross-legged and stooped, and I realized the gypsy wasn't a woman at all — it was a man. Dressed up in a skirt and everything. Stubble on his chin, chest as flat as dirt.

"You're the Tripnotyst?" I said, like an idiot.

The gypsy just winked at me as he tapped a control pad, a few of the buttons giving him trouble as he jabbed and poked with spindly fingers.

What air was in there was stale and thin and I felt about as strangled as when Frost had sat on top of me. I glanced down at Zee's mother, her tattoo eerie in the electric blue.

The woman's face was shut down, her muscles loose and her jewelry dusty. Her eyes were guarded by a pair of goggles, the lenses made of old wires and bits of metal.

"Put those on," the gypsy said, his voice as reedy as he was.

"What you gonna do?"

"Just put the goggles on. Ain't neither of us got a choice about it."

"You gonna drug me up?" I said, staring at the limp body beside me.

"Going under or not, that's up to you. But once you start remembering, you'll most likely want to shut down."

The gypsy had me lie back on top of Frost's wife. I tugged the goggles off her and started yanking them down over my own head.

"Try to relax," said the Tripnotyst, which was about the dumbest thing I'd ever heard. I struggled with the goggles, my elbows whacking at the steel walls. And then I glimpsed the patterns drawn across the blue ceiling.

I stopped working at the goggles and just squinted up at the image that was stretched above me, floating and shaking, drifting in and out of focus on the screen.

It was a wall. A massive, cement wall. A thin section close to the ground had been scribbled on, blackened with graffiti, but the top of the wall was all hidden by clouds.

I knew it was the South Wall, though I'd never seen it before, not even in pictures. It runs all the way across, from the Surge on one side to the Surge on the other. Was built before the Darkness, to keep people in the south stuck behind it.

"Put your goggles on," the gypsy said.

"It's the South Wall," I whispered. "Ain't it?"

"Nope." The gypsy punched a switch and the image disappeared from above me. "It's just a memory."

The goggles sealed tight and pinched my skin, blocking out any drop of the blue light. My face felt sticky and I tried to keep the panic within me, but I was blind now. Blind as well as trapped.

"Keep your eyes closed," the Tripnotyst said. "Less you want to lose your eyeballs."

I squeezed my eyes shut and held my breath as a thousand tiny spikes pricked my eyelids. I yelled out in horror but the needles stopped right where they were, not coming any closer, just locking me in place.

"Don't move," the gypsy said, his thin voice softer now, almost soothing.

Then music started. Strange, pulsing music. Gurgled beats and squelching bleeps and belches. The sound of bells rose up from the medley and I felt like I'd been stuck inside a wind chime, ringing and spinning and all blown to pieces.

"Welcome to the vibration of sound," a voice said. It was the gypsy's voice, but it had changed, each word booming now, bathed in echo. "Relax and let it ferry you away."

Every part of me screamed to stay present, but I felt myself unraveling, the music opening me. Untying me. I tried to focus my thoughts on Frost, on escape, on getting myself out of this weird coffin and setting myself free.

Free.

That was how I felt as I slipped into nothingness. Better than sleep, better than dreaming. I tried to fight the feeling for a moment, but then I gave up.

I mean, who doesn't want to be free?

I saw trees. Everywhere. Great labyrinths of shiny metal. Every forest me and Pop had ever built. All our trees grown tall and unruly and not a rusty spot between them.

At the center of the trees, my father was a hundred feet high, perched atop a strip of scaffold. And I was on his back, buried in a blanket, the fabric tied to his shoulders and wrapped around his waist.

My father was building. He was hammering out finishing touches. Bending at metal so the sun caught right. I felt his arm swinging the hammer, watched sweat beading on the back of his neck. When he welded steel joints, I saw hot sparks fly. And as he descended the ladders, I bounced and jostled and giggled.

On the ground, my father stared up at the canopy and I stared at it with him, listening as the wind blew tunes through the branches, watching as the breeze shook rhythm from the leaves.

I heard the gypsy's music again.

And then I was older. Curled up in the back of the wagon, eating popcorn and listening to my father read.

He told me stories of faraway places that had once existed. Tales told by countless fathers before him. Stories of bears and wolves and salmon and streams. The smell of wood on a fire. The sound of birds singing and the brush of their wings.

My father spoke me to sleep and I dreamt of waking to a real forest, our trees grown shaggy and breathing.

Bark and moss and twigs and spiders.

And in the dream I tried to wake my father so he could see the trees, but the sky grew fierce with the sound of locusts. And when silence returned, every tree was thin and crippled. Black and cold. And as the wind blew, the trees began falling upon us, each one of them tumbling and snapping, until I began catching the trees and planting them in ashes.

The music rose again. And with it, the trees I had planted all faded, and me and Pop were sat in the dust out past the cornfields. We had our backs to the corn, and we watched Vega glittering in the distance, like a light someone forgot to switch off.

One more day and we'd have reached the city. But then it was night and Pop was waking me, telling me there were voices outside. And the dust storm was raging and sucking the sky inside it, and I wanted to go find Pop but I was too damn scared. And it was too late when I finally crawled out of the wagon. There was no trace left after the storm had quit. No footsteps or shadows. Just dirt stretching ahead of me, all the way to the walls of the Electric City.

Pop was gone.

Taken.

Vanished like grass.

I could see myself twisted in the back of the wagon. My face smudged with dirt and swollen with tears, all of me shaking as it sunk in how alone I was now and always would be.

And the rest was all blank.

CHAPTER FOURTEEN

When I opened my eyes again, I felt damp and shivery. The goggles were gone and I was back outside the steel box, piled in the corner of the tent with Frost's boot heel digging in my ribs.

"That was it?" Frost said. "All of it?"

"Everything," said the gypsy.

I blinked up at the two of them but lay still, trying to figure out some plan to escape.

"He's no good to me," Frost spat. They'd been watching the screen inside the box, the lid flipped open, but the Tripnotyst punched the thing closed, sealing my memories back inside.

"Usual payment?" Frost said, and the gypsy grinned as Frost pulled a pouch from his back pocket and threw it on the dirt. Then Frost squatted close to me and pulled the knife up to give me a good look at it. The dirty pearl handle had been patterned once but was now worn smooth. The blade shimmered in the neon light.

"Old man ran off and left you, did he?" Frost faked a frown.

"He didn't run off," I said, teeth clamped tight. "He was taken."

Frost laughed. He ran a stubby finger along the edge of the blade.

Then he knelt on my chest and put his hand on my face, forcing me down as I struggled against him.

"Tell you what, Mister B. I catch up to that old man of yours, I'm gonna give him your best regards."

"Leave him," Crow boomed behind us, his voice like thunder as he burst into the tent.

Frost paused, the blade pressed at my windpipe. I tried not to breathe.

"Any news?" Frost said, staring up at Crow.

"Aye. There's one in Vega. And the truck's ready to go. So leave the boy. Miss Zee is back and you don't want his blood on your hands."

"You know what, watcher?" Frost struggled to his feet. "You're absolutely right."

He threw the knife to Crow.

"You do it," Frost said, stomping out of the tent. "And maybe next time you won't be so careless."

I glanced around the tent. The Tripnotyst was nowhere to be seen. And neither was Zee or her mother.

Just me and Crow, then. Just like old times.

Crow shook his head as he came over to me. I scrabbled to my knees, glancing toward the street but keeping an eye on the watcher as he stepped closer. I took too long to make a move and there was no move anyway. And then Crow was right above me, fingering the knife and bouncing the weight of it in his hand.

"I told you not to go messing, little man." Crow was still shaking his head, making out like he was real solemn about having to kill me. "So why you want to go messing for?"

I didn't say anything.

"Should've stuck to building," Crow said, staring at the door to the tent. He held the knife above his head and then cast it down. The blade spun and blurred, and then it sank into the dirt beside me.

Crow squatted down and yanked the knife from the sand. He wiped the blade on the fabric woven through his beard and he fixed me with his brown eyes. Then he pulled his shades down and stood.

"See you in the next one, little man," Crow said as he stepped to the door, and I watched as he threw the flap open and disappeared into daylight.

Couple seconds, maybe. That's how long I lay there with my heart beating a hole through my chest. Then I shot up and bolted to the door. I slid on the sand and tugged at the tent flap, pulling it high enough I could peer out at the world.

Everything was still there — sun, dust, and wind. I pulled my goggles on and choked on the dirt clouds. I could see strugglers down the street, scurrying away as a truck bellowed and smoked and grew small in the distance.

"Come on out." The Tripnotyst was lounging in a plastic hammock on the corner, smoking a crystal pipe.

"That how he pays you?" I said, scrambling up and striding over. I pointed at the pipe full of poison.

"Good shit, my friend. But there ain't enough to be sharing."

"He ever go in there himself?" I said.

"Fatty?"

"Yeah."

The Tripnotyst shook his head. "Just the pretty lady. And her girl."

"Zee?" I said. She'd either betrayed me in the tent or she'd been trying to buy us some time. Either way, I was on my own again. "What did she see?"

"Listen, friend. I might be high as one of your metal treetops, but I don't go dishing out beta on clients. Not to bums with no way of paying."

"She see the Wall, too?" I said, squatting down next to him.

"The Wall?" The Tripnotyst laughed, then he started coughing. "That's just the start, brother. Now give up. And relax. Neither of them girls make a damn bit of sense anyway."

"How much is it?" I said. "For a session."

"More than you can afford, bro. I don't deal in forests."

"What about a book? Would you take that?"

He studied me for a moment. "Depends on the quality," he said. "And the size."

"You can read?"

The Tripnotyst nodded, his eyes glazing over now from the crystal. "What you want to remember?"

"It's not for me," I said, standing up. "But give me two hours. I got someone ready to trip his balls off."

CHAPTER FIFTEEN

When I got back to the scrap farm, the Rasta was sitting on top of my wagon and singing a song about Babylon. Old One Eye raised both eyebrows at me as I walked back to where I'd stashed the car. I just nodded and smiled like this was business as usual. Then I climbed on top of the wagon with my new crazy pal.

"I need you to tell me where you saw my father," I said. "I need you to remember things."

The Rasta stopped singing and stared at me. "Oh, I remember, man. Promised Land. Across the ocean."

"But how'd you get there?"

The old guy just grinned and pointed north, then south, east, and west. "The King."

"The King," I muttered, and I studied the Rasta's wrinkled face. "We gotta take a trip," I said. "You and me."

"Right on, sire. Right on."

I helped the old man to his feet and the two of us balanced on top of the wagon, sticking out of the rust and scrap that stretched all around.

These people were like tickets, I thought. Zee's mother with her tattoo. The Rasta with his skin made of bark. And though Frost figured the woman was his golden key, I reckoned this old fool might prove more valuable. And Frost didn't even know the Rasta existed.

Not yet, anyway.

I thought about Zee and wondered whose damn side she was on. Guess I hoped she was on Frost's side, tell you the truth. Because if she wasn't, that girl was in a whole world of trouble.

The sun was setting by the time I got back to the Tripnotyst's tent. I peered through the door but was wasting my time – the gypsy was right where I'd left him, sleeping the crystal off, wound up inside his hammock and covered in dust and debris.

I shook him awake and he pulled his shawl over his shoulders, shivering at my touch. "Want another fix?" I said. I held my book at him. "You can read it or trade it."

The gypsy sat up and snatched the book. "'The Journals of Lewis and Clark,'" he read off the back cover. "'The first report on the West, over the hill and beyond the sunset, on the province of the American future.'" The gypsy stared at me. "True story?"

I shrugged.

"This buys you one trip," he said, standing. "One."

"Fine," I told him. "One's all we need."

The old Rasta's eyes grew huge as the door to the steel box began sealing us inside. Me and him were squeezed together, facing up at the blank screen.

“Don’t worry,” I told him. “You’re gonna love it. Just do what the man tells you is all.”

The Rasta made a hollow smile and the Tripnotyst sneered at me from the other end of the box, his face telling me just how big a waste of time he thought this would turn out to be.

“Direction?” he asked, the blue light flashing on above us.

“Zion,” I said. “The Promised Land.”

“Pick one.”

“The Promised Land, then.”

The gypsy punched it in on his keypad as I pulled the goggles onto the Rasta’s head.

“Relax,” I told him as music bathed the inside of the booth, but then the Rasta’s face drooped and his tongue wound out and I knew it had started.

I leaned back and stared up at the screen on the ceiling.

Blank.

I glanced at the Tripnotyst, but he just held a hand at me and punched something else at his control panel.

And then it began.

The trees were starting to look familiar — the tattoo, the photograph. And now this.

The Rasta’s memory swam across the screen, and I watched the leaves rustle and the limbs flow as the trees bent back and forth. I stared down at the base of the white trunks and peered high in the branches. But I saw no one. Nothing but forest.

When the trees faded they were replaced by water, and I should’ve seen that coming, but the sight still blew me away. The water stretched as far as the horizon, and it was calm enough you could count the ripples upon it.

Deep, still water. Soaking up the sun with the color of night. In the water, the Rasta watched his own reflection and his face was younger, his beard shorter, less patched with gray. A face appeared beside him. A hairless face. Pale skin taut on jagged bones. And that face kept multiplying until I could no longer see the water, and even the Rasta's reflection was squeezed from view.

The screen went white. Blank again but for a single word. A word even I could read. The word plastered on every box of corn, every bottle of liquor. Every gallon of fuel. Same word that grows across each kernel of corn, purple letters embedded in those juicy, yellow stumps so you can never forget who grew them.

The word seemed to buzz on the screen but then stayed still, glimmering at me till the screen turned black.

"GenTech," I muttered. "GenTech."

CHAPTER SIXTEEN

"I don't know if it matters," the gypsy said, punching at the control pad and shutting down the machine. "But Promised Land didn't do much for him. Typed in Zion to set him adrift."

I stared down at the Rasta, still splayed out inside the box. Then I set to shaking him, shoving around at the old guy and pulling off his goggles. But the Rasta wasn't going to wake up.

Not ever.

I could tell by the way his tongue had turned limp and his eyes were rolled back in his head.

"No you don't," I whispered. But it was useless. I tugged his eyelids closed and dragged him on my shoulders, and I was glad the gypsy had his back turned because all of a sudden I busted out crying as I stumbled for the door.

I moved like I was floating and my throat got thick. I breathed in the stench of the Rasta's dreadlocks and felt his body, stiff and warped. It was my fault — forcing the old guy into that box. It had been too much for him. He was dead and I'd killed him. Must have been the oldest person I ever had seen.

And he'd known my father. Somehow. In some insane way. They'd both been taken someplace together.

And now the Rasta was dead.

But this was the gypsy's doing. That's what I told myself. He was the one that should've known better. The damn freak had ripped me off.

So after I'd stuck the body in the back of the wagon, I quit sniveling and wiped my face with a rag. And Pop always said I was a builder, not a fighter. But Pop weren't there, was he? So I grabbed my nail gun and strode back into the tent.

"You killed him," I said as the Tripnotyst spun around to face me. I held the nail gun up at him. "You junkie son of a bitch."

"What the hell you gonna do with that?"

"That's up to you," I said. "I can pump you full of nails. Or you can give me back my damn book."

On the sand flats outside of town, I burned the Rasta, and the stench about made me sick. But not as sick as I'd felt carving the bark out of the old man's belly.

It'd been about an inch thick and his skin grew thin beneath it. I had to shave the wood off in pieces and ended up with one good chunk. The other scraps I burned and I listened as they popped and hissed and I watched as they smoked and flamed. Then I drew on the sand with the ashes and waited as night fell heavy upon me.

The bark was soft and spongy and I ran my fingers on it, rubbing the last bits of flesh from beneath it. Skin and bark. A piece of man and a piece of wood. It turned my guts, tell you the truth. But I couldn't stop fiddling with it.

I leaned back in the dirt and stared across to the city in the distance. It was a warm night, no wind blowing and the air about as clear as it ever would get.

I peered up at the stars, thinking about Pop. I felt the piece of bark between my fingers, knotted and rough and smooth. And I figured if that chunk of wood was as close as I was going to get to a real tree, then I was about as sorry a son of a bitch as you could find. I had clues up the ass. Knew I did. Just had to find some way to piece them all together. And by the time the fire died, I knew I had to head west.

West was where my father had been stolen away from me. Out past the cornfields, near Vega — the city juiced off the corn GenTech keeps hoarded. And the Electric City was where it sounded like Frost and Crow were now headed. There's one in Vega, Crow had told Frost. But one what? What could help them find the trees they wanted so bad to sell?

Zee was right. Folk would pay a fortune for a forest. The last trees left growing. Food and fuel and who knew what other riches? It was either a place without locusts or the trees there could somehow withstand them. And either way, everyone would want in.

Thing is, no one could pay like GenTech. Not even close. Not even Crow's old tribe in Niagara, though they make good off the water they sell. Sure, some say the Salvage Guild's still got a load of old world prizes, but I doubt it's as much as the stories make out. GenTech, though, they could make a man rich if he had the right information.

Or they could get the information they wanted and then cut that man's throat.

The last job we worked together, before Pop took us out west, we'd watched a client get dragged from her own home, and this agent with a giant scar said the woman was scum, said she'd been bootlegging corn all throughout the southeast. He took his spiky club to her till her screams turned to silence, and when it was over, Pop made me finish the woman's plastic pine and we buried her beneath it. When I asked him what bootlegging was, Pop said it was just another word for getting yourself killed.

But I found out about bootleggers. They're good people. Brave. The rare kind of rich folk that try and help others. They give corn away or sell it off at a discount, and GenTech doesn't like that at all.

As I sat there thinking, I started to figure those trees mightn't be for sharing, anyway. Maybe they were just somewhere to run and stay hidden, not to be stamped with some logo. Just a place to forget all you'd left behind.

Hell, maybe the trees were Zion. The Promised Land that everyone spoke of and no one could find. Grass and animals and clean water and air just right for breathing. Just like in the stories. But I told myself none of that could matter. Not yet. Because no future would matter unless I could save my old man.

Everyone's got to have something to believe in, that's what Pop always told me. He'd spent his whole life trying to make the world worth living in. And I was damned if I was going to let him die someplace alone.

My guts were all set to take off, drive west, but I needed supplies if I was heading onto the plains. I needed corn and juice and I had not a single cent to pay with.

And that's why I figured I should make one more visit to the Frost residence.

• • •

I loaded up the nail gun till the thing was fit to burst. Brightest, shiniest nails I had. Three-inch spikes. I buried the piece of bark in my pocket so it was close to me. And then I drove back to Frost's place. Before sunup.

I checked the house from a distance with the telescope I'd gotten for showing off canopies. Then I strode up to the storage shed on the side of the house and I shot the lock through with the nail gun. Inside, the bio kit where Crow brewed their juice was missing, and that meant they'd gone west already. Just as I'd thought.

I found a bucket of fuel and five more like it. Then I ran to the back of the house and thumped at the door, hanging at the side of it with my gun ready — just in case I was wrong, just in case Crow or Frost came rushing outside.

But the night stayed silent. I knocked again, beating the steel door like a drum, hitting it so hard I thought my fist might break.

Still nothing. No one.

I pulled the wagon around and took the blowtorch and carved a hole big enough to just slice the locks right off the back door. Then I kicked in what metal was left and pulled my goggles up and I ran through every room in the house with my nail gun ready.

Empty. Each damn room. Frost's study had been completely ripped clean.

I filled my arms with bags of popcorn and threw them in the back of the wagon with the buckets of juice. I buried my book and the piece of bark in a box of nails, and when I had everything packed, I pulled the wagon into the lot and tucked it out of sight amid the stacks of scrap metal.

The sun was almost up and I'd not slept for two days and as many nights, and I took the nail gun and a hot bag of corn and wound my way up to the bedroom where I'd found Zee. I stretched out on the bed, a real bed, and I ate the corn before sleeping a little.

But when I opened my eyes, Sal was sat on the bed beside me. And my nail gun was clamped tight in his sweaty hands.

CHAPTER SEVENTEEN

The sun had already cooked the house rotten and I was sticky on the sheets. I stared up at Sal and gazed at the nail gun, and you can bet that I didn't even blink.

"What the hell you doing here?" I said, eyeing his chubby finger on the trigger of the gun.

"This is my house, tree boy. The question's what are you doing here?"

I grinned at him, tried to give him the sense we were friends, like maybe he was crazy for forgetting how much he liked me. But Sal didn't smile back. He just squirmed around on the blankets and fidgeted with the nail gun.

"You know, Sal," I said. "I guess I just needed a good night's sleep before I set to finishing that forest of yours."

"Sleep, huh? You needed some juice, too?"

"Was running a little low."

"And some corn?"

"Right."

"Just a filthy big thief, aren't you?"

I started to say something but Sal jumped off the bed and pointed the nail gun between my eyes.

"Easy," I whispered, freaking out about now. "Easy."

"My dad hired you to build some trees, that's all. Not run off and steal our supplies." The kid pointed the gun up and let one loose, clanging a nail against the metal ceiling. That got him laughing, and he fired off another shot as he yelled, "You know what the red spot's for? The big cross in your forest?"

I shook my head.

"My daddy's going to be planting a real tree right there in the middle of your copies."

"Is that so?"

"You bet it's so. And we're going to be more rich than you could even imagine."

"I don't know," I said. "I can imagine a fair bit."

"Then try imagining how much GenTech's going to pay when my dad has real trees for selling. Real trees. Not like your stupid statues."

"That where he is now? Hunting you up some trees?"

The kid made a slobbery grin and pointed the nail gun back at me. I put my hands behind my head and tried to look relaxed about things, trying to get the kid to lower his guard.

"Your dad must love you a whole heck of a lot," I said. "Man could get himself killed looking for something that everyone wants and nobody has."

"No," Sal said quietly, then he threw the nail gun on the floor with a horrible clunk. "He always said he'd take me with him. But they're gone. All of them. Everyone except me."

"Maybe they wanted you to keep an eye on the place. Keep things safe."

Sal made a face. "Maybe they just didn't give a damn about me."

I went ahead and stood, walked over and grabbed the nail gun off the floor. The fat kid just watched me do it.

"You feel like doing a little tree hunting yourself?" he said, fixing me with a look.

"Tree hunting?" I shoved the nail gun in his chest and pushed him to his knees. "Ain't a good idea to go waving this thing around 'less you're gonna use it, son."

"I ain't your son," he whispered, his pale cheeks quivering, his eyes about to cry.

"Take it easy," I said, pulling the gun off him. "You got enough corn to last all winter. Wait long enough and your dad'll be back along. Though he might be empty-handed."

I went to leave, but Sal stopped me. His whiny little voice calling up from the floor. "You're right," the kid said. "He'll never find them. He's screwed. Completely screwed."

"Yeah?" I said, turning back to him. "And why's that?"

"Because he's looking in the wrong place."

Frost had left behind a case of corn liquor, and Sal helped himself to a bottle as he sat amid the pots and pans on the counter downstairs. I still had the nail gun in my hand, but the kid was talking plenty without me pointing it at him. And that was good. Swinging that thing around at people leaves a bad taste in your mouth.

"She's got numbers." Sal belched on the whiskey, acting like some shrunk-down version of his old man. "On the tree. Numbers on every leaf."

"So?"

"So you ever heard of GPS?"

I shook my head.

"It's like a map," Sal said. "Or a compass. Plug in the coordinates you need to find and the GPS tells you where it's at."

"And you believe that?"

"They say there's things up there," Sal said. "Orbiting out of view. Moving across the night. Satellites, they were called. It's them that tell the GPS how to get there."

"And you just punch in those numbers?"

"Leaves pointing up give you the north coordinates. You add them together, then subtract the ones that point south, down toward her you know what." The kid laughed hard, snorting out his nose like he'd just stopped breathing. "You get the easting coordinate the same way. The sideways leaves."

"How do you know?"

"Crow's been looking into this for years, that's how. He knew the story long before he found the woman."

"So it's a story, then. Don't mean it's true."

Sal rolled his eyes at me. "Of course it's true, tree boy. If GenTech believes it. But Crow never knew about the last tattoo, that's his problem."

"The last tattoo?"

"Oh? You didn't find it on your little midnight adventure?" Sal scrunched his face up, his skin all sweaty and gross. "The last tattoo's on Zee, you idiot. Small and hidden. She probably doesn't even know it's there herself."

He plopped off the counter and turned his back at me, stabbing a pudgy finger right above his ass crack. "Base of her spine," Sal said. "Right here. And that leaf points all the way down."

"How the hell'd you see it?"

Sal turned and winked at me. "Told you she ain't my sister."

Should've left right then, right?

But the kid kept talking.

"So they're going to be too far north. Without the correction. But you get us a GPS, and I can get us to the right place."

"You can't know all them numbers."

"Wrong again, tree boy. Wrong again."

Sal led us back to Frost's empty study. I stared at the clean desk, the cold TV screen, but Sal dug me in the ribs and pointed at the ceiling.

"She's something, isn't she?" Sal whispered, and I wasn't sure if he meant the woman or the tree, but up there, plastered on the ceiling in a jigsaw puzzle of photographs, Frost's wife was stretched out with her eyes closed and her top pulled off and the tattoo about as alive as it could be.

"So many numbers," I said, squatting down and craning my neck.

"And I got them all locked right here. Zee's, too." Sal tapped his greasy head. "But I say we bring the pictures with us."

"With us?"

"I told you. Get me a GPS and I can find us the right place."

"Sure. GPS. Anything else you might need?"

"If Crow found one, we can find one."

I thought about it. "Only one place worth looking."

"Vega."

I stared at the ceiling, studied the tree. "How about you just tell me the number?" I said. "The correction."

Sal shook his head. "I'll never tell you." He glanced at the nail gun. "That's why you've got to take me with you."

"Take you with me, huh?"

"That's right." His voice got scratchy. "You need me. Like I need you. And together we can catch us some trees, Banyan. That's what you want, isn't it?"

He was right. It was all I wanted. That forest could give me my old man back and a whole new life and a future like that's all the Promised Land you need. I knew I'd do anything to get there.

Anything at all.

PART TWO

CHAPTER EIGHTEEN

The forty is the only road west, and it takes you all the way to Vega. If you're lucky.

Head across the plains in the hot months and the locusts will strip your bones once you hit the corn. So you wait till winter falls and the corn has been zapped by cold. Locusts don't hatch again till spring so the forty should be good to go. All you have to worry about is pirates. And poachers.

Plus you got to pray that you don't get taken. Sure, folk go missing all over. Most places you go there's someone disappeared without trace. But it's worse on the plains. Just like the sun burns worse and the dirt blows worse and the hazard winds don't ever seem to quit.

Bits of the forty are solid, old tarmac sticky beneath the wheels. But mostly the dust slows your tires as it clouds up your windshield. And sometimes you got to drive blind.

Sal had found the camera and the bag full of photos, right where Zee had stashed them below the passenger seat. Now he kept messing with the camera, shooting pictures at the brown sky as we drove west.

"Shouldn't waste it," I told him as he held up another blurred image.

"Why?" He turned and snapped a picture of me with my hands on the wheel.

"'Cause it ain't yours."

"Whatever. What kinds of trees do you think are growing there, anyway?" The kid had the camera up his shirt now, taking pictures of his belly.

"Who cares? I don't reckon beggars can be choosers."

"I read books all about them. Apple trees and banana trees, mangoes and limes. Walnuts and cherries and peaches and plums. Hey." Sal shoved the camera in my face. "Smile."

I grabbed the camera from him and shoved it beneath my seat. And it wasn't long before Sal had grown bored enough that he was curled up and napping, the road bouncing his head against the car window, his mouth all scummy with spit.

The bag was open at Sal's feet and I leaned over and riffled through the images we'd peeled off Frost's ceiling. The tattoo coordinates all mapped out on skin. Then I flicked through the pictures Zee had taken. Shots of Crow and Sal were mixed in with ones of me rigging the understory. And I hardly recognized myself in those photos, my face lost in concentration, my hands buried in their work.

I checked the fuel gauge and we were doing pretty good considering how much weight I'd added, what with the juice and the corn and slobber boy. Another day or so and we'd be across the plains and heading into the cornfields, that shimmering zone of thirty-foot plants and crop poachers and field hands and GenTech agents. But the cornfields couldn't be counted on. Not yet. Because up ahead, through the dirt clouds, I began to spy our first signs of trouble.

Pirates.

Whole damn bunch of them.

There were two trucks. Built like tanks and feasting on a group of strugglers. God knows what the people had been doing trying to cross the forty on foot, but then I guess they'd probably not started out that way. Take the long road and anything can happen.

I tried to gauge the numbers, their distance ahead, but the dirt swarmed back and sealed the future from view.

"Wake up," I said, loud enough for Sal to bang his head on the ceiling. "We got company."

He couldn't see through the dust clouds so he just stared at me. "They don't look like traders," I said. "And we look pretty ripe for the picking." I pulled the wagon off the road.

"So what do we do?" He was panicked. "You think they've seen us?"

"They've seen us. Pirates tend to pay attention to things on the road."

I jumped out and pulled my goggles down so I could see. The dust was bad. Real bad. And that was about the only good news out there.

I yelled for Sal to get his fat ass out of the wagon, and I showed him how to shovel at the sand with his fingers.

"Quick now," I told him, trying to peer through the dust clouds. "Quick as you can."

As Sal scraped at the side of the road, I set to work on the engine, snapping hoses free and switching pieces out. Then I unloaded the buckets of juice and half the corn, found my book and the bark and stashed them with the pictures and camera inside Zee's bag. I buried everything in the channel Sal had scooped out. I worked at the ditch with my bare hands, clawing as deep as I could go. Then I poured the sand back on top of the supplies and pounded the dirt flat.

I watched the road ahead.

Still nothing but dust.

I checked the nail gun.

"For all they know, it's just me that's out here," I said. Sal just squinted and pointed his face in my direction. "So I'm saying you should run," I told him. "Scram. Out there off the road, and lay down low. Just don't go too far. You'll not find your way back."

Sal didn't budge. I was pretty sure he was going to start crying. Hell, he was probably already crying.

I grabbed him my extra goggles out the back of the wagon, yanked them down over his head. "Pull your shirt up so you can keep breathing," I said, the dust blowing worse now. Got so you couldn't see past your nose. But we could hear engines. Two of them. Growling up closer with every stupid moment Sal stood waiting.

"Go on," I yelled. "Scram."

And finally he took off running, fast as his stumpy legs would move. I watched him trip and fall, scramble up and keep going. Then I lost all sight of him at all.

I slammed down the hatch to seal up the wagon. I ran to the front where the hood was still gaping wide. And right before I turned back to the engine, I spotted the silhouettes of those two pirate vehicles, their oily color leaching through the dust storm, looming closer with every second.

CHAPTER NINETEEN

I had the nail gun tucked at my waist and my shirt pulled down over it. And I kept faking at the engine as the pirates rumbled closer. They had music blasting, a regular party rolling up. The electric sound of guitars split the air as the first truck sank to a stop.

The wind went soft and the dust eased a little. I turned from my engine and made a big deal of peering up at the truck closest to me, flashing the dumbest grin you ever seen. I yelled out, about as loud and cheery as I could manage. Act like you got nothing to worry about. That was my plan.

Each one of those tankers had nine sets of wheels and a solid box on the back, guns spiky off the top and pointy out the side. I studied the lifted tires with rubber knuckle tread, the graffiti, and tinted windows.

The music stopped and the engines sighed, then fell silent.

I waded over to the truck closest, waving my hands in the air, and just as I reached the cab, its door came flying open and all I could see was legs.

Thighs. Holy shit. As strong as they were pretty. The girl leapt out of the cab and stared down her broken nose at me.

Seen one pirate, you seen a hundred. The mohawks and the rubber boots. Three-foot hair and six-inch heels. If she was older than me, there weren't much in it, but her eyes showed the true mileage, if you know what I mean. A rifle of some sort hung loose off her shoulder. Goggles dangled from her neck, like the dust didn't bother her a bit.

"Something wrong with your wagon?" the girl said, crossing her arms as she looked me over.

"The power converter." I shrugged. "Think the fuse is fried."

"Where you heading?"

"Vega."

"Alone?"

"Why? You want to come?" I pushed my goggles up and squinted in the dust, as if I might match her in some way. "I could use a little company."

The pirate threw her head back in the storm and laughed, her breasts rocking inside her fuzzy pink vest. Then she stepped closer to me and lifted my shirt up. "So what's this for?"

"It's a nail gun."

"You always carry it shoved in your pants like that?"

"Not always."

"Just a regular joker, huh?"

"Just stuck on the side of the road, sister," I said. "Any chance you got parts for a trade?"

"Why? What you got in the back?"

One of the trucks began blasting its horn at us, voices yelled through the dust. But the girl just raised her hand to silence them. She threw open the back of the wagon, peering in at my bag of tools, the scattered bags of popcorn. I was pretty sure I'd left enough in there to look realistic. Bit of food. Bucket of fuel.

"Grab that," she said, pointing at the juice.

"What for?"

"You're bringing it with you. Your tools, too."

I reached for the nail gun. Panic coming over me. I tried to pull the gun up, point it at her, but the pirate just crushed her knee in my chest and I felt my arms go floppy. She grabbed the gun off the ground and shoved it at my arm, lodged a nail there so fast I'd no time to scream.

I staggered back. Fell. The pain surged through me like my arm had caught fire. My body writhed in the dust. The pirate girl snatched me up with one hand, grabbed my bag of tools with the other, and then she dragged me across the road to the back of her truck. My heels scraped through the dirt, my arm was ready to explode. I just stared back at my wagon, and for some reason, the worst of it was that hatch left hanging wide open, the car filling up with sand. Like the wagon had rolled its last mile and the world was telling me that nothing lasts forever.

Nothing, Banyan. Least of all you.

"Watch out, ladies," the pirate yelled into the belly of the truck as a hundred eyes blinked shiny from its depths. "This one's a charmer."

She hoisted me up and hurled me inside the tanker.

And the tanker was full of bodies.

Nothing but skin and bones, wound tight with terror, painted in piss and vomit. They were slumped in puddles of sweat on the floor. Stinking like week-old shit.

Every lousy part of me screamed and jerked and hustled, and my arm pulsed and my head spun. But there weren't no escape.

I screamed till my mouth was frothy. Tried to bolt. But the pirate pushed me back until I felt flesh beneath me, fingers clutching me, the slimy mob absorbing me in its gristle.

As the door slammed shut and sealed in the gloom, I squirmed and wriggled and gasped for air. The smell almost stopped me from breathing, but I fought to stay conscious, wrestled with myself to keep my eyes peeled.

For what?

Nothing to see but broken teeth and yellow skin. Nothing but bony flesh. I wound my way up to a wall as the wheels began moving. The music cranked on in the distance, and the squealing guitars knifed through the moans that whimpered out of my mouth and out the mouth of every sucker in there. Every now and then, a voice rose up or a fist pounded at the metal – one of the newer captives, I guess, one of the ones I'd seen stumbling on the road. But mostly the fear suffocated the sound out of everyone. It kept us pressed down, muffled in the dark.

What now? I thought. What next?

I shuddered. Broke out cold and sweaty. I was captive. The wagon would rust. And my book would crumble and the bark would fade and every one of Zee's pictures would turn blank like bits and pieces of nothing that ever mattered anyway. And my father would fade, too. Just like a photograph. He'd be killed in the spring and I'd be killed before him and there'd be no one to remember either one of us in the end.

I turned my face to the wall and sobbed. I clutched the nail in my arm and wished only to be numb. There was nowhere further to drop.

But then it was worse.

Because then the truck stopped and the door groaned open a little. "This one with you?" a woman called in at me.

I couldn't turn. Couldn't look at all. I just felt Sal grab a hold of me and hold on tight, the poor little bastard screaming so loud I could barely hear the door clanging shut behind him.

CHAPTER TWENTY

They played the same damn album. Over and over. Cranking up the volume at all the same places until we got wherever it was we were heading.

All I wanted to do was black out. Disappear. But I knew I had to stay awake and pay attention. So that's what I did — eyes closed but my ears pricked. And I counted that album cycle through four times before the truck stopped. So I figured we'd been driving about four hours. And at this speed, off-roading it, I guessed that put the wagon at a day's walk. If you knew the direction.

When the wheels stopped rolling, voices broke out inside the tanker, wobbling and whining, choking on bitter sounds. I tried to picture something safe in my head, something good, and I imagined I was back in the Tripnotyst's memory box and trees were growing all green around me.

Eventually, I heard the squealing of latches, the sound of steel on steel, and my eyes watered as daylight poured in like ice water.

Sal's arms were locked tight around my waist and I pried him off as I slithered to the doorway. I tried to stagger to my feet. But one by one, the pirates appeared. Silhouetted black against the setting sun. I counted their mohawks, their broad shoulders, the hips laden with pouches and guns. There was too many of them. Way too many.

I fell out of the truck and the mud was slimy on my face. Dark and sweet and wet. I let the stuff ooze inside me, tried to breathe it in and scrub the stench of the truck from my mind.

Bodies were stacked around me, on top of me, and I felt hands clutching at me, tapping frantic on my back. Spinning up, I could see it was Sal again, reaching for me. I stared up at the glimmering sky and wiped spit from my mouth, tried to croak some words to the kid, to comfort him.

But no words would come.

Between the two trucks, the pirates had racked up at least a hundred bodies, and god knows where they'd gotten them all.

The ones who couldn't wake or walk were picked up or dragged as the rest of us limped forward, following the pirate who'd caught me, the one who strutted like she was the biggest badass ever seen, her tall rubber boots splashing in the mud.

Alpha. That's what the others called her. And I reckoned that was the word stitched crooked in the back of her fuzzy vest, too.

I took Sal by the hand and led him through the slop, doing my best to stand upright, doing my best to see where in the hell we were going.

The air was as sticky as the mud and it pressed your skin, daring you to breathe it. The sun was low now, puke orange, but the day showed no sign of cooling. And it was still. No wind. No flutter or breeze. So we'd dropped south, I reckoned. Somewhere south of the forty.

Up ahead, an ancient settlement sat on stone stilts above brown water. There were bridges and walkways strewn between flat buildings, everything crumbling and patched with plastic.

The pirates pushed us up a ramp that led over the slime and deep inside the settlement. A rubbery banner frowned over our heads.

"What's it say?" I said, nudging at Sal.

"Old Orleans," he muttered, glancing up at the curly letters. I stared down through the slats and stone, watched the water move like sewage.

It was like being stranded in the devil's own shantytown, the world dissolving below you, leaving you in the refuse of days gone by.

Buried a half mile inside the town was another ramp, but this one led downward. The pirates kicked and prodded us into a watery corral, then they yanked rusty chains to pull the ramp over our heads, blocking out the near darkness of the sky.

I peered around at my fellow prisoners as they splashed and sat and buried their faces. I felt at my arm, the flat end of the nail solid beneath the festering wound.

"What are we gonna do?" Sal whispered. But I just peered up at the walkway, listened as the women went stomping away.

Somewhere in the enclosure a baby began wailing, and the whole world seemed to silence at the sound of it. Then the ramp started to lower again and we scurried from its path. A single pair of boot heels swaggered down the ramp, and I spotted the pink vest and the broken nose, watched as Alpha found the baby and took it in her arms. The infant fell silent as Alpha rocked it upon her hip, hushing and cooing the child and bundling it in rags. Weren't something you'd think would look right. But it did. And her tenderness sure stuck out in a place so ugly and torn.

"You people are safe here," Alpha said, and the whole place froze still. "For now. Some of you will be traded. The rest will be set free."

A murmur rippled through the enclosure, then cut short. I wanted to say something, shout out loud, but all I did was watch as Alpha held the baby close and strode up the ramp away from us, leaving those who could manage it to holler and beg.

Traded. That's what she'd said. Traded like an old world Benjamin or piece of salvage, a jug of water or a gallon of juice. But what was our value? I stared at the filthy bodies surrounding me, the ragged bits of skin in the moonlight.

What good were we to anyone but ourselves?

It made me get to wondering if this was how Pop had been taken. But him and me had been out near Vega, the other side of the cornfields, and pirates don't go messing where GenTech is at. Besides, all the racket they made, I would have heard pirates coming. Whoever stole Pop away had been stealthy. Because Pop had heard voices, but I never heard a damn thing.

I finally gave up standing and sank down in the sludge. Sal slumped beside me, waiting, I'd no doubt, for me to tell him how come we were pinned inside the leftovers of a city, trapped by buildings rooted in mud.

"They'll take him for sure," a raspy voice said behind me, and I spun around to a beady set of eyes. The man's head was smudged silver in the moonlight, his cheeks hammered hollow and thin. "The fat one," the man whispered, staring at me.

"What you talking about?"

"He's young. And there's plenty of him."

"For what?" Sal said in a small voice.

The scrawny dude scrunched up his shoulders. "For whatever they like."

"Shut it," I said, turning away. "Don't you listen to him."

But Sal was already sobbing, his fists squeezed tight.

I felt at my arm where the nail stung and throbbed, and I knew much longer and I'd have to claw the damn thing out with my fingers. At sunrise, I told myself, pulling away from Sal and hunkering down to sleep. I needed to rest, if I could. I couldn't do anything now. Not until the sun came up.

But when the sun came up, I was caught in a sickness, wrapped inside a fever that painted the brown world red.

CHAPTER TWENTY-ONE

I'd not hardly opened my eyes and I was throwing up what little was inside me. My head swirled, and I clutched the mud as if I could stop the earth from moving. I felt hands on me, stroking the hair from my eyes. I was wriggling around and shivering, my skin all thorny and pricked.

"He's burning up," Sal yelled, his voice piercing through the blur.

The pain howled in my arm, and I reached slippery fingers to where the nail had worked its way deep.

Eyes closed. Eyes open. It didn't matter. My guts twitched and I heaved again, and not a single drop squeezed out.

In a different world, I could hear the ramp cranking down amid a stampede of boots and voices. Then the smell of old leather filled me with nausea as hands grappled hold of my shoulders and grabbed at my feet.

"How many more days we got to keep them?" said the woman at my legs, her fingers sharp on my ankles.

"I quit counting," the voice right above me shot back, and the sound vibrated through me as the pirate woman sank my head against her chest. Her breath reeked like smoke she'd swallowed a thousand years prior. "Flip him," she said. "He's gonna lose his lunch."

Lunch.

The word jabbed at me as they turned me facedown and rushed me up the ramp. And I could almost taste burned corn and warm water, feel the breeze atop a finished forest. Me and Pop and a meal fit for kings. My old man trading me kernels so as to double my rations. And if I died now, then there'd be no one to go looking for him. No one to care.

In the distance there was music, a guitar stopping and starting and the sound of women singing. I strained my ears to listen. Blinked my eyes open.

I was stretched on a lumpy cot beneath a corrugated ceiling, little bits of sky poking through the metal, revealing the pink of a sun giving up or a sun coming back.

I shivered. Ran my hands on my tender skin. Naked. I clutched my stomach and it felt swollen and sticky. I tried to raise up my head but a hand eased me back.

"Rest," the girl said.

It was her. Alpha. The one who'd plugged me with the nail in the first place. I struggled against her and felt at my arm. The wound was bandaged now, the skin puffy.

"Pulled it out," Alpha said as I squinted up at her. "Can't have you dying on us."

"Shouldn't have shot me, then," I whispered, feeling a searing pain up the back of my skull.

"You tried to shoot me first, bud. Remember?"

She swabbed a damp cloth at my chest and I tensed as the water dripped and tickled. I remembered how this girl had looked with the baby on her hip — like someone who hadn't had all the sweetness beat out of her. And then the pain came tearing at my eyeballs again, and I blacked out hard and cold.

Went on like this for hours. Rolling back and forth on the cot, coming to, then passing out again. The voices quivering in the distance, singing and laughing. And Alpha returning to bathe me and check on my wound.

The holes in the ceiling became plugged with night, then turned pale with morning. And I didn't think of my pals down in the mud pit. Not even once.

I'd been left alone and was drowsy and spent when the door came open and a new girl came in. She pulled a sheet across me and sat beside me on the cot.

"Alpha tells me you're a tree builder," the girl said. She looked young, and much too small for a pirate.

"Used to be," I muttered, turning away from her. "Lost all my tools."

"I don't think it's the tools that matter. Either you are something or you're not."

I stayed silent.

"Let me see your hands," she said, not giving me much choice in the matter. She studied my fingertips, felt at my palms.

"I want you to build something for us," the girl said, looking satisfied. "To finish something."

I tried to sit up on the cot but was too weak, so I just blinked at her. She was handsome, in a stern sort of way. Her braided hair was blond, and cleaner than it had any right to be in a town so full of filth.

"Who the hell are you?" I said.

"You can call me Jawbone. Though most here call me Captain."

"Thought Alpha was in charge."

"Alpha answers to me."

"You don't look much like a captain."

She smiled, all patient and shit. I started to say something else but she cut me off.

"You should feel honored. Your work will leave quite the legacy." The girl spoke smart, like she'd been schooled or something, not grown up here south of the forty.

"You'll have to excuse me not giving a damn," I said.

"I imagine you give a damn about one thing. Yourself."

"You can imagine all you want."

"If you build for us, then you'll go free."

I stopped cold at that, felt my guard slip.

"Another few days and King Harvest will be here," she went on. "You can be part of our trade with him. Or not."

Build or be traded. Easy enough choice.

"I got a friend, though," I said, surprising myself with the word. "Little fat kid, down in your pit."

"You can take my terms or reject them. But they're not to be altered."

"Then you'd better let me sleep," I told her. "I'll start building once the heat wears down."

"I'm sorry about your friend," the girl said, standing. "I'd like nothing more than to free all of them."

"So why don't you?"

"Because King Harvest requires we meet our quota. One way or another."

CHAPTER TWENTY-TWO

At sunset, I was strong enough to stand, and I took to the walkways with Alpha on one side of me and Jawbone on the other.

We worked our way wordlessly through Old Orleans, pausing only when I needed to rest, my arm still swollen and aching, my whole body drained to its core. I'd lean up on the metal railing and study the strange, dustless sky or examine the foundations of buildings that had once stood tall. The brown water sat stagnant below us, filling the air with a dampness as sour as it was soft.

The pirate women gazed at me as I passed them, some of them winking or smiling, their faces blurring into one. Jawbone walked with her mouth stern and the women gave way as their captain hustled by. But Alpha joked with her compadres, slapping at their outstretched hands.

In the distance, I heard generators growl and the music started again, guitars crashing and drums surging and each one fighting the other for control.

"Here we are," Jawbone said finally. We were right in the middle of the city and on the edge of a clearing, an empty stretch of concrete and mud. And in the middle of that clearing was what they'd brought me to see.

I stopped dead and felt dizzy just trying to take in the sight of it.

It was incredible work. Stunning. Even though the years had caked everything in rust.

A low canopy of copper ferns mingled with cypress. Palm leaves, carved from tin, dangled from crooked spokes. The shortness gave the forest a softness, a sweetness I'd rarely considered, always striving for the biggest, tallest trees, always climbing as high as the scaffold would take me. But the lack of height had another purpose. It served to accentuate what had been built at the center.

I stumbled as I stared up at the unfinished statue. I fell against jagged shrubs, and Alpha grabbed me, pulling me so I could lean against her.

"What do you think?" said Jawbone, peering with me at the rusty masterpiece.

I didn't know what to say, and I didn't say anything.

"Can you finish it?" Alpha asked.

I nodded.

I could finish it. Or at least I would try. Because there, in the middle of the forest, rising up a hundred feet high, was something prettier than any tree I'd ever seen. A statue of a woman with arms spread wide and one leg lifted like she was dancing. And not just any woman, either. I knew it even though the head was unfinished and the hair was missing. I knew it deep down in my bones.

The statue was the tattoo woman. Zee's mother.

Frost's wife.

Whoever had built the statue had got the proportions perfect, not selling her short by making the boobs too big or the legs more curvy.

They'd been true to the slope of her shoulders, the delicate way she held up her neck. But what really got me, what blew me away, was how they'd captured the tree.

They'd built a separate installation for it, then woven one statue with the other, bending the steel branches so they gripped the woman's waist, the leaves hanging loose so they'd turn in the breeze, shimmering where all else was rust. I studied their texture.

Brass. Of course.

Thin and shiny and perfect. And I knew I'd have never thought of brass. Not in a million years.

"Used to light up," Alpha said. "Switch different colors, till the wiring got messed."

"Where'd it come from?" I pushed myself forward.

"Came from right here," said Jawbone. "We had a craftsman. An artist. This was before I was born. Back when the pirates were still united. When we fought as the Army of the Fallen Sun."

"And this army had a tree builder?"

"He built the forest here, some others we lost in the lowlands. Swamps, people would have called them. Once upon a time."

"But what about the woman?"

"She was found not far from here, down near the South Wall. Our women say she came from the Other Side."

"You ever seen the Wall?" Alpha said, and I nodded, picturing the memory screen. "Then you know that's impossible."

"Myth. Legend." Jawbone waved her hand in the air. "The story goes that she was beautiful and the tattoo she wore was more beautiful, still. Our tree builder fell in love with her, began building this to honor her. And I like to think, to honor all women. Just as he'd honored life through his building of trees."

"But he didn't finish?"

"No. He and his muse vanished. Just before the city was destroyed by the Purple Hand."

"GenTech?"

"It was the end of our resistance. And that's where the story ends. Until you. Finish the statue, and you're free to leave the city."

I stared up at the curves of the woman and the steel limbs of the tree. "What else do you know about the tattoo she wore?"

"There were numbers on it," Alpha said, and Jawbone rolled her eyes. "They say if you could play those numbers in Vega, you'd strike it rich."

I watched the tarnished brass leaves turning. I'd never heard about pirates fighting GenTech. Never thought anyone but the Soljahs had tried to make a stand. It made me wonder what else might be buried out here beneath the plains. What battles had raged on the mud? What cities had sunk under the sand?

"Okay," I said. "I'll work at night. Right through till the sun gets hot. I'll need a scaffold, though. And my tools. Every bit of scrap you got. You got spare hands, I can use them. Wire can clean the rust right off that metal, and you should keep at it long after I'm gone." People think you just build up some trees and you got yourself a forest. But you got to tend it. Just like everything else.

"Alpha will help you any way you need. I'll send others as necessary." Jawbone extended her little hand and I shook it.

"Your lucky day," Alpha said, nudging my ribs as Jawbone slipped away. Then Alpha handed me the nail gun, fixed me with a grin. "Best be careful, though," she said. "Don't want that luck running out."

"What was the name of the woman?" I said, still staring up at the statue. "The woman from the South Wall?"

"Hina," Alpha said. "That's what we call her, anyway."

"Hina," I said to myself, like I was trying to see if it fit. And now she wasn't just someone's mother or somebody's wife, a map or a statue.

Now she was someone with a name.

CHAPTER TWENTY-THREE

I left the face blank. Only not. I figured if I was building something for all women, then I should somehow try to reflect each one of them. And that's what I did. I broke glass and mirrors into pieces the size of my hand, then glued those chunks all across the metal sheets I'd beaten to the shape of her cheekbones and the fullness of her lips. I put the shiniest blocks in diamond patterns where her eyes should've been and I cast her gaze downward as I soldered the face to the frame my predecessor had left behind.

I worked through till sunrise and left the head coated in a plastic tarp, exhausted as I slipped down the side of the scaffold that Alpha and me had set the evening before.

At the bottom of the final ladder, Alpha was stretched on her back, staring up at the statue. She spread her arms and moved her legs, mimicking Hina's pose as I dropped from the scaffold. I ran my fingers at the wound on my arm. Seemed like this pirate girl could act more like a girl or more like a pirate. And I reckoned the girl was a whole lot more to my liking.

"How's it coming up there?" she said, eyeing me.

"What do you think?"

"I think we got ourselves a real tree builder, that's what I think."

I stared at her as she stared at the statue. And for a moment, I wondered what she'd do if I was to try running right then. I'd not get far, I reckoned. Even if I could make it to the city walls, there was no way I'd get over.

"You born in this city?" I said, collapsing onto the dirt beside her. She rolled over so she was looking at me, and I studied her eyes for the first time. Before I'd been sort of blinded by the mohawk or the way that she moved, but her eyes were golden and brown and real pretty, too. Like sunlight on a muddy river.

"What's it to you, bud?" Alpha said, and I'd nearly forgot I'd asked her a question. Hell, I was still gazing into her eyes like a damn fool.

"Just wondered if you're a local girl."

"Why? Where are you from?"

"Nowhere," I told her. "Nowhere at all."

That day I hardly slept worth a damn. I kept waking to the strange sounds of the city, wanting to head back to the forest but then drowsing off again. Slipping in and out of dreams like I was waiting for something. And I reckon I was waiting on Alpha to come get me. But Alpha never showed.

At sunset, I made my way outside, figuring a route that put me right above the mud pit. With the ramp raised up, you could hardly see the bodies twisted below, but I squatted on the walkway, checked to make sure I was alone, and then stared down at the squirming rags.

"Sal," I hissed, peering under the railing. "It's Banyan."

A face glanced up from the shadows. The scrawny dude I'd spoken with before. "Got better, did you?" he called.

"You seen my buddy? The fat kid?"

I heard Sal calling, scrabbling into view. "Banyan," he yelled. "Banyan."

"Right here, kid."

"What are you doing?"

"Getting free."

His face turned red and tight and he clenched his fist at me. "What about me?" he screamed, and I stood to make sure no one was paying attention to his ruckus.

"Keep your voice down," I hissed. "Someone'll come."

"Don't you forget about me," he yelled as I sauntered away, and I could hear him calling after me. "Don't you forget, tree boy. I got the number. The number you need."

When I reached the forest, I got caught up in my tracks again. In patches, the trees were still rusty. But many were now sparkling in the dusk.

I watched the women working at the leaves and branches, scraping with wire and steel wool, just as I'd said. Alpha hooted and whooped at the sight of me.

"You like it?" she called, her whole body coated in sweat. And the forest looked great, but I tell you, that girl looked even better. She strutted and shook on the scaffold, her body like a smokeless fire. Her skin slippery and gold.

A pirate with green hair said something to Alpha that made all the women bust out laughing, and they kept staring at me as I pretended to be busy, checking their work. My face burned up red as they watched me. And that just made them laugh even more.

Ahead of me, Jawbone dropped from the scaffold where she'd been working at Hina's thigh.

"Hell of a job," I told her as she came toward me.

"Yeah," she said, smiling. "You, too."

That night, I got all the rebar curved how I wanted and then welded it together just right. Way I did it, the hair was shorter than Hina wore it, but it'd work better that way, putting the focus more on her face.

I worked with Alpha beside me. She was good with the blowtorch, and the sparks shone in her eyes as the soot stained our skin. We welded till the sun was too high and then rolled back into the city, swelled by that good kind of tired when your body's been worked to the bone.

"So you build a statue," Alpha said, as I knelt to drink from a rusty pipe. "And then you never see it again."

I splashed the dirty water on my face, the back of my neck. It was still early and the streets were empty.

"Me seeing them ain't what's important," I said. "Just so long as somebody can."

"And you make enough to keep drifting, one place to the next?"

"Better than robbing folk blind and hauling them off the forty."

Alpha knelt beside me, cupped her hands under the pipe. "It's called surviving, bud."

"Gotta believe in more than that."

She rubbed water over her arms, smeared the soot off her legs. "Like what?"

"Like what you leave behind." I pointed back toward the forest. "The statues, they're like stories. They keep things from getting forgot."

"You believe what the Rastas say? That there's still a place where real things grow?"

"I don't know. They say it's over the ocean. And I've seen the Surge." I nearly felt bad for lying to her. For not telling her there were trees growing someplace. Trees people were fighting to find.

"So you like statues and stories," Alpha said, making to stand. "What about old world songs?"

"Never had much in the way of music. Though I guess I never had many stories, either."

"That's what you get for just drifting." She grinned. "Come on. You better stick with me."

I scrambled up, and we started along a broken path. And as I followed behind her, I felt like I was being tugged toward something. Like how the needle on a compass points north.

In a far corner of the city, we reached a crooked stone building, and the dirty flag raised above it showed a falling yellow sun. Alpha banged at the door, then pushed it open, leading me inside.

"Captain?" she hollered into the silence. "You here?"

There was no answer. We were alone, out of the sunlight.

And we were surrounded by hundreds of books.

I stared around at the walls, the shelves full of pages and dust. All that paper. All those words.

A plastic desk sat in the middle of the room, and in the corner there was an old bathtub full of CDs. Piles of books had been stacked like towers across the floor. It was beautiful. Cluttered and sealed off from the world. My old man would have loved it.

"Where'd you get these?" I said, rushing to the shelves and running my hands along the soft covers, the cardboard spines.

"They were passed down to Jawbone," Alpha said. "Along with the right to read 'em. I'm not even supposed to come in here. But she's a good one, the Captain. Reads to us all the time."

"Yeah?" I grabbed a book and started thumbing at the pages. "You heard Lewis and Clark?"

"Don't think so." Alpha stared at the book in my hands. "You can read?"

"My dad used to."

"Where's he at now?"

I stayed quiet. I felt sort of pissed for bringing it up at all. It was none of this girl's business. And even if the books had blown me away, wasn't this just a waste of my time?

"Said you were heading to Vega," she said.

"I am." I slammed the book back on the shelf. "Once I get the hell out of here."

"Don't worry, bud. I'll help you finish it. Soon as the sun goes down." She came over and straightened up the shelf beside me.

"You could let me run now. If you wanted. You could show me which way to go."

"What's the rush? You got a girl waiting?" She said it half like she was joking.

"Ain't got no girl, damn it. It's my old man. He's in all kinds of trouble."

"Then I tell you what, you finish the statue like the Captain wants, and I'll drive you back to the forty. First chance we get."

"You would?"

"Sure." Alpha leaned against the shelves and studied me. "Most folk are just busy trying to keep alive. Seems like you're different, bud."

"Thought you were just about survival."

"I thought you said there's something more."

It was like she wanted to believe it. Or she wanted to believe in me, maybe. I picked up a book and glared at the cover, my brain all jumbled and fried.

"I know how it feels," Alpha said, her voice soft. "My mom raised me here and left me here and I used to wish for a whole lot different."

"And now what?"

"I quit wishing, that's all. There's folk who think the pirates are gonna come back together. Bring down the Purple Hand. But that's just dreaming. I had a baby sister, and I used to whisper her promises and they all ended up lies."

Girl made my dizzy. First she'd shot me, then she'd healed me. And now she was going to tell me the things that lay heavy upon her?

"Hard to be alone already," she said. "Ain't it?"

I looked into her brown eyes like she might blink me inside them. And the room seemed to turn for a moment, as if the world was trying to spin me toward her.

"I ain't alone," I said, losing my balance and knocking over a stack of books on the floor. "Not as long as my old man's alive."

I was exhausted all of a sudden, and I sank to the ground.

"What's he like?" Alpha said, sitting beside me.

"He's smart. Real smart. And he can be funny as hell."

I wanted to say more, but I remembered the night Pop got taken. I pictured myself shut inside the wagon as the dust storm raged, strangers creeping around outside. I'd been frightened. Too frightened. And I'd just stayed in the wagon, safe, waiting on Pop to come back.

I put my head in my hands.

"I gotta finish that statue," I whispered.

"Then you'd better go get some rest."

She was right. Outside the sun was too high and too hot, and I let Alpha guide me back to the shack. She left me alone, and I sprawled on the cot. But my mind worked too fast to quit.

I kept picturing myself in that room full of stories, surrounded by the beautiful books. And where was my old man? Trapped and alone somewhere. No books. No pretty girls to make eyes at. Did he even remember the future we'd mapped out together? The forest we were going to build of our own? I imagined us in a house with ragged tin walls, surrounded by cast-iron branches and leaves we'd change in the fall and the spring.

Usually spring comes before the killing. That's what the old Rasta had said. And now those words just stuck to my brain.

Murderers, the old Rasta had told me.

Murderers, the lot of them.

I headed back to the forest before the sun even started to drop. Told myself I had to stay strong. Had to keep my head in the game. Had to finish that statue, get Sal, and then get us to Vega and find that damn GPS.

It was near dawn by the time I'd wrapped the finishing touches. Alpha was working below, and the sun had just started to blur the horizon, painting the eastern edge of the earth with a smear. I watched the pink embers grow and hover, the sun bubbling up.

"Here it comes," I yelled down. And I drew the tarp back from the face that was now cloaked in iron threads, watching as Alpha studied her thousand reflections in the splintered rays of dawn.

She pulled herself up the ladders and scaffold, moving effortless and alive. And when she reached the top, I could smell the taste of her sweat mixed with leather and steel.

"Can I touch it?" she said.

"Go ahead."

She ran her fingers over Hina's glittering face and tapped each one of her reflections, laughing when she glimpsed me behind her.

"It's incredible," she said.

"I like seeing you in it." It was like the words got spoke before I'd thought them. Like my mouth had played a trick on my brain.

"That so?" Alpha turned to face me.

My skin prickled, being right up close to her. My bones felt heavy and loose. And my mind started racing and my heart beat fast, hard to know which was quicker.

"So," she said. "You're done."

"I reckon."

"You reckon." It was like she was bitter about something. I started to speak, but she cut back in. "Relax, bud. I'll get you back to the road and you can keep on drifting."

"I ain't drifting," I shot back at her. "I got a father to find."

Alpha laughed again, but her laugh had lost its juice. She went and sat on the edge of the scaffold and peeled off her boots, dangling her feet over the top of the forest. And I stood where she'd left me, staring down at where the ferns gave way to the crumbled old streets.

"So you're always gonna live here?" I said. "In Old Orleans?"

"There's worse places."

"You seen 'em?"

"Not unless they're between here and the forty."

"So you never really been anywhere."

"Where else is there to go?" She said it like she was all done talking, but I thought about the sprawl and the Surge and the endless miles of dirt between them. And I thought about the electric lights, the skyline of Vega, like concrete mountains all sparkled and bright. And above it all, just the steam rolling down and the ash blowing off the lava that pours out of the Rift.

"Niagara's worth seeing," I said. "The Soljahs got a whole city built behind waterfalls. It's something to look at, anyway. Though with the water crashing, you can't hardly hear yourself think."

For a moment, I thought about telling Alpha about the trees and Pop and the old Rasta with the bark in his skin. The GPS numbers and the Promised Land. But how could I trust her? I reckoned she'd be loyal to that captain of hers, and there wasn't room in this for an army of pirates. And besides, I didn't want to become just Alpha's ticket to something. She'd offered to help me out, get me back to my wagon. And it had been since Pop had been taken that I'd seen a helping hand.

"So what happened to your sister?" I said, sitting down next to her, trying to get her to look at me.

Alpha let the question hang for a moment. "Starved."

"Shit."

"She'd barely started walking."

"You couldn't get her nothing to eat?"

"It weren't that. Corn made her throat swell tight. Once my mom was gone, there wasn't a thing I could do."

"So it weren't your fault."

"Don't make it easier."

"My mother starved," I said, not knowing what else to say. "I was just a nipper. Our wagon broke on the Thousand Mile Road, and my dad was gone too long trying to scavenge up parts. Said he staggered back to find my momma starved to death and me just barely breathing. And sometimes I think about what she must have done. Giving herself up so I could keep hanging on. Gotta be that's the worst way to go."

"All the ways are the worst way," Alpha said, and it's probably true.

I waited for her to say something else, shoot me a glance. But she just stared down at her toes and the treetops, her face glum.

I watched the sun come higher. I turned to the west where the world was still black and shadowed. But then I froze. Because there, creeping out of the edges of night, was the biggest damn vehicle I'd ever seen.

It was like a city on wheels. Trundling toward Old Orleans on tires that looked too big to ever be in a rush.

"What the hell is that?" I whispered, standing.

"Looks like you're staying another day." Alpha knelt alongside me. "Can't be out on the plains when they're prowling. They'll be here by nightfall, though. Every year, son of a bitch is right on time."

"Who?"

"Who do you think? King Harvest. Ready for the trade."

"What is it you trade him for?"

"Our freedom," she said. "Give him enough bodies so he won't take our own."

CHAPTER TWENTY-FOUR

I knew it was a day of endings, one way or another. The sun already seemed too high, like it was arcing too fast. And there was not a damn thing I could do about it. By nightfall, King Harvest would be at Old Orleans, and I had till then to rescue Sal, or there'd be no knowing the right place to go. No way to find Pop.

I followed Alpha off the scaffold, unbolting and tearing apart our metal tower as we descended, my work finished. Almost.

"You said she used to light up," I said.

"Used to."

"Then I better see if I can wire her right again."

Alpha set to scrubbing the shine back to a mess of ferns, and I laid fresh cable through the undergrowth, running it from an old generator to the base of the statue. Hina's foot was arched up with the heel high, and you could access the inside by crawling up through the ball of the foot. I grabbed wire and tape and my headlamp, scooting myself inside the metal and searching for circuits to patch.

I pulled myself up, tracing the curve of her calf, the straight line of shin, running new wire where she needed it, taping her electrics back together like they were veins in her skin.

As I climbed through the statue, swinging between her hips and crawling down along her dancing leg, following the tunnel through her outstretched arms and working my way up where her brain would be, I came to know the work in a whole new way — seeing the statue from the perspective of the creator, learning the steps by which she'd been built. The seams and the joint work, the weld marks and support beams.

And there was something routine about being inside that statue. Something familiar about it. Every builder has their own way of bending the rules, each takes their own risk with their rhythm. And I knew the work I was studying. I knew the caution, the passion and style.

Of course I knew it.

I'd seen it mirrored in my own building. Reflected in every tree I'd ever built.

And as I lowered myself down, descending the thigh and dropping to the ground, I was sure of it. Sure as you can be about anything.

The statue could only be the work of one builder.

And that builder had been my old man.

When I crawled back out into the forest, I felt like my blood had drained out and grown thick in my shoes. I stared up at the sky but the sun was gone, disappeared behind a layer of gray that billowed and curled and smudged the world with its fingers.

"Rain clouds," Alpha said, watching me. "We should head back."

"What all do you know about the guy who built her?" I said, when I could speak again. I tried packing my tools with my hands all shaky and weak, but then I gave up and left the tools piled at the base of the statue.

"Some people say he took her to Vega," said Alpha. "To play those numbers and strike it rich."

"He didn't care about striking it rich."

"How the hell would you know?"

"Just a feeling," I muttered, avoiding Alpha's eyes. "I mean, you love something like that and you're already rich." I pointed up at the statue.

Alpha watched her reflection bounce and shatter in Hina's face. "Guess it's like the Captain says. Just a myth. A story."

"A story that keeps things from getting forgot."

"Just all about remembering, ain't you?"

"Only the things that matter."

"You gonna remember me?" Alpha said, her eyes still fixed on the statue. But before I could say anything, she spun around and started walking. "Come on, let's go back. You look like shit."

"No, wait. You gotta see something."

The storm clouds had bunched up enough to mimic twilight, and on the far edge of the forest I cranked the generator and flipped the breakers on.

Small lights blinked on the branches, and for a second Hina stayed colorless in the half-light. But then she broke free. Purple. Blues and reds. She held each shade for a moment before switching to the next one. She became green and yellow, then gold and pink. And the brass leaves bounced the colors back at her, bringing the whole forest to life.

As the rain began to fall, Alpha turned her face to the heavens and sang out with laughter, stretching her arms to the sky.

"It's so beautiful," she cried, her voice just like music, all the sour notes drained out and washing away.

And it was beautiful. More beautiful than anything had a right to be in this crummy old shell of a world. The statue was finished, and the finishing was a beginning. And I knew it was by far the greatest work Pop and I had ever done.

CHAPTER TWENTY-FIVE

We ran back along the walkways as the thunder cracked and the rain beat our skin. I sensed lightning and felt it flash, but I kept my eyes on Alpha's pink vest before me, slicked flat now, sopping like everything else.

We found the shack and burst inside, and Alpha locked the door behind us as the rain hammered upon the roof. There were drips and leaks and the cot was damp, but she climbed upon it, her mohawk tied back in a slippery tail.

I fell beside her and lay watching the back of her neck and the backs of her legs, and hoping she'd roll over and face me.

"What are you doing?" she said, her back still turned.

"Just looking at you."

"Don't get any ideas. I just wanted to get out of the rain."

"Sure you did."

She rolled around to look at me. "It ain't happening."

"Why not?"

"'Cause you're leaving." She shut her eyes and turned away.

But that just made me want her even more. I wanted to touch her and feel her against me. I wanted her above and below me, my arms wrapped around her. I wanted to lose myself for as long as I'd stay gone. But I knew I had to keep focused. I needed Alpha to take me north, soon as the trade was over. And I still had to figure out how to get Sal out of the mud pit. I needed that coordinate if I was going to find my father. I had to rescue the fat kid before he got traded away.

Got hard to concentrate, though. Lying beside that girl's rubber and curves and the sound of her breathing. It was like my whole body was soaking up what hers was pushing out. But my eyes finally shut. And then all the wanting got stolen by sleep.

I woke to the sound of a fist pounding the door to the shack, and I sat up with my brain spinning. The whole shack rattled as the door bounced, but Alpha was still sleeping. She'd curled up close to me and I just sat there, staring at a little scar hooked on the side of her forehead, wishing to hell whoever was at the door would just go on away.

The fist thumped louder.

"Hang on," I yelled, getting up.

"I don't need you," Jawbone spat when I'd cracked the door open. She leaned into the shack and pointed at the cot. "I need her."

If anything, the rain was coming harder now, but Jawbone didn't seem to notice as she led us along the walkways to the edge of the city, stomping her stiff little legs through the puddles and sludge.

I cupped my hands full of water and blew my nose in it. One thing about rain like that, it clears you right out, blasts all the dust off you until you never felt so clean. But my clothes were heavy and chafing as I trudged along, wondering where in the hell we were in such a rush to get.

Then I saw it.

I saw it before we'd even reached the outer walls of the city. The tip of that huge vehicle I'd watched rumble out of the night. There it was, towering above us.

It was as much steel as I'd ever seen in one place. Hard to even imagine it moving, now that I could see it up close. It seemed bigger than Old Orleans itself.

Strange lettering marked the side of the hull, and I pointed to it. "What's it say?" I yelled above the sound of the storm.

"The Ark," Jawbone called back, her face solemn. "It's what Harvest calls his slave ship."

I couldn't understand why the transport had come so close to the city, practically leaning on the crumbling walls like it might break them once and for all.

"They're supposed to wait a half mile from here." Jawbone pointed. "Out on the mud flats is where we hand the people over."

"Maybe it's the rain," I offered. "Maybe they don't want everyone getting wet."

She glowered at me. "If your work's done, tree builder, then you're free to go."

"I reckon," I said. Beneath us, the brown water was rising as the rain bounced upon it. I had to get Sal out of that pit. And soon. "Just thought I'd stay through the trade."

Jawbone shook her head. "Not part of the deal. You should cut out while you still can."

"He can't leave in this," Alpha said, pointing as the storm clouds sank and swelled.

Thunder rolled in the distance, farther now, sparking up some lightning before fading away and leaving nothing but the downpour. The huge transport just sat cold and silent. As if it were empty. Or chock-full of ghosts.

We scrambled up the city walls so we were level with the deck of the ship and about twenty feet from the guardrail that ran its length. At the far end of the deck rose a cockpit, black with windows and crowned with guns. The weaponry dwarfed any I'd seen. Made the pirate trucks look like toys. We stood there, waiting on someone to show.

Until finally somebody did.

Took me all of two seconds to place him. The smooth white skin and jagged bones.

It was the man from the Rasta's vision, the floating face from the Tripnotyst's screen.

The King, the old Rasta had called him. The King.

CHAPTER TWENTY-SIX

"That's him?" I said. "Harvest?"

"That's him," Alpha muttered, hands on her hips.

Jawbone just stood with her arms crossed and the face of someone ready to cut any deal she needed. Something about her eyes told me she'd spent a long time counting on the worst that could happen.

"It's good to see you again, Captain." The man strolled up to the edge of the deck and leaned against the guardrail as if he was just checking out the view. He wore a gray plastic jacket with the hood left down, and water dribbled all over him. Like he was made out of rain.

"Is it?" Jawbone called back.

"But of course." The man spoke all fancy, like a rich freak from Vega. "A year is far too long to go without seeing something as charming as you lovely ladies."

Jawbone leaned and spat in the rain. "Then what's taken you so long to get out here?"

"Running numbers, my dear. Calculating how many we still need." He gestured down at the hull. "And how much space we still have."

"Been busy, have you?" It was Alpha who spoke.

"Yes." He gave a wink. "It's been quite the season. I'm sad to see it come to an end. But who's your young friend? Someone ready to be traded?"

I returned the man's stare. If this face had been in the Rasta's vision, then it had something to do with where the Rasta had been taken. And that meant Harvest had something to do with my father being chained to those trees.

"This is our tree builder," Jawbone said. "And he's not for sale."

"My dear, everyone's for sale." The pale man chuckled. "But if he's been working in your forest, then you must have him come aboard. I've something I imagine he'd very much like to see."

I felt Alpha go tense beside me.

"Come, my young Captain," King Harvest called, stretching out his hands, rain bouncing on his fingers. "We've much to talk about."

"Lower the plank," said Jawbone.

"No," Alpha whispered. "I don't like it."

"Don't worry," Jawbone said. "Your boyfriend's coming with me."

"You don't have to," Alpha said, turning to me.

"Yeah I do."

"Why?"

"I think that man took my father."

"Join the club," she said. "He took my mother. Ten years to the day."

I followed Jawbone across the warped metal plank, our feet slipping in the rain. "What does he do with them?" I said, muffling my mouth close behind her. "With his slaves?"

"Turns a profit, I suppose." Jawbone shrugged. "What else?"

Harvest was still alone when we reached the deck, and he made a big deal of smiling and shaking our hands. "Come, come," he said, gesturing across to the cockpit. "Let's get you out of the rain."

I stomped across the giant puddled platform, glancing back at where Alpha was still stood on the wall of the city. But she seemed so far already. Out of reach.

Inside the cockpit, you could barely hear the storm, the roar of water silenced to a hush. The room was full of plastic charts and gadgets, lights blinking on control panels. Whatever the guy was doing, he was squeezing some serious cash.

"Superfood?" Harvest said, showing us a steaming bowl of popcorn. I took a handful and munched on it, staring around the cockpit and wondering where Harvest had hidden his crew.

"So where do you head next?" I asked, but he ignored me.

"Come along," he said. "This way." He led us deeper into the transport, winding down dim corridors until we reached the top of a ladder that went nowhere but down.

"What are we doing here?" Jawbone snapped, her voice echoing along the tunnel.

"Bear with me," he said. "There's something I want you to see."

We descended the ladder, down into the vast hull of the transport, where the walls had been smeared in green phosphorescent, the insides of the ship painted in an oozing glow. And as we got lower, I began to hear voices. Muted at first, then growing spiky and loud as we sank deeper among them.

The ladder ended on another steel walkway. But this one was surrounded by cells.

Jawbone stood close to me, her arms tight and her face showing the first strains of fear. Guess she didn't like being on this side of the slaving business.

People were pressed at the bars and groping at us, fingers scratching in the air. The moans and wails reminded me of being in the back of the pirate truck. The smell, too. I studied the thin faces between the steel bars, the dirty hair and blank eyes. I thought about the Rasta, his skin spliced with bark. And I wondered if my old man had once been stuck down here somewhere.

Was this it? The boat across the ocean? Didn't look much like a passage to the Promised Land. Looked about as far from the Promised Land as you could get.

"I don't believe you've ever seen the holding level." Harvest grinned at Jawbone, his pale skin stained green by the phosphorescence. "And yet you've sentenced so many to its depths."

"Show us what you want us to see," I said.

"Oh, yes, tree builder. With pleasure."

We walked narrow and hunched, avoiding the grip of the fingers that stretched through the bars toward us. And I practically slumped into Harvest when he pulled up short at a cell door.

"Here we are," he said, working a combination lock till the door pinged free. I stood in the doorway, studying the faces that hung suspended in the dark.

Then I leaned into the cell, shuffling forward, hardly believing my eyes.

"Banyan," a voice called. "Banyan?"

I rushed forward and all of a sudden Zee was embracing me, her body reeking of piss and metal, her eyes wet against my cheek.

“Someone you know, builder?” Harvest called from the doorway. “How touching.”

“Who is it?” said Jawbone. She came up behind me. “Banyan, what’s going on?”

“And there was me thinking it’s the other one you’d want. The one like the statue. The one with the tree.” Harvest cranked on a flashlight and scoured the cell with it, illuminating the sorry pieces of flesh, one body at a time.

I spotted her in the corner. Bundled in filthy rags and all the sparkles plucked from her hair and skin. She raised her face up to meet the torch beam, and it looked to me like Hina had fallen from everything that statue had come to mean.

“It is her, isn’t it?” Jawbone whispered. She could still see it, I guess. Beneath the filth, the grace still present. That same poise that danced above the forest, a hundred footsteps high.

“Harvest,” I called, turning to face him. “These women should come with us now. Part of the trade.”

Harvest just laughed. A drawn, cruel sound. Not a drop of humor in it. “Trade?” the man said, sealing the cell door shut behind us. “What trade?”

“Wait.” Jawbone spun and clutched at the bars. “What the hell are you doing?” she yelled. “Let us out.”

“Sorry, Captain,” Harvest said, shaking his head like he really meant it. “Time’s up. Last orders. I’m cashing my chips in. All of them. I’ll be taking everything.” He bared his teeth, smiling in the dark. “And everyone.”

CHAPTER TWENTY-SEVEN

Jawbone stood at the cell door, fingers clamped on the bars like she might snap them in two. I watched her through the murk, studied the straight edge of her back, the blond hair matted tight on her skull. And I knew there was not an ounce in her that could give up. It was killing her, I reckoned. Her people were in danger and there was not a damn thing she could do about it.

Zee was still trembling against me. Hina still cowered at the wall. Footsteps echoed down the walkway as Harvest disappeared, but then all trace of the man was gone, swallowed by the moan of the prisoners and the coughs of despair.

"I thought you were dead," Zee whispered against me. Her chest was wheezing worse than ever. "They said they killed you. In the tent."

"Where's Crow?" I asked her. "Frost?"

"Crow's here, I think. Somewhere. Frost bartered us all away."

"He traded you up?"

"We'd just reached the corn. I tried to run. Into the fields." She punched at her chest as she started coughing.

"Where's Harvest taking you?"

"We don't know," Zee said, her voice cracking.

"He's taking them to be sold," Jawbone said from her vigil at the cell door. "It doesn't matter where."

"Did you go back to the house?" Zee said through the tight sound in her chest.

"Yeah. I went back there."

"I told Sal I'd take care of him."

"He's here."

"He's okay?"

"Not for long." I peered back at Zee's mother again. The woman my father had loved. I had questions for her. But no time now to ask them.

"Banyan," Zee whispered. "I heard they run a meat trade. In the Electric City."

"Yeah," I said. "I heard it."

These folk were too scrawny, I told myself. But then I reckoned they could be fattened up if they got stuffed full of Superfood. Didn't make sense with what the Rasta had told me – the trees, the boat across the ocean. But none of that made much sense, either.

I pulled myself loose of Zee but she followed me to the cell door. "What do you think his next move is?" I said to Jawbone.

"Depends how big his army is."

"So what's the plan?"

She smiled a little, her eyes gleaming in the dull green light. "The plan's the same as it's always been," she said. "Since old Harvest parked his ship too close to my city."

Jawbone pulled off her soggy boots and plucked a string of wires from inside them, spilling her wares across the floor.

Explosives. Whole reel of them.

"Hope you're ready for a fight, tree builder," Jawbone said, staring at me. "We're going to gut the bastard from the inside out."

Zee gathered up the rest of the people in the cell, shuffling them tight to the far wall as I helped Jawbone set a small pack of plastics on the door.

"You know how big this'll blow?" I asked, watching her hands working a short fuse, her fingers full of fury.

"Big enough," she said. "The rest we slap on a live fuel line. Then I suggest you get above deck, fast as your friends can move."

"What about the other folk? The rest of the prisoners?"

"You want to waste time down here, go ahead. I'll be trying to save the rest of my people. Alpha included." She let her eyes linger on me a moment longer, watching to see what I was going to do. But there was no way she could read me. Because I had no idea my damn self.

Jawbone reached down the front of her pants and retrieved a gold lighter. She flicked the thing open and waved it at the fuse.

"Ready?"

I backed up. Stumbled and fell. Then I rolled over and leapt to the back wall, the crazy girl with the bombs coming right on behind me.

I heard the blast an instant before I felt it. And when I did feel it, the shock wave lifted me off my feet and hurled me at the wall. I crashed into steel. Choked on smoke. The heat scorched my throat and I crouched there with my eyes watering.

I staggered up and bent forward as the smoke lifted. I screamed for Jawbone. But she was already gone.

• • •

Out on the walkway I peered through the patches of smoke, panic setting in as I realized I'd no idea which direction Jawbone had headed. I called her name again, loud as I could, but other voices had risen up now, and the screams all joined together.

I sprinted back into the cell, grabbing Zee and her mother, suddenly furious with their lack of speed. But then I saw Zee's face. She was choking up, and each time she coughed a little splatter of blood sprayed on her hands and dripped down her chin.

"Listen," I said, trying to get her to breathe. "They got this room full of books in this city. We get out of here and you can just sit there and read each one." She blinked at me, wiping the blood off her fingers.

"Makes you feel better," I said. "Remember?"

I turned to Hina. "You gotta run." I pointed in the direction Harvest had disappeared. "At the end of the walkway there's a ladder. Go up. Far as you can."

"What are you going to do?" Zee said, her mother pushing her forward.

"I'll be right behind you," I lied. "Start running."

I watched them for a moment. Then I turned and bolted down the corridor, heading deeper into the hull.

I slammed at the cell doors as I ran alongside them. But it was useless, each one was padlocked shut. My best guess of our location made me figure any sort of fuel lines would be at this end of the transport. And I knew if I thought the juice was this way, then Jawbone would be betting the same thing.

I'd no idea what I'd do if I caught her. No plan. No options left.

But there had to be a better way. A better answer than letting all these lost souls disintegrate in the bowels of this horrible ship.

Hands reached through the bars at me, swiping and clutching. Voices begged me to stop.

"Jawbone," I screamed, like the name had torn its way outside me. And for a moment I saw her. But then she was just blowing right through me, sprinting back down the walkway as I sprawled on the floor.

She turned and called back, never losing her pace. "It's too late," she yelled. "I found a hot spot. Run with me."

"Better do what the lady tells you, little man."

I spun around at the voice. Crow's voice.

He reached through the bars and gripped my neck in his hand, dragging me to my feet and pulling me close.

I stared into the cell and the whites of his eyes. I studied his beard, his dreads, limp now, all matted with filth.

Crow grinned his glittery teeth through the blackness. "You get out of here, little man, you catch up to Frost, you say hello to him for me."

I nodded, the watcher's hand warm and rough, squeezing my windpipe. Then he let go and my feet dropped back to the floor.

"I and I be seeing you," Crow said. "In the next one."

I scrambled down the corridor and away from him. Not ever once turning back.

When the first charge blew, it made a broken sound. A crack, then a boom. I was almost at the damn ladder, had almost made it. I felt the heat as I slid forward, and I watched the fireball tear down the tunnel behind me like it was being sucked through a straw.

The flames rolled like the sun, and I tugged at the low rung of the ladder, heaving myself up as the air itself seemed to melt.

I crawled into the pipe as the fire surged and ruptured, the force of it pushing me higher, propelling me up, burning the soles off my shoes.

Top of the ladder, I rolled onto the walkway. Black and smoking. Flames spiraled through the darkness as I leapt to my feet.

I kicked off my melted shoes as I sprinted back into the cockpit, and right away I could see through the window why the ship had seemed so empty of crew.

They were out there. All of them. An army, like Jawbone had said. An army of gray men in gray plastic jackets. And each one of those men looked exactly same. Even from a distance, I could see it. Their faces as identical as the clothes they wore. The same hairless skull. An army of copies. A thousand King Harvests.

They were crawling over Old Orleans, rounding up pirates or mowing them down. It was a war zone. Chaos. And there in the cockpit was Zee and Hina. Waiting on me.

But Jawbone was straddling the control panel with a gun in her hand. And pinned beneath her was Harvest himself. The one man who might hold all the answers. The one man who knew where the slave ship was bound.

CHAPTER TWENTY-EIGHT

Jawbone fired before I could even holler. Before I could do any damn thing at all. She had the pistol rammed under Harvest's chin, and the bullet splattered bits of his brain across the sparkle of the control panel, his blood spraying at the monitors and levers and knobs.

Someone was screaming and I realized it was my own voice, the sound rising out of me with no warning.

Jawbone stared at me, brushing the bits of skin out of her hair as she leapt off the console. "Relax, Banyan," she muttered. "The man wasn't worth crying for."

She lowered her gun too soon and the cockpit door sprang open, and a man who looked just like Harvest came sliding in with the rain.

He was packing artillery and he let the bullets fly, unloading a round clear into Jawbone until her little body ripped and shuddered and was pinned lifeless against the console. Then the man was done with her. And he turned on Zee.

I leapt across that room like there were two of me, one standing still, watching. The other nothing but speed.

I slid into the man, knocking him from his feet as he squeezed at the trigger and his gun pointed at the ceiling and drilled it with holes. Suddenly, I had hands helping me. Zee and her mother. The four of us all tangled together like our bodies had been joined and only one brain could rule.

I scratched and clawed at the man's waxy skin, yanking and squeezing at that gun until it was in my hands, my finger on the trigger. I got on my knees and sank the weapon into his face, making sure he could see it, making it all nice and clear.

"Where did you come from?" I screamed at him, scaring the girls clean away.

The man just stared at me. His features bloodless and blank. He looked like Harvest. Hell, he was Harvest. But he wasn't. Not quite. Not in the eyes.

"Where do you take them?" I said, leaning down into him and forcing the gun at his cheek.

"He can't tell you."

I spun around. My mouth open. It was Hina who spoke, and I'd never heard her make even a sound.

"What do you mean he can't tell me?"

"They can copy the body," she said. "But not the mind."

I stared down at the man. I glanced at Zee, then back at Hina. "How do you know?"

Her gray eyes stared deep into mine. "Because your father told me."

I didn't know what to say. But it didn't matter. Because right then the transport cracked and moaned beneath us, the cockpit shuddering as somewhere deep in the hull, the fuel tank began blowing itself to pieces.

• • •

The second explosion threw the four of us to the ceiling, pinning us there as the floor reared up. The control panel flared and each window shattered. I lost track of my prisoner. And then I lost Zee. Hina, too.

I scrambled and bounced as the transport shook, broken glass puncturing my skin, smoke billowing around me. I plunged forward, picking my direction based on nothing but the sound of rain. There it was again. I could hear it. Closer now. I stretched an arm forward. And then I could feel it, slippery and warm on my hand.

My body wriggled into daylight and I rolled on my back, the platform all warped and quaking. The plank that had led off the deck was long gone. But as the transport swayed, it reached close to the city walls, bashing at concrete and knocking it loose.

I squatted amid the steam and sparks. I peered back into the rubble and saw limbs moving.

"This way," I shouted. "Follow my voice." I kept yelling as I pried my way back into the remains of the cockpit. I caught Hina in my arms and tugged her free. "Where are you?" I screamed for Zee. "I can't see you."

No answer.

"Zee?"

It was useless. I hollered again. But we were all out of time.

I grabbed Hina around the waist as the transport toppled. She strapped her arm across my shoulders as I ran and jumped.

Must've been a good ten feet and it felt like twenty. We hit the wall and it broke powdery beneath us, but it held as we sank our arms across it, our feet scrabbling up the concrete blocks.

The transport let out a groan as it tumbled to the mud, and it sank and flamed and split. Gashes all down the side of it. The top all full of holes.

The rain had quit and the air crackled with gunfire. I crouched on the wall and stared down into the city, where the pirates had clogged the walkways but the Harvesters showed no sign of retreat. Middle of the city, I could see the walls of the mud pit, the ramp still raised. And beyond it was the forest of cypress and fern, and the woman in the middle of it, still dancing above the rest of the world.

I don't know who detonated the generators. But those juicy suckers damn near scorched the sky. Was like the clouds themselves were burning, and I heaved in the black fumes as I staggered into the middle of the forest.

Hina didn't weigh much, but I dropped her like a sack of stone when I reached the statue, everything taking too long as I scrambled in the undergrowth and wrestled the panel free. She was barely conscious as I dragged her to the foot and squeezed her up through its entrance.

I groped in the mud where I'd left my tools. I found the nail gun and loaded that sucker full. I stood. Stared back at Old Orleans and watched it burning. I needed to find Sal. Get that damn coordinate for the GPS and get the hell away from this city.

But I had to do something first.

I had to find Alpha.

One good thing about a world made of stone and steel, that world can't burn for long. Once the fire had eaten through the juice, it fizzled into fuming stacks, molten piles of rubber and plastic. But the smoke was almost worse than the flames had been. Black and toxic, steaming in the brown water.

Just like the fire turned to smoke, my sprinting turned to stumbling. I had the nail gun held before me and my shirt pulled across my face. The concrete was doing a real number on my feet now, shredding me to pieces one step at a time.

I stopped running, stared ahead through the streaky blackness. Coming out of that smoke were two of Harvest's commandos, a pair of washed-out twins with vacant stares, sub guns rattling before them as they darted through the fumes.

I dropped to one knee and steadied the nail gun in both fists. My first shot hit before they'd even spotted me. But it didn't do much good. The nail just lodged in the one man's shoulder and it didn't slow him down a damn bit. I fired again, higher this time, though aiming at the head left less room for error. But I hit him square on.

Nailed him, you might say.

The guy went down with a choke but his buddy was ripping off a quick round in my direction. I rolled too hard across the walkway. Lost my grip at the edge. And then I was tumbling down into the darkness, disappearing beneath the city.

I lost the nail gun on impact, splashed into the mud and just kept on going. Heavy and deep and holy shit I wasn't stopping.

This weren't mud, it was water. And I wasn't swimming.

I was drowning.

CHAPTER TWENTY-NINE

Almost drown once and then try drowning a second time. It's so much worse than the first. I knew what was coming before it even happened, my mind one step ahead of my body as my eyes started pulsing too hard and my throat seized up. My limbs thrashed. Twitched. And then stiffened.

I didn't want to give up and keep sinking, but after all your shit stops working, there ain't much else you can do. I'm not going to tell you my life went flashing before me, because it didn't. Something about the way my arms stretched out, though, it's crazy, but I swear I felt like I was dancing. And I never danced once in my whole lousy life.

It was like I became her for a moment. Hina. The statue. And then my feet started kicking all over again. As if my heart had just remembered to beat.

Didn't do any good though. Just another round of pushing and splashing. But I got a hand out the top of the water and for a moment I felt the air and tried to hold on. Then I was sinking again. Darkening. I know I blacked out for a second because there was a moment where nothing happened but a murky drift.

Then I was being lifted. Hands clutched at my shirt and my pants, tugging me up through the gloom.

My face broke the surface, but I still couldn't breathe. My jaws were clamped shut and my eyes fluttered, water sticky inside me. I blacked out again. Came to on a stretch of mud. Then my lungs kicked back in like a frozen engine and I shuddered with every breath.

The underside of the walkways formed a concrete sky above me, a patchwork of stone woven with steel. I tried sitting up but stayed resting. And Sal squatted there beside me, like he was waiting on me to speak.

You never seen someone float like Sal could. Son of a bitch was unsinkable. Took him all he had to keep plunging down below the surface, groping around for the nail gun like I'd asked him, his feet sticking up in the air, then disappearing before he came up empty-handed. Over and over again.

"I can't find it." Sal sputtered and gasped as he paddled back to the mud. "It's too deep." He stretched out on the bank and shook his head at me.

I stared up at the city, feeling like I was just shit in its pants. I knew I had to get gone. Far away and quick about it. I thought about Pop. The trees.

But then I thought about Alpha.

"I'm heading back up there," I said.

"You're insane. The women have gone loopy. And those men, you've never seen so many guns."

"Where's the pit?"

He pointed. "Full of water now. And bodies. You can't go that way if you don't know how to swim."

"Then follow me," I said. "We'll head back to the forest. From there I can double back around."

"There's a forest?" Sal said as we began slipping through the mud.

"Yeah," I told him, glancing up through the slats in the walkways. "And that ain't all."

Beneath the ferns, I found a pillar we could climb and I pushed Sal out of the mud, shoving at him till he was clear to the top. He stared at the statue of Hina like his brain had stopped working.

"It's her," the kid whispered.

"Wait till you get on the inside."

I pushed him off toward the statue, told him how to get up under its foot. And then I turned back to the city.

The bullets had faded to a dribble. Just the occasional burst of gunfire breaking the silence. Smoke had cleared off the walkways, and as I ran through the mess, the clouds began to open again, washing away the remains, turning the piles of bodies into mush.

At the center of town I'd still not seen a soul, and finally I began to holler for Alpha, screaming her name at the top of my lungs.

I heard her long before I could see her, and when I saw her I barely knew who she was. She was stood atop the walls of the city, her legs wide and her head thrown back. And she was making a noise like a creature that had just figured out it could fly.

I stared up through the smoke at her. She was like something you'd try to build, if you could. As if she represented something no words could say.

She was slick with mud and her vest had been matted stringy, soaked with the blood of others. I watched as she raised both arms in the air, waving her gun above her head, still whooping that battle cry that no soul could have taught her.

When I finally found nerve to call up, she spun and stared down upon me and I felt naked beneath the wildness of her eyes. I felt alive. Unknown. And I knew then that the world contained so many things I would never understand.

I ran up to her, though she stood still. And when I reached her, I held her the way I longed to be held. She folded into me and I gazed across the top of her, staring out at the plains where the remains of Harvest's troops had scattered in the mud.

The transport lay split and smoldering below us, and I studied the broken shell that just a day before had seemed to me like a city that could move.

"This is the way the world ends," Alpha whispered, her head slippery on my shoulder.

"No," I said, squeezing her against me. "There's more."

It didn't take much time to persuade her. As the rain poured down and the darkness gathered, I told Alpha everything. All of my secrets. All that I knew. I told her about the tattoo that pointed to a place that was different. A place that wasn't just locked in an old story or stuck inside an old world song. I told her about my father. And I told her about the trees. About how beautiful they were and how they were more even than that. How they were something built for survival. Something that might put food on the table and burn bright the dark. And as I talked, I wondered if my father had once made a promise as he sat on the walls of this city, his arms holding the world through a woman, his eyes straining out at the mysterious night.

"What if we don't find them?" Alpha said, shivering in the rain as it mingled with the blood on her skin.

"Then I'll keep building them," I said. "Best as I can."

She studied my face, like she was reading something.

"Where my dad was taken," I told her. "Could be that's where your mom got dragged off, too."

"Been a long time, bud." She stared down into the city. The pirates had begun to gather below us, waiting for a new captain to call.

"I don't think they can come," I said, looking down. "If you're coming with me."

"I'll go with you, bud. They'll call me queen of every pirate army, I come home with trees to grow and fruit to eat."

I stared at her. Wanting her. And I wanted to be more than just her means to some end. I wanted to be someone with which she'd become rooted and tangled.

I leaned into her. And I would have kissed her. Never mind all the guts on the ground, never mind her face being covered in filth. I would have kissed her. Tried to, at least. But I heard a voice rise up from the city below us. And the voice belonged to no pirate.

"That you, little man?" Crow called through the darkness. "That you?"

CHAPTER THIRTY

My heart sank in my guts as I staggered back down into the city. It was pitch black now, the clouds plugging the stars and painting the moon. The rain had settled into a drizzle. Harvesters lay broken on the ground, and the surviving pirates were huddled in stooped patches. But Crow stood tall and wide, towering above everyone. And everything.

He'd lost his beard. All the hair on his head had been singed off, replaced by blood and blisters. His clothes hung off him, torn and frayed, as if he'd been trying to shed them but had given up halfway through.

Crow's grin split the dark as I approached him. "Happy to see you," he said. "Though you look about as bad as I feel."

"You got out," I said, as if saying the words might make me believe them.

"Aye. With bodies before me. And bodies behind." Crow studied his hands, his forearms. "Can still feel the poor bastards sticky on my skin."

"Are there more?"

"Don't know. Was a mighty big split in the hull. But Miss Zee was in there. Her mother also."

"How'd they catch you?"

"In the corn."

"Poachers?"

"Agents."

"Agents don't grab folk off the road."

"They do now."

I thought about what that could mean – GenTech agents handing off slaves to King Harvest. And I thought about how it made heading west now seem a whole lot more dangerous, seeing as the cornfields are never short of those bastards in the purple suits.

"What the hell was he gonna do with all those people?" I said.

"I don't know." Crow shrugged. "But a ship that size, I'd say whatever he been doing it for, he been doing it a long time."

"Wait," I said, remembering what Zee had told me. "You used to work for GenTech. Before you worked for Frost."

Crow laughed that low rumble of his. "Indeed I did, little man. Indeed I did."

"You were looking for trees."

He quit laughing and his eyes changed. "Looking?" he said. "No, I wasn't looking. But they found me, you might say. And now I think you'd better take me with you."

"Take you with me?"

"Miss Zee said you hell bent on finding the Promised Land, in which case you need what I need. Vega's the only place you can find the GPS. So you best head west. And that being so, I'd say you need me."

"Why?" said Alpha, coming up behind me. "So you can get caught by agents again?"

Crow turned to her. He licked his broken lips. And then he turned back to me. "The cornfields are a maze, tree builder. Big as the South Wall. And the forty ain't the only way of crossing it."

"There's another way?"

"GenTech got plenty of ways. Some of them unguarded. Some of them unwatched."

"Then why not just head there yourself?"

"Oh, I would, little man. I would. But where's my wheels? Know what I mean? You get us moving, and I can show us the way."

"What makes you think I got wheels?"

"The pirates got trucks. And this pirate girl likes you." He stared at the two of us, lifting his chin as if that single motion made him in control of everything. "Course she does," he said, his melted face suddenly bleeding he was grinning so hard. "Told you before, little man. You're crazy cool."

A mist rolled in from the south, and at the forest it was too dark to see. Just gray clouds moving through the metal, drizzle sprinkling at the trees. Alpha and Crow were passed out sleeping in the city, but I'd come back to retrieve Sal. And Hina.

I stepped through the slippery undergrowth, a dead Harvester's plastic boots on my feet. I knocked at the base of the statue, called for Sal, but when there was no reply I rummaged through my soggy tools, found my headlamp, and then shimmied under the foot and pried the panel free.

They were all the way at the end of the outstretched leg, Sal curled up against Hina and both of them crashed out cold. There was a sweetness they held in sleeping that neither of them showed awake. They looked peaceful. Calm. I lowered my headlamp and rested against the curve of the statue.

I tried to conjure some feeling for the mother whose arms I'd once slept in. She'd been from the northern lands, Pop had told me. And she'd starved to death before I was able to remember her. But she'd taught Pop to read, which I'd always thought a real good gift. I guess you got to take what you can get.

I leaned back and tried to picture what had happened between my father and this woman who now slept across from me, her arms held tight around her adopted son. Pop must have loved her real fierce to build such a statue, and I reckoned that meant she must have loved him in return. But I'd really little idea about the way of such things. And whatever had happened, whatever had been felt, their paths had got split in the end.

Hina wound up gambled away and ended up raising a daughter with a fat junky bastard. And my father met my mother and then dragged me around the Steel Cities, faking nature in a world where none survived.

Or did it?

I thought of waking the woman, staring into those silver eyes of hers and asking her what she knew. Ask her about my father. About that tree curved around her belly. Because it seemed strange that this tattoo Pop must have known so well now led to the same place he'd been taken.

The night felt heavy and my eyes drooped. And before I could think anymore or get up or move, I was sleeping, my headlamp still shining, its batteries burning, and by the time I woke up the thing was useless.

But it didn't matter. When I woke up, the sun was back out and I could hear Alpha calling my name from the forest.

"Where's Crow?" I asked Alpha as I hurried out through the base of the statue, squinting at the sky.

"Still sleeping," she said. "Like a dead man. If the dead could snore."

"Good." I didn't want Crow to see the forest. Or the statue. I figured anything I knew that the watcher didn't, just might prove useful somewhere down the line.

Sal crept out behind me, all sweaty and pale in the heat of morning. He slumped down, yawning.

"Your friend?" said Alpha.

"I guess."

"So where's the woman?"

As if she'd been summoned, Hina crawled out of the statue, all matted down and her muscles straining. I tell you, it was like watching that statue give birth to itself. And I remembered what Zee had said, how Frost had gotten this woman hooked on the crystal.. So I reckoned Hina was now facing the worst kind of sober. Along with the fact that her daughter was dead.

"We're heading to Vega," I said, helping her to her feet. "And I reckon you should come on with us, but I ain't gonna make you if you don't want to go."

"I can't stay here," Hina said, keeping her back to the statue. She seemed to shrink as the sun beat down. But her eyes were as cold as ever.

"You said something," I said, dropping my voice. "About those fake Harvesters."

She stared at me. Not blinking.

But I couldn't talk to her about my old man. Not in front of Sal. He was someone else I might need advantages over, somewhere on down the line.

CHAPTER THIRTY-ONE

Every vehicle the pirates owned had been torched and left to smolder on the clay, their giant steel carcasses still steaming.

"We're stranded," muttered Alpha, staring out at the smoky wreckage.

"No," I said. "My wagon should work, if it's still where we left it. We'll just have to find it on foot."

We filled a couple of canteens with rainwater, salvaged a pocketful of cornmeal between us. And then the five of us headed north. Back toward the forty.

Must have looked like a right family of freaks out there, shuffling along the plains with our boots sticky in the mud. Old Orleans dissolved in the haze behind us, and ahead of us we couldn't see a whole lot at all. Just the endless dirt and the washed-out sky.

Alpha took the lead, guiding us toward where we hoped the wagon would still be. And I hung back, behind the group, trying to figure out what the deal was between Hina and Sal and the man who'd once been their watcher. Hell, I guess I was trying to figure out which one of them I could trust.

Crow spent most of the morning switching between Hina in his arms and Sal on his shoulders, both of them too weak to walk too far. The fat kid had gotten real quiet when I told him about Zee. Caught him crying, too. But now he was warbling on about what happens when you die and if you go on to someplace different. Asking if we thought you head someplace better. Or if you wind up someplace worse.

But the kid should have been saving his energy — no one was paying him any mind. Probably they were too busy mulling how they'd wound up out here in the first place. And no one was more silent than Hina. She was grieving hard, and it got to me, seeing the pain etched all across her. But Zee hadn't had much time left, that's what I told myself. Not with how bad her lungs had gotten.

Truth is, part of the reason I kept pulling up the rear was because I thought Hina might drift back there with me. Figured I could comfort her. Talk to her. But slow as she moved, she always seemed to pick up the pace a little when she felt me getting close behind.

She was valuable, that's what she was. And she was more than just a map. She knew about my father and maybe about the place he'd been hauled off. In that head of hers, there were answers. I tell you, I would have traded my last drop of water just to see what she had hidden inside.

So there we were, stumbling along. I'd told Alpha to make the weapons scarce and not let the pirates give one to Crow, no matter how many times he kept demanding one. So Alpha strode out in front of us stragglers, two pistols rammed down her belt and her rifle slung across her back. The only one of us who was armed.

Her tall boots made quick work of the mud, and her mohawk had returned to its former glory. Hell, even that fuzzy vest of hers was coming back to life. And I knew if I let myself, I'd do nothing but want her, and the wanting would turn thick inside me. But that would have to wait, I reckoned. Like everything else I was after. It'd have to wait.

Around noon, Sal got sick of walking and sat his ass in the mud. "I need a rest," he mumbled when I caught up to them.

"Can't you carry him?" I said to Crow, who had put down Hina and was rolling his eyes at me.

"I been carrying him half the morning. You carry him."

I didn't have it in me, and I whistled for Alpha to stop. She squatted down right where she was, fifty yards ahead.

"How's your skin?" I said to Crow.

"Parched and broken." He squinted at me, and I reckoned he was missing those big old shades of his right about now.

"You want water?"

"No. Give mine to the lady."

I glanced across at where Hina was kneeling down in the mud, her face turned eastward. It was hot out there. Damn hot. I mean, it was supposed to be winter and all, and we sure could have used a little nip in the air down south of the forty.

"Hina," I called, but she didn't turn her head or anything. "You thirsty?"

"I'm thirsty," Sal moaned. "But more I'm starving."

"You ain't starving," I told him. "You don't know what the word means."

I trudged over to where Hina was sat.

"You should drink some." I held my canteen to her. Her eyes flickered at me, held my gaze a moment. Then she took the canteen and knocked it back, taking a good long draw. She screwed the cap back in place and set the water on the ground.

"Thank you," she said.

"I finished that statue," I told her. "The way my old man would have wanted."

She froze.

"The pirates said he loved you," I went on, but Hina shook her head.

"He left me," she said. "I wasn't enough for him."

"They said you both went to Vega."

She opened her mouth as if to say something. She stared up at me. But then she dropped her eyes again and I'd lost her like the sun going down.

"How did he know about the Harvesters?" I said. "About how they got copied?"

She stayed blank, like I wasn't even talking to her.

"Shit," I said, picking up the canteen. "I get that you're suffering. And I can't even tell you how sorry I am. But you know something about where it is that we're heading, you'd do well to spill it to me."

"I try to remember," Hina said. "I do. But all I see is that wall, the concrete rising up into clouds."

"The South Wall. Yeah. That's where they found you."

"And I remember the statue. I remember your father building it. But more I remember him angry. And afraid."

"Afraid of what?"

She buried her face in her hands.

I tried to touch her shoulder, but she flinched like I was some sort of devil.

"I'm sorry," I said. And I just stood there for a moment, watching her rattle and cry.

When I got back to Crow, his face was smug. "You ready?" he asked, getting up off the dirt.

"Waiting on you, tough guy."

"Just as long as you're all taken care of." Crow glanced over at Hina and then fixed me with a look.

"What's that supposed to mean?"

"Is it lunchtime?" Sal asked, tugging at Crow.

"Ask the boss," Crow said, still staring at me. "He be the one in charge."

"Get up," I said. "We're walking."

But we walked until nightfall. And we still had not found the road.

CHAPTER THIRTY-TWO

"The stars are all I need," Alpha said, pointing at the night sky. "We keep north. Keep moving."

"Thought it was a day's walk," Crow said, looming over my shoulder. "You getting us lost, sweet thing?"

"It is a day's walk," she said. "If you keep at the walking. And call me sweet thing again, I'll chop you in two."

Crow chuckled. "Your little man here mightn't like me and you get to wrestling."

"Cut it out," I said. "We'll be at the wagon soon enough."

"Soon enough? Soon enough for what? Ain't no prize for seconds. Not in this race. How you think we gonna beat Mister Frost to the punch?"

"Depends on your shortcut."

"Didn't say it were no shortcut. Just said it was safe."

Alpha pointed at where Sal and Hina were already curled up, passed out on the mud. "We're gonna have to rest a minute. Or the two of them ain't gonna make it."

"Fine," Crow said. "Rest. I'll do the watching."

"I ain't sleeping," I said.

"That right?" Crow laughed as he sank down on the dirt. He stretched his arms out, and stared at the stars. "Sleep with one eye open, boss man."

I went and sat on the other side of Hina and Sal, trying to keep my back straight so my head wouldn't fall.

"We can't trust him," Alpha whispered, kneeling beside me.

"I know. But he needs us if he wants to find the wagon."

"And then what?"

"Then we'll have to keep our eyes on him."

"I'm keeping my eyes on him now."

"So am I."

And I did. For about five minutes. Then my head plunged and my eyes sealed up and I was lost in a shadowy sleep.

I dreamt about Zee, and a nightmare is more what it was. She was on my back and I was crawling out of the Surge, soaking wet and my lungs tight, limbs all made of mud and crawling for the high ground. I held Zee on my shoulders, in the middle of a dusty city, and she began building, her hands weaving my hair in her fingers and tying my hair to the trees.

When she'd finished, she began on something different and I sensed someone watching us, but I couldn't see who it was, and then Zee's trees began falling, one by one, only I couldn't catch any one of them because my hair was all tied in the branches and they were pinning me in place as Zee wandered free.

I could see now she'd been building a statue, broad shouldered and faceless. It grew a beard and it was Crow, and then its belly sagged and it was Frost. But then its body was Frost and its face was me and finally the statue was my father, and he was staring down at me as if he were sorry for something.

And then the statue fell in pieces on top of us and I watched as Zee was crushed beneath the steel and wires, her face howling silently and my hands reaching for her. And I wanted to tell her something.

But she was already dead.

When I came to, the stars were so bright it was like they'd pricked me awake. But it wasn't the night sky that had caused me to stir. Alpha was stood above me, her face peering into the distance. And Crow was right beside her, his eyes so focused it filled me with fear.

"What is it?" I whispered.

"Don't know," Alpha said, and I could hear the sound now, faint but growing louder. The sound of an engine, something moving. A vehicle out on the plains.

"The forty?" I asked, standing beside them.

"No." Alpha cocked her rifle, jutted her head. "Forty's that way. This is out of the south."

"From the south?"

"That's right, bud. And if I had to guess, I'd say it's coming straight out of Old Orleans."

Soon as we could see it, we knew it was too big to try messing with. It was taller than it was wide and the whole thing seemed to be spinning, a broad beam of light arcing off the front side, setting the mud flats ablaze.

"We should get down," I said. "Take cover."

"Take cover in what?" Alpha said.

"In the ground."

We woke Sal and Hina and had them stretch flat on their bellies as we scooped at the clay and smeared it upon them. Then we dug in the dirt and laid ourselves flat, painting our faces and squirming down till we were drenched in the soil.

Alpha stretched the rifle out, pointed it right at the vehicle that was now just a hundred yards away. It was trundling and buzzing right along, angling itself to the right of us, heading northwest, I reckoned. And I hoped with all I had it'd just keep passing by.

"You ever shot a gun before?" Alpha shoved one of the pistols in my hand. "One that ain't full of nails?"

I shook my head, and she grabbed the gun back and showed me how to pull the safety off and get the thing ready to fire.

"There's one more of those," said Crow. "I'd say it best go to someone who can use it."

"Forget it, Rasta," Alpha muttered, and then we lay there, still and silent as the engine grew louder and the vehicle spun close.

There was this moment when that big moving shadow seemed to alter its course right for us, and I couldn't understand it, but that's what it did. We'd not made a move or a sound and it was dark as all hell out there, but I swear it seemed like the thing was coming dead on. Damn near was going to be right on top of us.

"Give him the gun," I said to Alpha, fear seizing me up inside.

"What?"

"Give him the gun. It's no use if we're dead."

I heard her scrabble for the last pistol and then she threw it at Crow. And now all three of us were armed.

Crow clicked off his safety. But then the vehicle turned again, steering itself westward, the engine screaming and grinding and us just watching as the thing sailed by.

It was a wheel. A giant wheel. Giant tire tread churning up mud as it rolled through the night. And inside of that wheel, suspended so as not to be spinning, was a cockpit built for a few dozen people.

There was only one thing big enough to spin wheels like that one. Only one thing I'd seen, anyway. The Harvester transport. The Ark. And that's where this damn thing had come from. No doubt in my mind. Some kind of escape pod. Get out clause. Transport all blown to hell and that wheel just rolling free, moving fast, jetting off in the night.

"Holy shit," I said, sucking myself out of the mud, staring into the distance where the Harvest wheel grew quiet and its torch beam got small.

"Give it up, Rasta," Alpha said, and I turned to see Crow shoving his pistol in what was left of his pants.

"I ain't no Rasta, sweet thing," he said. "Not technically speaking. But I do believe in the Promised Land." Crow grinned, patting the butt of the gun. "And we all be heading there together. Ain't that right, little man?"

CHAPTER THIRTY-THREE

The mud turned to sand and the sand turned into the forty, and when we hit that old strip of tarmac we turned west.

"The wagon's this way," Alpha said. "If it's still out here at all."

Dust clouds picked up around dawn and for an hour we had to hold on to one another as we choked and stumbled through the dirt. And then, when the winds quit, the sky just started cooking. Sweat ran down my face and stung my eyes all grimy and swollen. Both canteens were dry. But the five of us just kept on walking. Looked like we were made out of sand.

My old brown wagon had dissolved into the dirt, and it wasn't until we were almost to it that I spotted the thing, half-buried in the earth.

I broke into a run and exhausted myself, my pistol jabbing me as I jogged down the road, the sun burning like winter wasn't ever going to come. My skin was crispy and my limbs were sore but you can bet I had the biggest damn grin on my face. No soul's ever been more happy to see a junky old pile of metal. I could hardly believe it. My old jalopy. Still there, waiting on me like a friend I didn't deserve. And it was only after a half day of digging we came to realize the wheels were gone.

We'd worked right through the afternoon and I'd discovered early that the inside of the car had been stripped. All the doors were open and the corn and juice had been taken. The passenger seat had been yanked right out and someone had peeled the nylon off the inside of the doors. But the engine seemed as intact as I'd left it looking, and we worked brimmed with hope until Crow scooped out around the first wheel and found it missing. I clawed the dirt out from beneath the rest of the car and uncovered the same sad story. Sons of bitches may as well have hauled off the whole damn thing. What good's a wagon without wheels?

"So what do we do now?" Sal said, plopping down in the dirt. The sun had done the kid no favors – beneath the dust, his bloated face was a chapped shade of purple, blisters puckering his skin. Still, he was nothing next to Crow. The watcher's burns had shriveled and glazed in shredded patches, like he'd decided to just unpeel his flesh and start over.

"We wait," Alpha said. I'd given her my dad's old sombrero and she'd punched a whole through the lid so her mohawk stuck out the top. You'd think I'd have minded, her messing up my old man's hat. But I didn't. I liked seeing her wear it.

"Someone comes along, we take their wheels off 'em," she said. "Shouldn't be too long. Not this time of year."

"Guess you'd know, pirate." Crow grinned.

"If it goes against your moral code," she said, "then you can make a better plan."

"Moral code?" Crow leaned back on the wagon and it shifted beneath him. "What moral code?"

• • •

I'd only salvaged a few of my tools in Old Orleans. Just some spanners and ratchets, a spare set of fuses. But I'd grabbed the telescope. The thing was on the heavy side but I figured it might come in handy, and it came in handy now, all five of us hunkered down and sweating inside the wagon, Alpha checking the road through the scope.

One of the scavengers had tried to pry out the microwave and they'd tried so hard, they'd messed up the wiring. I got it patched back together, but the water was a tougher fix. The tank had been drained empty.

"One bit of good news," I said to the others. "We got corn and juice buried on the side of the road."

"Yeah," Sal said. "And we got the pictures."

"What pictures?" Crow was stooped and squashed in the back of the wagon, his frame much too big for the space.

Sal pointed at Hina, gesturing at her belly like the woman was no more than a picture herself. "We got shots of each one of them. Every leaf. Her whole body."

"We need water, though," I said, not liking the way the conversation was heading. Hina crossed her arms across her stomach and gazed at the floor.

"How you get those pictures, little man?" Crow stared at me, eyes bugging off his melted face.

"You left them behind." I shrugged. "With your boy."

"I didn't leave no one behind."

"Just wanted me to keep the house safe," said Sal, peering up at Crow. "Right?"

Crow didn't say a thing. He was too busy glaring at me and I couldn't figure out what had gotten him so worked up. Then he turned his gaze on Hina, and I imagined he was thinking that if we had the

GPS numbers, then we didn't need the woman. But Frost had headed off with Hina and Zee along for the ride. Did he need them for something? Why else would he have brought along two more mouths to feed? Even mouths as pretty as theirs.

"Banyan," Alpha said from behind the steering wheel, her eye pressed at the telescope. "We got company."

Could have been anyone. Just a slate gray cruiser with a flatbed trailer off the back, rolling out of the west in no particular hurry. I wondered if they'd already seen us, but I doubted our wagon looked like any reason to slow down.

I peered through the telescope at the tinted windows, tried to imagine what face was staring back at me. Then I studied the tires, the good thick tread. Off-road tires. Oversize. They'd be perfect. But they weren't mine. And here I was getting ready to take them.

"You flag them down," said Alpha. "I'll be on the other side of the wagon. Waiting."

"Right," I muttered, concealing the pistol down the back of my pants. "What about the others?"

Alpha glanced at the rest of our crew. "Stay down," she said. "But keep the hatch open. And be ready."

"Oh, don't worry," said Crow, cocking his weapon. "I'm ready every second of the day."

I popped the hatch and climbed out, wondering how I was going to get out of this one with a new set of wheels but without having to shoot somebody. I got the hood up and faked messing with the engine again, thinking about the last time I'd done that and how it had played out.

The cruiser crept up the road behind me, the tread of its tires clacking at the tarmac. Out the corner of my eye, I could see the barrel of Alpha's rifle, pointed right across the engine, angled straight into the road.

Wasn't long before the growl of the cruiser was at my shoulders, brakes tapping and squeaking to a stop. I turned around then, watched the wheels make their last rotation before they eased to a standstill. I stared into those black tint windows. I grinned and waved. And then I just stood there and waited.

Seemed like a month and nothing happened. I glanced at the trailer, but the thing was almost empty. If they'd gone west looking for salvage, then they'd not done too good a job.

"Banyan," Alpha whispered from behind the wagon. "Go say hello."

She was right. Standing around was getting me nowhere. So I amped up the grin and waltzed up to the driver's door. And I'd almost reached the cruiser when the window slid down a crack.

I stopped dead.

The window buzzed a little lower. And the smell. Oh, man. The smell was so bad it made my belly squirm.

"Hello?" I called, not wanting to move an inch closer. "Got a little engine trouble here."

I heard a voice croak something from behind the wheel, but I still couldn't see a face through the shadows. I acted like I was scratching at my back but really I was getting the pistol ready. I took a step closer and was sweating like crazy now, and that combined with the sick feeling in my stomach and that awful stench wafting over me, I felt like when I was ill in the mud pit, back stuck in that filthy fever.

I went to say something, but before I got the words out, I saw the driver's face bobble into the sunlight.

His skin was almost green and his eyes had clouded over, the marks on his face were like moldy bits of corn. The man was trying to speak but his mouth was too thick with spit, his lips too cracked and bleeding.

"Holy shit," I whispered.

Then I shouted for Alpha.

She came running up behind me as I covered my mouth with my shirt and stepped closer to the cruiser. I peered in at the rest of the man's body — his clothes soiled with sweat, his right arm missing below the elbow. He'd tied his shirt beneath the stump and it was soaked black with blood that was still dripping. I almost puked right then, but that was nothing next to the far side of his neck. The skin gnawed all the way to muscle. Bits of bone poking through.

Alpha groaned behind me.

"What is it?" Sal squeaked from the wagon. "What do you see?"

"Nothing," I shouted. "Don't you come out here."

Crow, of course, was already on his way.

He hollered at the stink then made a sound like he was laughing. "Not bad," he shouted, throwing open the doors to the cruiser. "Today be our lucky day."

"Lucky?" I muttered, staring inside at the carcasses stacked on the rear seat. It was the man's family, I guess. Three smaller bodies and a bigger one. Nothing left to bury but bones and patches of hair.

"That's right, little man. Lucky." Crow held his nose as he slammed the doors shut. "Got ourselves a new set of wheels and didn't even have to kill no one to get it."

He was right. We'd take the wheels, though not the cruiser, not as greased with death and poisoned as it was. But as the man went to switch his engine back on, to keep on toward who knows where, I felt Crow shoving me in the rubs.

"Spoke to soon," he said. "You better take care of business."

I snatched the pistol from out the back of my pants. But that was as far as I got with it. Sure, I'd waved the nail gun around before, even taken out one of the Harvesters with it, but there was some new thing needed now to pull a trigger in cold blood. And I remembered what my father had told me. About me being a builder. Not a fighter.

"Come on, bud," Alpha said, stepping past me to fire a shot through the driver's skull. "It's just putting him out of his misery."

She was right. The guy had been all out of time. But that didn't make killing him weigh any less heavy. He'd been just pushing down the road, I reckon. Just trying to do the right thing. And now he was slumped over his steering wheel. Dead.

"What happened to them?" Sal whispered, running up. His hand clutched at me, and his legs wobbled as he stared into the car.

"Locusts," said Crow.

"It should be too cold," I said. "It should be good crossing season."

"Should be, little man." Crow opened the driver's door and wound the window up, then slammed the door shut to seal the stench inside. "But should don't mean shit."

He was right. It don't.

And it weren't long before Sal went and threw up all over my boots.

CHAPTER THIRTY-FOUR

I worked the rest of the day getting the wheels off the cruiser and rigging them up to my wagon. I even salvaged two extra tires off the dead man's trailer and I strapped them across our roof. The water in their tank smelled bad and tasted worse, but it kept a hungry mouth from getting thirsty.

The sun was dropping and the wind had stayed down, and we were all famished by the time we uncovered the stash Sal and me had buried. I had to keep Sal from shoving all the corn in the microwave so we could cook it and eat it all right then.

"Gotta pace ourselves," I told him. "Got a ways to go yet."

But how far were we heading? I'd no real idea. To Vega, first. That was the plan. We had to get ourselves a GPS by trading something. Or someone. I watched Hina as she chewed her rations and licked her fingers clean. But you can't go trading people, I thought. You do that and you'll end up the one not worth a damn.

Still, we'd have to do something. Without the GPS gadget, we couldn't plug in the numbers that were supposed to lead us to the Promised Land. My father and the trees.

By nightfall, there was only one thing left to be dug back up — Zee's bag where I'd squeezed my book and the bark, along with the camera and pictures.

I'd deliberately worked around the spot, kept it hid. Problem was, Crow was always around. Always paying attention. And I reckon that made him a real good watcher, but right now it just made him a huge pain in the ass.

"We got to be careful," Alpha said as I siphoned off the last of the cruiser's water. "Now he's got his wheels, what's he need us for?"

"He needs the numbers."

"So he takes the woman."

I glanced over at where Hina was sitting. "I can't get through to her," I said. "But she knows things. She knew my father."

"Just keep focused on finding those trees."

"She ain't distracting me."

"Good."

"She's got nothing on you."

Alpha eyes flashed, and for a moment it was like I could feel the electricity howl inside her.

"You sure know how to make a girl feel special," she said.

"Oh, you're special all right."

"Yeah?" She laughed. "For how long?"

"Stick around," I said.

"No one sticks around, Banyan. Not for a feeling. Not in the end." She was grinning when she said it, but I saw her smile disappear as she turned to walk away.

• • •

I'd pieced the engine back together and had the wagon ready, but I let them all rest awhile longer. I paced the tarmac with my telescope in one hand, my gun in the other.

Alpha was stretched on the sand and sleeping, and as I watched her I wondered what it'd be like to stroke that crazy mohawk of hers. Or run my fingers across her dirty pink vest. And then I thought about just lying beside her, resting my face on her dusty skin.

It was a clear night and the big old moon was low. The stars looked so close you could touch them. I stared up at the sky, half looking for one of those satellites Sal had said were still up there. Then I shuffled closer to the wagon, to see how the crew was getting on.

Hina and Sal were curled beneath the wagon, huddled in their usual position, her wrapped around him like a mom who'd not realized her baby had grown too big too quickly. I thought about how Sal had talked about Zee when she was living, how he'd gotten crude, said she wasn't his sister. And Hina sure as hell wasn't his mother. But he looked pretty peaceful there, all curled up against her. And I figured as little as I knew about love and such matters, that poor chubby bastard must have known a whole lot less.

Of course, who I'd really come over to take a look at was Crow. He was sprawled on top of the wagon, his feet propped on one of the new tires I'd tied to the roof. I pretended I was just pacing the tarmac, but I was really trying to catch a glimpse of his face.

"Your sweet thing sleeping?" he said. I was on my fourth go-around of the pacing business, and Crow rolled on his side and stared at me. "Got yourself a real firecracker there, little man."

"Take it easy."

"Think you can trust her?"

"More than I trust you."

"That all?"

"That's not what I meant."

"Sure it is. You take my advice, little man. Don't go trusting no one but yourself."

"That's what you do, I guess."

"Only ones I trust are the ones I know what they're gonna do before they do it. Like you, little man, I can trust you pretty good. Real good, matter of fact."

I started to say something, but he cut back in.

"Where are the pictures?"

"What pictures?"

"Pictures of the tree. The GPS numbers. The pictures Sal said you took from the house. I not seen you dig them up yet. Which makes me wonder what else you got buried."

"I got a book," I hissed at him. "That what you want to know?"

"A book?"

"Yeah."

"Good. Gets cold one of these nights, we can burn it."

"We ain't burning nothing. I call the shots."

"Really?" Crow said, laughter in his voice. "Between me and the firecracker, I'd say you're just firing on empty."

I crawled beside Alpha and dug Zee's bag out of the ground.

"What are you doing?" Alpha said, coming awake in a hurry.

"Nothing," I told her. "Just go on and sleep."

She rolled over, and I unzipped the bag and counted out the pictures of the tattoo leaves. I lay the pictures flat on the dirt so I could see that tree again, and then I gathered up the photos and slipped them in Alpha's vest pocket.

Flicking through the rest of the bag, I found a picture of Zee and pulled it out, thinking I could give it to Hina. I studied Zee's face in the photograph. And then I stared at the trashed bits of tarmac in the moonlight, the road people built when the world was still growing, before the earth was just rubble and stunted, before everything became punctured and blank.

I left Zee's picture in the dust. Just didn't see it doing Hina any good to pass it along. I reckoned some things you do best to remember. But some things it's best to forget.

I tied the piece of bark around my waist with a plastic cord, and I had my back turned so none of them could see what I'd got there. Then I strode up to the wagon with the book in one hand and Zee's camera in the other, and I shoved them beneath the driver's seat.

I jammed on the horn, leaning on it way longer than necessary.

Sal and Hina crawled out from under the wagon with their hands over their ears. Crow stared at me from the roof, the giant moon bright behind him. And Alpha gave me a strange look as she came up, brushing the sand off the back of her thighs.

"Me and my wagon are taking off," I shouted, yelling to all who'd listen, my voice echoing in the empty night. "You want to find Zion, then jump right in. You got other plans, that's fine. I'll leave your ass. Right here in the dust."

CHAPTER THIRTY-FIVE

Five bodies full but the wagon zipped along pretty good. I wasn't in much mood for talking and was glad to be behind the wheel again. Gave me something to focus on – plowing through the dirt clouds, keeping steady against the winds. Dodging the deep sand and ditches. This road led to Vega. It'd take us right through the corn, and right past the place where my father had been stolen away.

Took the whole day to reach the cornfields and when we did the sun was red behind them. The wind had mostly quit and we watched as the crops appeared on the horizon – a thin strip of yellow against the colors of evening sky.

No one said anything. We all just stared.

The plants stood dense and tall and ordered, running as far as we could see from north to south. They barely seemed to sway in the breeze.

When my father had taken me west, we'd stopped in the cornfields, camped on the side of the road beneath the crops. It was dead of winter, good crossing season, and Pop had dug in the snow and pulled up a plant, shown me roots that plugged right into the ground. He told me a tree's roots could reach a mile deep, that the corn was nothing, just a fluke made by people who'd done nothing but play a trick on nature. Except nature got the last laugh, I guess. If that's what you can call a never-ending plague of locusts eating every damn thing in sight. I don't know that you can. But those people had done such a good job of twisting the corn into something indestructible, here it still was, food and fuel and a gold mine for the ones who owned it.

The cornstalks became silhouetted black against the sky as the sun sank farther from view. And I pulled the wagon off to the side of the road, right at the point where the plains gave way to crops.

We stood out of the car, our feet in the dirt but our eyes on that dusty wall of corn ahead. The thirty-foot plants.

GenTech designed the corn to withstand frost and drought, bad winds and big temperatures. Hell, if the crops flooded, I reckon that corn could probably grow arms and swim. The one living thing the locusts couldn't feast on, the one thing to grow back after the Darkness. And now nothing could kill it. All GenTech had to worry about was poachers, and it was hard to imagine the poachers even made a dent, burrowed in their underground colonies, hidden from the locusts and the agents, buried away from the sun.

These crops on the edge were full grown and just turning ripe. You could see the biggest cobs near the top, where the thick leaves rustled. Another week and GenTech would have the dusters down here, blading one crop and reseeding for the next.

You can't steal the corn for planting, on account of the purple logo on the kernels. People steal the corn, they eat it. Hungry people. People like us.

"The perimeter's the safest spot," Crow said. "Locusts nest on the insides, keep to the core. And agents figure most folk ain't got the balls to do their poaching out near the open."

"So what's the plan?" I said, annoyed at Crow being the expert.

"What plan?" Crow laughed. "All we need right now is a knife."

Alpha had a blade stashed down her boot, so we pushed into the first rows of plants, looking for food, all pressed up in the cornstalks because they plant that stuff so damn close together. Beneath all the dust, the leaves were dark green and crunchy. I tapped at a stem and it made a hollow sound, like a tube of plastic. Hardly even felt like a living thing.

Alpha climbed Crow's back and settled in on his shoulders, sawing her blade at the ears of corn, dust raining down as she worked. Crow had his big hands clasped on those pretty thighs of hers, holding her in place, and something about his fingers pressed tight on her skin made me feel all queasy inside.

"Can't you go a little faster?" I called up at her.

"Going as fast as I can, bud."

"You should keep watch, little man," Crow said. "Out by the wagon. We're not gonna spot no agents all bunched up in here."

He was right, but it pissed me off to admit it. Pissed me off him calling me little man all the time, too. Little man? Son of a bitch. We can't all be seven-foot watchers.

I forced my way back through the plants, their lousy leaves all covered in sand and whacking me in the face. And I was about to bust free when I stepped right on top of Sal.

Kid was on all fours, trying to eat his way through a stem, really gnawing at it but getting nowhere. "I'm so hungry," he said, taking a break to stare up at me, spit hanging out of his mouth.

"Just don't you get lost in here," I said, stepping over him and pushing my way outside.

Hina hadn't joined us in the cornfield. She was sat in the dirt, arms around her knees and her head bent on her shoulder. She was facing away from the sunset, staring east where the sky was nothing but black.

I sat down next to her, our backs to the corn.

I saw goose bumps on Hina's shoulders and thought of taking my shirt off to give it to her, but I had the bark tied on my skin, so I left my shirt right where it was. She trembled a little in her thin top, and there was a distance in her eyes that reminded me of my father. That faraway look that said no matter where you were staring, you were seeing some whole different world.

"Gonna eat soon," I said. Hina didn't say anything but I thought I caught her glancing at the car. "I know," I said. "Gonna be kind of cramped. Once we enter the cornfields there's no going outside the wagon. But all goes well we should be through these crops in a day or so."

"And then what?" she said, startling me. She never spoke enough for her voice to be something I got used to.

"Well, then I reckon we're gonna find us your trees."

She smiled, but it was a thin, bitter shape. "They're not my trees," she said, her hands going to her belly.

"You remembered anything?" I said.

"Like what?"

"Like about my old man."

"Just bits and pieces." She stared east again, scratching at her arms. "Guess I'm no good to anyone without the gypsy's memory box."

I watched her blink three times before a tear rolled out and ran down the side of her cheek. I thought I ought to say something. Do something. But I didn't know what.

"You find your father," Hina whispered. "Then you can ask him what happened." I felt her lean against me, and I suddenly wished I'd kept that picture of Zee to give her, this woman with a brain like a broken sieve. But I just sat there, leaning against her, until the others came crashing back through the crops.

Hina went rigid and I stood, turning to watch Alpha come busting into the open with a whole stack of corn in her arms. Crow came after her, stupid big grin on his face.

"We gonna eat good tonight, people," he boomed. "Miss Alpha ain't a pirate no more. She's a poacher."

CHAPTER THIRTY-SIX

"Ready to head south?" Crow said as I jumped behind the wheel and fired up the wagon.

"South?"

"Follow the perimeter until you see the fourth service road. We'll follow that west and start winding our way through the maze."

"The least watched way."

"That's right, little man. Crow here gonna steer you right on through."

I pulled off the road and the wagon sank into the sand as I pointed us south. I flicked the lights on, but Crow had me turn them off again.

"Just go slow," he said, leaning over my shoulder and peering with me through the windshield. "We'll see the service roads. Night as clear as this."

We drove silent through the dark, nothing but the soft hum of the engine, and cruising south somehow felt like we were going downhill.

The first service road surprised me.

"It's huge," I said, studying the broad path cutting through the crops. Unpaved. Just packed dirt, the walls of corn towering on either side.

"Gotta be big enough for the dusters," Crow said. "Get them in the right spots to start harvesting."

"The dusters are that big?" I'd heard stories, but that service road was massive.

"Oh, they're big," said Crow. "Getting bigger every year."

Hours passed. I counted two more turns, and at the fourth I cut right, pointing us west again.

"Here we go," Crow said. "No more plains. Anyone needs to take a leak, you get one minute out of the car. Max. In fact, I need to take a piss, I might just be hanging out the back window, know what I mean? This here is locust country, people. Bad as it comes."

We turned south. Then west. Then south again until we cut east. And by dawn we'd made so many damn turns that the only way I knew which direction we were heading was because the sun was coming back up.

"You get sleepy, I can drive." Crow said, his head at my shoulder.

"I ain't sleepy."

"Just an offer, little man. No need to be so tough all the time."

"You're all heart. But you can stick it. It's my wagon. And I'm the one who drives her."

"Fine. I'll stick to navigating."

"Feels like we're going in circles."

"Aye," Crow said. "Does feel that way, don't it? Always does. Out here in the corn."

"How the hell you end up working out here anyway?" I asked him.

"Oh, I worked all over."

"As an agent?"

"Special agent, you might say."

"Looking for trees?"

"Sort of. GenTech wants them trees bad, little man. They reckon there's food growing in Zion."

"And all that time you were looking for Zion, you ever heard of folk getting dragged off there? You heard of folk being chained to the trees?"

Crow stared out the window. "I saw the same picture you did."

I watched the corn get its color as the sky grew light. Deeper into the fields, the crops got less dusty. More green.

"So how'd you end up with Frost?"

"Mister Frost had something I needed."

"The tattoo."

"Said if we found those trees, he'd split whatever GenTech gave us. Split it right down the middle."

"And you trusted him?"

"Much as I trusted anyone," Crow said. "And you could say I figured I'd have a little more leverage on old man Frost than with GenTech Corporation."

"Didn't work out too good, I guess."

"It did and it didn't. See, I'm not just aiming for the money. I want to bring me something back home."

"Home?"

"To Niagara."

"Thought you'd have given up being a warrior."

"You born Soljah, little man, then you die part of the tribe."

"So why'd you leave?" Sal said, from the back of the wagon. "If you just want to go back there."

"You must know, I got myself thrown out of Waterfall City."

"Banished," I said. "Who'd have thought?"

"Bring a tree back, though," Crow went on, "like a nice little fruit tree. I be back in the good graces then, no? Give the Soljahs something to trade besides water."

"Reckon I'll bring me one back to Old Orleans," said Alpha. "An apple tree. Like in the stories."

"You can't go wasting apples in that shit hole," Crow said, laughing.

Split up all the trees, I guess. That was the plan.

"What about you?" Crow said, fixing me with a look. "What you aiming to do?"

"He's my father," I said. "The man in the picture. The man chained in the trees."

"Your daddy?"

"That's right."

Crow grinned. "And you don't think he's dead?"

"He ain't dead in that picture."

"True that," Crow said. Then he pointed. "Here. Take this left."

I made the turn and we started down a thinner service road, the dirt a little softer beneath the wheels.

And at the end of that road, not a hundred yards from us, towered a GenTech duster in all its glory.

CHAPTER THIRTY-SEVEN

I skidded the wagon to a halt, grinding up the dirt into a cloud all around us. The duster was as wide as the service road, twice as tall as the highest crops. And it wasn't moving. Damn thing was just sitting there. Facing us.

The huge, rolling blades were rested on the ground, and behind the blades were rows of metal teeth that fed the compactor and the sorting boxes. And on top of it all, painted in GenTech purple, was the duster's cockpit, windows bulging out the front of it like goggles on a steel face.

They'd seen us, of course. Whoever was up there. They were pointed toward us, staring right at us.

I cranked the wagon into reverse.

"Wait," Crow said.

"For what?"

"Running ain't gonna do us no good. And GenTech likes to keep its dusters moving. Check the grime on that thing."

He was right. The machine was covered in a fine layer of dirt — the blades, the engine, even the windows. None of it looked like it'd moved in a while.

"Shift over," Alpha said, climbing past Crow and squatting next to me. She had the telescope out, scanning the duster and the rest of the road. "Can't see nothing else," she said. "Nothing but that big hunk of steel."

"I say we go closer," Crow said. "See what we find."

"What is it?" Sal was trying to squirm himself a view.

"Ain't nothing," I said, and Crow pushed the kid back down.

Alpha flipped the safety off her rifle and lowered her window a crack, just enough she could ease out the barrel of her gun. Then I popped the wagon back into gear and rolled slowly forward.

As we got closer, I could tell just how big the damn thing stood. The blades alone were taller than the wagon, and the duster was so wide I could barely squeeze between it and the wall of corn at the edge of the road. I steered through the gap, me and Crow and Alpha all staring at the engines and sorting boxes, peering up at the cockpit.

I pulled past the blades and teeth, brought us alongside the flank of the machine.

"Wait," Alpha said. "Stop."

"What do you see?"

"Up there." She pointed at a ladder that stretched from the dirt all the way to the cockpit.

I stopped the wagon. Leaned across Alpha.

"You see it?" she said.

"Yeah. I see it."

"Well, what is it then?" said Crow, trying to push his face at the window.

"It's a body," I said. Though I'm not sure you could really call it that. Just bones is what it was. Blood dried black and baked in the sun. Little tuft of hair, maybe. But no flesh. No organs. Poor bastard was gripped on that ladder, and he'd been almost to the top of it, too. Almost back in the cockpit. Almost safe. But almost ain't enough. Not out here. Not with the locusts.

"And that," said Crow. "Is why we do not leave the vehicle."

"No shit," whispered Alpha. She glanced across at me, more fear in her eyes than she'd shown before. She pulled her gun down and cranked the window back in place.

I turned the wagon around the back of the duster, heading for the next crossroads.

"Which way now?" I said to Crow.

"Stop," he said.

"What?"

"Stop. Here. Behind the engines."

"Why? What'd you see?"

"Agents," Crow said. "Right behind us."

I spun the wagon back around, pulled in behind the bulk of the duster. Then I cut the engine.

"You think they're following us?" Alpha said.

"Most likely," said Crow. "Unless you seen someone else out here to follow."

"Maybe they're just checking on the duster," I said. "That could make sense."

"Well, I say we ambush 'em." Alpha peered up at the duster. "We got the high ground, after all."

"That means getting out of the wagon," I said.

"You want to sit here and wait, bud, you can go right ahead." And with that, Alpha popped her door open and leapt out of the car.

Me and Crow just stared at her as she strapped the rifle on her back and began crawling her way up the duster, hoisting herself atop the rear wheels, then working her hands and boots along the engine.

"Told you." Crow shook his head. "Girl's a firecracker. A real live wire."

"Not much of a plan," I said.

"No it isn't."

"Guess today's your lucky day, though."

"How's that?"

I threw my door open and climbed outside. "'Cause you get to drive."

They say you can hear locusts a moment before you see them. A big buzzing rush of noise. The sound, I guess, of their countless tiny wings. So that was good. Because right now everything was silent. Except for the sound of my breathing as I hauled my way up that grimy machine.

Alpha was ahead of me, almost to the cockpit, clambering her way along a section of purple tubing, carefully remaining blocked from the other side. I scrambled to the top of the engine, getting a good look down at the sorting units — cobs in one, husks and stems in the other. Cleanly done. Efficient.

I was pretty high now, a good forty feet up. And I could see out above the rows of plants, see the waves of crops shimmering in every direction until they just merged with the sky.

"Take my hand," Alpha whispered. She was just above me, hanging off the back of the cockpit, and she gripped my wrist and hauled me alongside her. We stood with our feet on a thin metal ledge, our hands grabbing hold of anything we could find.

"You see them?" I whispered.

"Yeah. Here." She pulled me past her so I could poke my head around the cockpit. And there they were. Agents.

There were three of them. Two men and a woman. Dust masks on, even here in the cornfields where the dirt can't blow so free. They were dressed identical – dark purple suits with the GenTech logo plastered all over in tiny white letters, as if the cloth had caught some disease. They matched their vehicle, too. A small round pod with fat purple tires and dark tinted windows, it sat fifty yards behind them. I watched the agents kneel and bend at the dirt, studying the tracks. Our tracks.

"You think there's anyone left in the car?" I whispered, swinging myself back behind the cockpit.

"Hard to say. One more, maybe."

"Well, you're the pirate."

Alpha grinned at me. "Here's how it goes down. Even if there's no one in their vehicle, we gotta immobilize it, in case they make it back there and try to get away."

"All right."

"So we wait till the agents are close enough for you, then you start shooting. I'll take out their tires with the rifle."

"Right."

"You got it?"

"Got it."

She worked her way into position, angling her rifle till she was all set and ready. Then she motioned me behind her and I kept low as I climbed around to the edge of the cockpit, holding on with one hand and laying out my pistol with the other.

The agents were pointing at our tracks and jabbing around at the corn, talking over something. Then the two men started for the duster. And the woman began jogging back to their pod.

"I'll take homegirl," Alpha whispered.

The agents pointed up at the cockpit, and for a moment I thought they'd seen us. My heart stopped but then thudded back into action — they were staring at the remains of the field hand, the bones must've been hanging right below me, just down the ladder on the far side.

"They gotta be in range," Alpha said. And she was right. They got much closer and I'd lose sight of them behind the blades. But I was trembling now, and not out of fear. I told myself it was like the Harvester I'd plugged with the nail gun. But it didn't feel the same. That was a war zone, and out here was so quiet. Those agents had no idea I was aiming to steal away their last breath.

"Banyan," Alpha hissed. I clicked the safety off, aimed the gun right at the nearest agent's chest, my heart pumping cold blood through my veins. I closed my eyes and pictured Pop needing me, his body wound up in chains and cuffed to the trees, and there was a gun at my father's head and he was starving to death. Just like my mother had starved so many years before.

I squeezed the trigger. I'd barely pulled it tight when the agent slumped forward and hit the ground. The second guy pulled his weapon and took a shot at me, the bullet clanging off the side of the cockpit. Awful damn close.

I ducked back. Alpha was firing at their vehicle and the noise of her gun seemed to shake my brain loose. I needed to get back up. Take another shot. But suddenly I wasn't real worried about it. Because there, beneath the boom of Alpha's rifle and the thud of bullets on steel, there was another sound. A terrible sound.

The sound of locusts.

CHAPTER THIRTY-EIGHT

I screamed at Alpha and begged her to move. I grabbed her by the vest and dragged her with me around the side of the cockpit. I stumbled. Slipped. Almost lost it. Hanging on by one arm, my face staring down at the top of the dead field hand's skull.

The noise was louder now, whining like a broken engine. I pulled myself up as Alpha yanked at the door to the cockpit. But she slipped back as the door flew open. And then she was hanging off the purple tubing below. Ten feet down. Ten feet too far.

The sun went black as locusts swarmed above us, spiraling out of the sky as I scrambled below the cockpit, inching out along a steel pipe, reaching down with my hand.

"Go," Alpha screamed, but I just kept reaching for her as the swarm closed in above us. And then I saw locusts below, pouring out of the corn and across the service road, rising up the sides of the duster like a flood.

Alpha stretched up with her fingers, high as she could, and the locusts grew louder, wailing and buzzing and filling the air.

I locked my hand on Alpha's wrist. Dragged her toward me, hauling her up. We slipped back along the pipe as it gave way beneath us, leapt for the cockpit as the locusts hit.

I felt their wings beat the wind through my hair and they bored through my boots as I shoved Alpha into the cab and spun around to seal the door tight behind us.

They hammered at the glass windows. They rattled at the walls. A black cloud. A blur of wings and sharp little mouths. We stamped dead the rogues that had made it inside, and then we pressed together in the middle of the cockpit, arms over our ears as we squeezed our eyes shut.

Then the roar became a buzz and it faded. Light broke back inside the cockpit. Sunlight. I opened my eyes. Stared out the window. I watched as the locusts drifted across the tops of the cornfields then swooped down all at once inside the plants, sinking into the crops like a stone. Gone to feast on some field hand, I guess. Or some other poor struggler who'd strayed into the corn.

"We're okay?" Alpha whispered, shaking against me.

"Yeah," I said. "We're okay."

I stared down at the service road where the bones of the agents were splayed on the dirt. If there'd been another agent inside the pod, then they'd not made it — Alpha had shot the windshield clean through.

"We should get back," I said.

"Wait," she said. "Look."

I peered west across the top of the cornfields and there, jagged and dark on the horizon, I could see the towering mess of Vega. The bulging skyline of the Electric City.

"We're getting close," I said. I turned to Alpha and her eyes were bright. Her lips were just inches from mine.

"You know what we're supposed to do?" she whispered.

"Just keep on till we get there."

"No." She made our noses touch. "I mean now."

She pulled me to the floor on top of her, and my heart was pounding and my mouth got thick. I felt wired up. Full of juice. And then we were kissing, something inside of me exploding as I felt her lips on mine.

She took my hands and wrapped my fingers beneath her thighs. Her legs were strong. Smooth. And she was so warm. I'd never felt anything near as soft as her skin. I kissed her jaw and her neck and then her mouth again, and kissing that girl was like the whole point of living.

Her eyes were closed and trembling and I closed mine too. Dark now. Like we'd been sucked inside some tunnel leading down through the earth.

"Damn, bud," she said, when I stopped kissing her.

I just lay there, breathing her in.

She reached to her vest and unclipped it, as if she was unlocking herself for me. I stared into her brown eyes as she took my hand and pressed it on her chest. I felt her heart beat strong. But then Alpha grinned, like being serious had suddenly become foolish.

I went to kiss her again, but she was already grabbing her gun and standing, buttoning back up her vest. "Come on," she said, pulling me to my feet. "They'll be worried about us."

She winked at me as she threw the door open, and then she slid down the ladder, blowing right through the bones of the field hand and kicking his remains into dust. I just stared after her for a moment, my body still hungry and light. Then I shot down the ladder and we hit the ground running, our eyes watching the sky for the darkness, our ears peeled for that horrible sound.

Crow shoved the door open and we dove into the wagon. Ended up in a sweaty pile on the floor by the driver's seat, Crow just staring down at us, shaking his head.

"Your car's tougher than it looks," he said.

I saw Hina and Sal cowered in the back, holding on to each other, and Hina was giving me some new look I'd not seen before.

"What's left out there?" Crow said.

"Nothing," I told him. "Just their vehicle."

He arched his eyebrows. "Their vehicle? Unattended?"

"Right."

Crow sparked the engine and backed up the wagon, pointing it around the far side of the duster.

"What are you doing?" said Alpha, and Crow laughed out loud.

"I be going to see what Jah has provided for us on this fine morning. A GenTech pod ain't salvage," he said. "It's gold. Solid gold."

Crow tore through the dirt and plowed the wagon through those three piles of bones, and what was left of the agents just fizzled like smoke. We pulled so close to the GenTech pod that the two vehicles were almost touching. Then Crow cut the engine and waited until everything was silent.

"We leave this door open," he said, pointing at the passenger side. "We're quick. And we're quiet. Anyone hears anything, the door closes in ten seconds. Right?"

"All right," I said, then I turned to Sal and Hina. "You two stay in here."

"I want to come," Sal said.

"You're too slow, kid."

"It's all right," Hina said, giving me that strange look again, like her eyes were trying to tell me something. "I'll watch him."

Alpha popped open the door and we fell into daylight, the sky blue above us and the corn a deep green.

The pod had sunk on busted tires, bullet holes riddled the paint job, and all its glass was shattered. We lifted up the side hatch. And then we dropped down inside a whole different world.

GenTech purple. Everywhere. Everything clean looking, shiny, like it had been snatched from a dream. They had gadgets down in that pod that you could tell were a whole different league. None of it was sprouting wires or had been taped together or was rigged backward and falling apart. These gizmos were tidier than the console in Harvest's ship. Sleek and small and silent.

"There it is," Crow said, kneeling on a seat, getting up close to a glittery console on the wall.

Alpha still had her head out the top of the hatch, watching the skies.

"What is it?" I said to Crow.

"This here's the main hub," he said. "And the readouts. But there'll be another one around somewhere." He yanked open some panels and rummaged inside.

"You see anything?" I said to Alpha, giving her leg a squeeze.

"Quiet," she said. "I'm listening."

I stared around the pod again. Picked up a foam hat with the GenTech logo plastered across the front of it.

"Fancy shit," I said.

"As fancy as it comes," said Crow, digging inside a box of tools. "Look in the back for their guns, little man."

I stuck my head back there and found a spare set of suits all neatly folded and stacked in place. And there, hanging off the ceiling, were two purple handguns that looked a whole lot better than the one I'd been using. The guns were clean and smooth, looked like they'd never even been used. I unclipped them, grabbed them off the ceiling, then I scooted back to the front of the pod.

"I got it," Crow said.

"What is it?" I stared at the small box in the palm of his hand.

"This," Crow said, his grin broad as I'd seen it, "is a GenTech Positioning System. Agent types in coordinates, it tells them where to go. This is it, little man. This is what we been needing. This right here is our GPS."

CHAPTER THIRTY-NINE

Sal couldn't believe it. His eyes grew as big as his whole head. Hell, I could hardly believe it myself. But there we were, heading west, winding through the service roads, weaving our way through that maze of corn, and when we popped out the other side, all we'd have to do is enter those numbers, the north one and the east one, and then we'd just glide right on through. My old man seemed close all of a sudden. Like he could be waiting around the next bend in the road.

Alpha wanted to enter the numbers right then, see how far away we'd be heading, but Crow just dangled the gadget off his fingertips, holding it away from us. Had to conserve the battery, he said. Better to wait till we were out of the maze.

I drove through till the sun went down, and when it got dark I pulled over next to the corn and shut the engine off. We couldn't risk using the headlights, and the absence of moon made it too dark to see.

The five of us clumped in the back of the wagon, all rammed together as we guessed about the future. Closest thing to family I'd known since Pop had been taken. A team, all of a sudden. A real team. Hell, even Hina seemed to be smiling, though she also kept stealing strange looks at me. I paid that no mind, though. We had food in our bellies and tomorrow on our brains. And the next day, and the next one. And every day after that.

"What do you think they look like?" Alpha said.

"Like that, you dummy," Sal yelled, pointing at Hina's belly and laughing. "What do you think they're going to look like?"

"But do you think there's just a couple?" she said. "Or a whole big stand?"

"There's a stand," I said, picturing the photo of my father. "Whole forest."

"You bet there's a whole forest. And I bet there are oranges and coconuts and almonds, too. Imagine the flavors." Sal let out a shriek. He slapped me on the thigh. "We're going to be so loaded. So rich we won't even know what to do."

Crow had stayed quiet mostly, but now he chimed in. "Just remember, Mister Sal, your daddy might be there, too." Crow stared at me as he said it.

"That's right," Sal said, nodding at Crow. Then the kid turned his face so I couldn't see it. I thought about the correction, the hidden tattoo.

And I thought about Zee.

Thinking about her made me solemn. Couldn't help but picture her in the back of the wagon with us, celebrating something we'd not yet done. And it made me think about what was going to happen when the journey ended. Would I really find my father in that stand of trees? Alive? The old Rasta had said Pop had until spring. And winter had only just barely begun.

So if my old man was there, what would come next? Could we build us a house in those treetops? Or had the trees already been cut down and sold? Was that what it came down to? Selling the forest like a bucket of corn? Something for the pirates. Something for the Soljahs. Who else? The Salvage Guild?

Still, as long as GenTech didn't get it. I thought about the endless rows of crops that surrounded us. Enough food you could feed every struggler. Or you could just get rich off your prices, and keep people low down and starved.

Soon we had eaten and talked enough to be sleepy. No damn air in the wagon that hadn't been breathed a thousand times over. We were drowsy. All of us. Even the watcher.

"Been awake since Old Orleans," Crow said, pulling my old man's sombrero over his face. "Believe I earned me some shut eye."

And one by one, our heads dropped till we were all passed out and sleeping. Reckon I was the last to go, pressed up against Alpha as her face twitched and her mouth hung open. I loved the smell of her, and I remember thinking that right before I fell asleep.

Before my eyes fell shut and everything changed again.

It was Hina that woke me. She was poking at my back, and I sat up and glanced around the wagon. Everyone was sleeping. Everyone but her and me.

She pointed at the hatch, gesturing that she wanted to go outside. The moon was up now, white on the cornstalks.

"We can't," I whispered. But she nodded. And I wondered if this meant she had something to tell me. About my father. About the trees.

I popped the hatch open, nice and quiet, and I breathed in the fresh smell of crops as I poked my head through.

Straining to listen, I climbed out of the wagon and held the hatch so Hina could come beside me. I stared around at the night, thinking about the locusts and that awful noise they made, thinking how Hina had better make this real quick. But she surprised me by clicking the hatch shut behind us.

"Come with me," she whispered, taking my hand. And then she led me inside the corn.

Our footsteps made a dry, cracking sound. We squeezed past the stalks until we found a sort of clearing, just enough space that we could stand facing each other. All I could hear was the thump of my heart. It was stupid being out there. I knew it was dangerous. But if Hina had something to tell me, I reckoned it was something I needed to hear.

"What is it?" I whispered.

"I remembered where it came from," she said, and as she spoke she lifted her shirt off her belly, showing me the leaves and branches of that beautiful tree. I could see her pulse through her stomach.

"I thought you were dead," she said. "When you climbed that machine and the swarms came. But you're strong, like your father. And I remembered it. How they sent me to find him. To bring him back home."

I went to speak, but she talked right over me, all the while stroking at the colors tattooed on her skin.

"He wanted to stop it," she said. Her voice was like she'd just come awake. "All of it. And now I have to warn you."

"What?" I said. "Warn me about what?"

But Hina just closed her eyes. Her fingers still caressing the tattoo tree but the rest of her like she was sleeping, standing on her feet but caught in a dream. And for a moment everything was silent. Everything was still. But then I heard the footsteps come crunching toward us. Closer and closer. Someone stepping through the corn.

CHAPTER FORTY

The poacher's face looked like it had once been broke open and then pieced back together wrong. He stood before us. An ugly shadow beneath the bright white of the moon.

"Get away from her," the man said. But I was frozen, like I was tangled up in the plants. "Move," he said, and this time he pointed a shotgun at my head.

I stepped aside, the gun following my every move, waving just inches from my face. I went to say something, but the man cut me off.

"Keep your mouth shut, boy."

He shone his flashlight over Hina, top to bottom, his mouth hanging open and stringy with spit, his eyes bulging out of his head. He blinked as he jabbed the flashlight at her skin, like he was testing whether or not she was real. Then he stared at me again and pushed the shotgun under my jaw.

The man turned his head and waved his flashlight in a figure eight. He knocked four times at a cornstalk.

"How many are there?" he said.

"Ain't no one else," I told him, my voice as shaky as the rest of me.

"In the car?" He jabbed the shotgun deeper. "How many in the car?"

"It's empty," I said. "Broken."

"You lie." He sneered. "But it'll do you no good."

I heard more footsteps in the crops, and the poacher gestured for me to start walking. I pushed Hina in front of me, keeping my hands on her shoulders and trying to block her from the poacher as he stabbed his gun at my spine and shoved us back toward the wagon.

When we stepped onto the service road, about twenty poachers stepped onto it with us. They slid through the stems and appeared in the night, like they'd bled right out of the crops. Some of them didn't even carry guns, just knives or hacksaws. They wore clothes made of corn husks, and all their feet were bare.

I studied the shriveled bodies and the faces in the moonlight. Dead eyes. More scars than teeth.

The poacher behind me prodded his gun at my head, pushing me against the wagon as he tried to peer inside it. Then he took the butt of the shotgun and pounded at the roof.

"Come on out," he roared.

The rest of the poachers had circled the car now. Heads stooped and weapons raised. The man pounded on the wagon again.

"We don't want you," he yelled. "Just the car and what's in it. So come on out. Or your friends here are gonna suffer." He stared at Hina as he said it and I felt her tremble beside me.

The man hammered at the roof until the rear hatch lifted as if the pounding had popped it loose. Sal's head stuck out and the poacher made a sound that was supposed to be laughter.

"Shit," the man said, pulling Sal out of the car by his ear. "Look at the size of this one."

It all happened so fast there was no time to think.

A gun fired out the back of the wagon, and the bullet sank into that brokeface poacher, launched him back about five feet. Then the rest of the poachers fell upon us. Some of them heading for Sal, but most of them cornering me and Hina and wrestling us into the corn.

It was chaos. A tumble of bodies charging through the crops, gunshots and voices screaming.

But then the world stood still. The night turned black.

And an ugly swarming sound filled up the air.

I'd never seen people disappear like that. Those poachers spread thin and then vanished, like they'd found holes in the world to stay hidden inside. They were gone. Just like that. And me and Hina were ten yards from the road.

I stumbled and thrashed through the crops, pulling Hina with me as locusts filled the air with a whining, desperate sound that filled your head and stopped you from thinking.

I crashed forward, losing my balance for an instant, and then I was down in the dirt and lost and Hina's hand was gone.

I spun around and saw her.

One last time.

She'd stopped running. She was just stood there, staring at me, and I watched as that frothy cloud descended upon her, buzzing and biting and coming down slow. Consuming her. Her head, her beautiful head. The swarm seemed to suck her inside it. It went down past her neck and over her shoulders, spun down her arms and low down her chest, pulling her in like a twister on the plains.

Her beautiful belly. That soft brown skin. The tree. All of it. Gone.

Ravaged. Every root and branch and leaf. Every secret inside that now would stay hidden.

And I howled at that swarm and the crops and the sky, and the stars should have quit because there weren't no reason to be shining.

The locusts were at her hips now, clawing their way lower. And I could have touched them if I'd just reached out my hand. But finally I felt my legs moving, pushing me backward. I was on all fours. And then I was running.

At the wagon every door was closed. I punched at the windows, smashed at the roof. And I felt the locusts buzz closer, tearing through the air toward me.

Alpha threw open the door as I felt the sharp mouths sink into my skin. I fell inside, pulled the door shut. But the locusts were still on me, gnawing my neck and the back of my skull.

Crow pushed me to the floor and leaned over me, swiping at the locusts, crushing them with his fist. They bit at him, and he lashed and cried till the last one was dead. And then he just crouched above me, his fists all bleeding and raw and the windows black with that swarm pressing in at us.

Then, finally, as the noise let up and the swarm drifted higher, I could hear the sound of Sal weeping. And Alpha's voice, quiet and muffled.

"What were you doing?" she kept saying. "What have you done?"

I stared at her as the moonlight spilled in. Her face was slick with tears and her hands were clasped at her stomach, pressing at the bullet wound like she might squeeze the blood back inside her.

CHAPTER FORTY-ONE

Alpha gazed at me through a face full of pain. She was quivering with it. But her eyes were still sharp. Focused. The veins on her neck twitched and her breath came short and shallow.

"Banyan," Crow said, but the word seemed to float past me. "Banyan."

He'd slid behind the steering wheel with his hands all mashed and bleeding. I stared at him, wondering what could possibly matter now.

Then I sensed the night shift color again. Brighten. But not on its own accord. I stared through the windshield and saw three pods in the distance. Bearing down the road toward us, burning us up with their purple glare.

Crow cranked on the engine and spun the wagon back around.

"You're gonna need to hold them off," he said, and for the first time, everything about Crow seemed out in the open. And he was scared shitless. Just like me.

I hauled Alpha into the back as Crow slid the wagon through a turn and began speeding back down the service roads. Undoing all the distance we'd covered. Losing ground all over again.

I got Alpha set so she'd not be shaking around too much, and she was staying silent now, but her eyes told me all I needed to know. Her hands were slick with her own blood, and I tried shoving my hands against her wound but the blood kept coming and the blood would not stop.

"Sal," I screamed, and I could hear Crow shouting at me. "Sal." I grabbed the kid by his neck. "Quit sniveling, you little shit. You gotta help."

I pulled off my shirt and had Sal shove it deep in Alpha's stomach, stemming the wound that kept gaping and frothing like some sort of mouth. Then I yanked the piece of bark off my torso and placed it over the shirt, strapping it in place so tight I was scared it might stop her from breathing.

Sal fingered at the bark.

"Leave it alone," I told him. "Take one of these."

I handed him one of the pistols I'd snagged from the pod.

"Come on," Crow bellowed, and I yanked up the rear hatch with Alpha behind me, and Sal at my elbow, ready to shoot.

"Fire," I yelled, and we let it rip. Just squeezing the triggers, letting off a round of those fancy bullets, a round that seemed like it might never end.

The GenTech pods didn't fire back at us. They just kept on coming, our bullets puncturing the purple steel but not slowing them down a damn bit.

"The glass," Crow called. "Aim for the glass."

I tried. Kept trying. But it was too hard to point straight, what with the wagon swerving every which way as we bounced through the sand.

Finally, I cracked one of the windshields and sent that pod reeling into the crops. The others opened fire now, keeping their bullets low, aiming for our tires.

“Keep shooting,” I said to Sal, but he held his gun up. Empty. I handed him what was left of mine and reached for Alpha’s rifle in the front of the wagon, stretching my arm out across her crumpled body, groping through the dark.

But my hand never found the rifle.

The duster appeared out of the crops in front of us like a wall of steel teeth. Crow seized up the brakes but we hit. We hit hard. The wagon never stood a chance. Those duster blades ripped right through the engine and gobbled it in pieces, clamping down every inch and dragging it inside the belly of that giant metal beast.

The blades chopped through the steering wheel, and Crow’s thighs exploded as the metal ripped them apart. I grabbed his arms and yanked what was left of him into the rear of the wagon.

But the duster kept coming.

Sal was gone, I remember. Like maybe he’d been hurled out the back on impact. Or maybe he’d scampered free. And Alpha was out cold. I dragged her on top of me with one hand and clawed toward the open hatch with the other. The sound of the duster was something beyond noise. So loud it seemed silent. Or perhaps I’d already gone numb.

Crow pulled his bleeding stump along with his fingernails. The three of us moving too slow. But then we reached the hatch. Pushed through.

My wagon thrashed and spun into tiny chunks behind us and I remember gazing back down the throat of the duster, watching my old life being digested and sorted into scraps. And the duster seemed to keep eating my wagon, long after everything had stopped moving, even after the blades had stopped spinning, after every engine shut off.

And in the same way, I don't think there was a time I stopped screaming. Crow all bloody and twitching, and Alpha all gone beside me.

I wailed and hollered and I wished I was dead.

Then the duster fired up a torch beam and brought that light down upon us. The color of a bruised purple sun. And the headlights of the pods all fused together, making things as bright as they were bad.

I heard footsteps. Doors opening and closing. I heard voices. Then they were taking Alpha from me. They had blood on their suits. Purple and red. And I couldn't stop them from taking her because they were taking me too. Needles jabbing at me, breaking my skin.

"Hold still," someone yelled. As if I was moving. Then I could hear Crow screaming and it was exactly what the Darkness must have sounded like. The twenty years of night.

"Not again," Crow roared, till his voice split in two. "Not again."

PART THREE

CHAPTER FORTY-TWO

When I came to, I wished to hell I hadn't. I'd lost Alpha. And Crow. Sal and Hina.

They'd been replaced by strangers.

We were on a road, and I knew that immediately. Being on the road's in my blood, I guess. It's hardwired into me. I felt the shake. The unpeeling feeling. I tried lifting my head but only my eyes would move. Drugged. Strapped in place. And back on the road, staring at the brightest sky I'd ever seen.

I peered at the strangers to the right of me, the strangers to the left. Their eyes were closed and I told those faces to just keep on sleeping. Ain't nothing to see up here anyway.

No more corn. The world had changed.

New smells now. Familiar smells.

Plastic. Steel and juice.

Ah, yeah. Juice. The smell of the road. Lifeblood to every set of wheels that's rolling.

When the first building passed over my head, I thought it was nothing but a shadow. I thought maybe I'd blinked. But those buildings kept popping into my sky, flashing past me, more and more of them until the buildings took over and the sky disappeared.

Endless shades of black and gray and silver. You never seen so many windows. Like glassy eyes. Buildings so high, they bent like a landscape, arcing all together, slivers of steel in plastic sleeves, pointing at the sun.

Then pointing at the moon. But then even the moon got blocked by the buildings. Even that massive old moon.

I could smell the fumes off the bio vats. The greasy stink of hoarded corn being brewed into juice. And that juice must have flowed through pipes as wide as ancient rivers, all tunneled through the streets like veins.

When the lights came on in the city, it made the drugs feel even stronger. First the windows sparked up, but that was nothing, just a simple orange like something burning. It was the fizzy billboard glow that got me. Lights of every color, you couldn't even try to count them. They never flickered, but they spun and I spiraled, orbiting in light like I was drowning in stars. It made it hard to swallow, and I chewed at my tongue and my cheek. Signs flashed at me. Saying what? Who cared? Not me. Couldn't read those suckers anyway.

Until the last one.

All the wealth in the world and this is what they do with it. Tall buildings and lights that burn twice as bright and all night long. So much juice, you'd wonder how there was any corn left for eating. But I'm sure they were eating plenty in that city that don't sleep.

No sleeping in Vega. No rest for the wicked.

But I thought maybe I could drift off now, the buildings disappearing, the lights going out. We were being sucked under the ground.

Deeper and deeper. Yeah, just go to sleep, that's what I wanted. Except, that last sign I'd spotted, it bothered me. Because I hated to think it might be the one word I could read, like it was the only word that mattered.

GenTech.

I don't even want to tell you what it was like down there. It was a place the sun didn't shine and no wind whispered.

They kept the lights low, and that was the one nice thing they did for us. They had a system, I guess. Though I had no idea what it was.

But of course they had a system. This was GenTech. They knew what they were doing. They knew what they wanted.

Sick bastards. Dressed in purple and marching about with their clubs raised high. And I don't know what they needed those clubs for. Most of the prisoners were still unconscious, and the ones like me were too drugged numb to fight. We were just bodies. Not even people. We were bodies that pissed and puked and moaned as the agents picked through our limbs and faces and dragged each victim one by one to a staging area in the middle of that nasty black hole.

I reckoned this was the lowest point to which all else tumbled. The end of the road for all those lost souls who'd been taken. The people plucked from the dust and sold off by slavers. The people like my father and the old Rasta and Alpha's mother and now me.

It was GenTech. In the end, it had always been GenTech. The purple fist crushing the last gasp from our crusty lungs.

But for what?

On the outside, I could still barely move my fingers. But inside I was a full-on riot. My mind not working right but all looping around.

And I thought again about the damn story about a meat trade, that the rich freaks in Vega liked to mix up their meals. But if it was meat they were after, then why were those agents testing each of one us by taking our blood? Because that's what they were doing – sucking the red stuff into small plastic tubes.

From what I could tell, there were two possible things that could happen once the agents ran their tests. Two options for all the bodies that had been taken.

First option was the agents grabbed your blood and ran the test, and then off you went. Gone. No idea where you were dragged to. But it was better than the alternative. Much better.

Because the second option was the agents grabbed your blood and ran the test, but then they just looked right through you.

And then they burned you.

Middle of the staging area they had some furnace sunk in the ground. A pit full of flames.

And that was option number two. So you can see how the first one became so appealing. Especially after you spent a day breathing in the ashes of all those poor bastards who'd been fried.

Could have been longer than a day. Could have been it was just an hour and each minute felt like twenty. The drugs we were on kept things silent. For the most part.

Every now and then a low moan would howl, escaping out of someone's lips like they were trying to wake themselves up.

I was awake enough already, though. On the inside. I was trying to figure out what the hell was going on as I watched the poor bastards who had to take their turns before me.

A woman with one arm tested positive and the agents dragged her away. Next up was a blond kid who failed, and I clenched my eyes shut.

And it kept going on like this. One after another. Those purple suits threading through the crowd and calling out numbers, hauling off bodies, and stoking that fire pit in the middle of the room.

It just kept on going, and what started off horrifying only got worse. Any wall that my mind had built or the drugs provided, that wall pretty soon got blown into bits, reality piercing like a razor on bone. It got so bad I started longing for my own turn to be tested, just so I wouldn't have to witness no more. Watching some kid get pulled from his mother, or some woman being took from her man. All these unknown faces. These strangers.

But then the purple suits changed even that. Because from out of a corner, they gathered up someone I knew.

It was Crow. His top half hadn't ever really healed from the burning, and his bottom half wasn't even there at all. Gone. Lost in the jaws of the duster. The agents carried Crow's torso to the staging area. And as they jabbed his arm with the needle and siphoned his blood, some twisted part of me wanted to shout out at him.

Hey, little man. That's what I wanted to yell.

Sick, right?

Must have been the drugs.

Crow passed the test and they hauled him out of view, and I wondered how they'd stopped him from bleeding out in the cornfields. I wondered where they were taking him now. But I didn't have long to sit there and think about it, because next thing you know, the agents had Sal up there, and I could tell by their faces that the poor bastard had failed the test.

The sight of Sal being hoisted toward the flames did something to me. It broke into my skull and shattered down the back of my mind, and I could move again. But as I stumbled up and staggered toward the purple suits, it was like someone was working my muscles for me, as if it wasn't my mouth that was screaming. As if it wasn't my friend about to be burned alive.

Is that what he was, then? My friend?

I honestly don't know, but yeah, I like to think that he was. Which is why it must have hurt him when his eyes recognized me for a moment but all I was shouting was "The numbers, the number. Tell me what it is."

And maybe that's all we'd been to each other, anyway. Not just the fat kid and me, but Crow and Alpha and Zee. The whole damn lot of us. All we'd wanted was to find those trees.

Something to believe in. To bring us back home. Something to make us free, maybe. Or just something to sell.

The agents were all over me, blocking Sal from view. But the strength I'd saved while I'd been under, it all came racing to the surface now. I pushed and kicked at some bastard in a purple suit that I'd never seen before, but here he was trying to control me. Trying to hurt me. Trying to murder my fat little buddy right in front of my eyes.

I must have been spitting, I was crying so hard. And for a moment I reached him, somehow Sal was next to me, we were breathing in smoke from the fire, gloved hands all over us.

That kid stared at me like his eyes were windows and he was trapped inside there somewhere, tired of hiding.

"The number," I said to him, or I tried to say it anyway. And what good was it? Now everything was lost.

But the kid surprised me. His voice popped out.

"There was no number," he said, the suits lifting him up, shoving him at the flames. "I made it up," he said, as he disappeared from me forever. "So you'd take me with you."

And then he was gone. Still high, I reckon. Because I never even heard him scream.

I felt the hands working me over, and I thought that was it. Thought I was just going to burn right then. And all I could think was how Frost must have already made it. He had his coordinates. His GPS. And somewhere, he was out there. And my father was out there, too. Surrounded by trees and murderers.

"Wait," one of the agents was yelling. "He should be tested."

They yanked me to my feet.

I didn't do a thing. I couldn't even feel the needle go in or the blood coming out. But I watched it, that deep dark red. And because of the blood draining out of me or my previous show of strength, whatever it was, I was suddenly empty. And as they pulled the needle from my skin, I sank inward as every light inside turned black.

CHAPTER FORTY-THREE

Weirdest thing about whatever they'd doped me up with — awake you felt like you were dreaming, but pass out and no dream would come. It was a void. The darkest night. Untouched by the motion of the world or the swell of whatever you kept hidden inside.

Sometime on the boat, though, they let us come around. And somehow I knew that meant we were almost there.

They fed us. Juiciest damn corn I ever tasted. They gave us water and then they stripped us of clothes and shaved off our hair. I waited. Still coming back to life. Shielding my eyes from the neon lights. But soon as I could, I stumbled across the giant cargo hold we'd been allowed to wake up in. I made for the exit. And I found my way onto the deck.

I don't know what time it was. Early morning, maybe. I stood alone, bony beneath the plastic sheet they'd draped across my shoulders. It was so cold out there, made me feel brand new and old as anything, both at the same time. The cold hurt, too. I almost turned back inside with the others. But I just bit at my tongue as the freeze enveloped me. I watched my hands shake and my toes turn blue.

I found my way to the center of the deck and I watched the water and I stared around at the boat. A cockpit sat on top of the cargo hold and above that was a gun tower. Everything black and silver. No purple. No GenTech logos. It sure wasn't the biggest boat I'd ever imagined, but it didn't need to be. The water was flat. And it stretched in every direction for as far as my eyes could see.

I pulled the sheet around me and hunched my shoulders in. My breath blew steamy, the same color as the clouds. Air was so cold it was hard work just to breathe it. But it helped my mind come back into focus, even if my body felt like it might snap apart.

I stared back at the steel walls of the cargo hold where my fellow survivors were now huddled together, escaped from the fire. Escaped from the burn.

But still taken.

I remembered Sal. Too high to be scared, robbed even of emotion as they'd tossed him to the flames. And I reckon I'd been a bastard to Sal, pretty much right from the beginning. I mean, what had he done? Other than live up to the way the world seemed to treat him. Father like Frost and what chance did he have? I pictured Hina holding the kid, giving him some sort of feeling, and I figured that was such a good thing to have done for someone. To give without wanting nothing in return. But Hina was gone, too. I shuddered as I pictured her about to tell me her secrets but then stolen away and lost in that swarm. And who was left? Me. Crow?

I stared at the cargo hold.

And what about Alpha?

I'd not seen her in the factory, or whatever you want to call that place. I'd not seen her since the cornfields. The back of the wagon, where she'd been dying in my arms. Dying from a poacher's bullet I might as well have shot from my own gun. May as well have killed them all with my selfishness. Running around without thinking, instead of doing what I'd promised and finding the trees.

And you know what? For a moment I didn't even care about the damn trees.

All I wanted was my pirate girl back.

I wanted her the same way as when I'd run barefoot through Old Orleans with my hands empty and my heart full. The way you want something when every part of you says that you ain't going to get it.

I was scared to go looking for her. So scared to know full out she was gone. She probably hadn't made it to the factory at all. And if somehow she had, then she'd likely been thrown like poor Sal into those hungry flames. And how could I stand not seeing her among the stolen and shaved sat huddled on this ugly barge? What would I do if she was ash and smoke when she should have been beside me with her voice soaring free?

Eventually, though, I staggered up to go try and find her. Because even when there is no hope, somehow you can still find a place to pin inside the things that you need.

I started across the deck but I tripped and fell. Landed on my face and began crawling, dragging myself through puddles of icy water. And as I tasted the water, I stopped crawling and just stared off the boat.

Water. Flat water. All the way to every horizon. And this water wasn't just flat – it was fresh. Like out of a river. Water you could drink, not salty like the Surge. We were on a lake. Cold and deep and wide.

The freeze in the air told me we were north. Way north. Had to be somewhere above the molten wastelands, this cold this early. Somehow GenTech must have figured a path through the steam and ash of the Rift. And I figured if this was a lake, then somewhere there had to be a shoreline. A place they were taking us. And some kind of reason we had been kept alive.

I crashed back through the steel doors and let the warmth and the stale air consume me, felt every bit of skin and bone I had come roaring back to life. I steadied myself against the door as I thawed out. And then I stared around the cargo hold.

There were agents stationed along the walls, their bright purple suits in contrast to the white paint and the pale neon blast. The agents were weaponed up, no doubt about that. Pistols on their belts, spiky clubs in their hands. But I tell you, those agents had nothing to worry about. My fellow prisoners might have been moving some, but they still looked like corpses.

Vacant eyes. Lips too tired for screaming. We were a broken crew. Silent. I thought again of King Harvest and his hull full of bodies. That's why they'd needed so many, I guess. That damn test they were running. Take some of us off across the water and burn up the ones left behind.

But what test had we passed?

I couldn't see us being meant for working. Or eating. Not the state we were in.

I stared around for Alpha. For Crow. Scanning those shaved heads and plastic sheets for a face I knew. I wandered between the bodies that were sprawled and twisted on the floor, stepped past groping fingers and patches of flesh half-covered in plastic. Voices rose up. People whispering to one another, moaning and holding on to the person beside them.

I kept walking. Stumbling is what it was. I kept an eye on the agents along the walls. Watched for Crow's melted skin or the stump his legs had left behind. And in my mind, Alpha didn't fit in with anything I was seeing. Like two worlds that could not meet.

Fingers gripped cold around my ankle. They tugged at me, squeezed at me, and then went limp. I looked down. And no part of me was surprised I had walked right past her.

I remembered when I found Alpha on the wall in Old Orleans, with her arms above her head and her vest all matted with blood. I held that image close inside of me, really lodging it tight so I'd remember. So I couldn't forget.

Because this time, Alpha wasn't towering above me, legs spread and head thrown back. This time she was crumpled. The fuzzy pink vest with her name etched upon it had been replaced by the white of her shoulders and the crappy GenTech plastic. They'd shaved off her mohawk, and it changed her whole face. Made her look younger. And older.

I squatted down to her. My hands on her hands. My feet touching her feet. We'd been stripped of everything and painted gray, but it didn't matter. Not in that moment. Not right then. I ran my hand over the stubble on top of her head, and she blinked at me like her eyes might work her mouth into a smile.

"I'm here," I whispered. "Right here. And I won't go nowhere. I promise."

She pulled my hand to her cheek and touched her mouth to my fingers. And we sat that way for a bit, comfort enough to just keep on breathing. But finally I wanted to tell her about the lake outside we were floating over. And I wanted to know if she'd seen the things I'd seen. If she'd been awake when we'd been pulled into the city, if she'd seen the buildings grow tall and the lights explode. I wanted to know if she'd seen the fire at the factory, if she'd watched as people were torn from the rest of us and the bodies were cast into flames.

But I couldn't bring myself to talk about it. Not yet. And I had another question, one that somehow seemed more pressing.

"Your wound?" I said. "You were shot." I pointed at my own belly. "Right here."

"Sealed up," she said, and her hands went to her stomach, clamping down on the plastic sheet.

"Let me see."

She shook her head.

"Come on," I whispered. "Show me."

She let her hands fall beside her and I pulled apart the plastic. And there, where the wound had been, a chunk of her skin was missing. And where there used to be skin, now there was bark. Not the old piece of wood I'd shoved there to stem the bleeding. This was new. Grown fresh to patch her together. It was pink and green and knotted. I tapped on it. That unmistakable sound of wood.

Alpha yanked the plastic back across her and turned her eyes from me, as if ashamed.

"No," I said. "It's beautiful." And I weren't lying. All the beauty I'd seen before was just a dream with her in it. I tried to kiss her, but she spun her head away.

"Where are they taking us?" she muttered, tears streaming down her face.

"I don't know," I said. But truth was, I was starting to think I did know. It was the same place the old Rasta had been taken. The place where he'd seen my father.

The place where he'd seen the trees.

CHAPTER FORTY-FOUR

We found Crow and carried him out to the deck so he could see the water. I didn't ask how they'd stitched him back together, because I already had a pretty good idea.

But why? That's what I wanted to know. What were they keeping us alive for? And what was so important that we'd been taken so far?

"You worked for them," I said to Crow as the three of us huddled together near the railing, shivering and watching the spray off the water. "You worked for GenTech. So what the hell do you think they're doing?"

Crow moved his head so he was staring away from me, as if any one direction held something the others didn't show.

"I worked for them," he said, first words I'd heard out the mouth of his new body. "I was security. The lower ranks started asking too many questions. I was supposed to shut them up."

"Too many questions? About what?"

"About what was happening."

I just stared at him. Blank.

"This." Crow pointed with his chin. "All this."

"What is this?"

"It's what happens to those that get taken. Project Zion, GenTech calls it."

"And what the hell's that?"

"I don't know." Crow shrugged. "I was supposed to stop the questions. Not find the answers. But I heard GenTech was desperate to find them some trees. And I uncovered a legend about a forest and a woman that could point its direction. So I started digging. GenTech tried to shut me down. They captured me, drugged me. But I escaped. Kept on digging, following clues. Till I tracked the woman down. Till I found that tattoo."

"And you think the trees are across the water?" I said. "I mean, what if they are? What if they're out here?"

"Here?"

"Yeah."

"Well, then I think GenTech should've charged me a ticket. Instead of slicing me to pieces."

"Think about it," I said. "Project Zion."

"Zion. Trees. You're talking about heaven, boy. We be heading to hell."

"I don't know," I said. "Could be one's really just the same as the other."

I watched clumps of ice appear on the water. And I pictured my father, chained to a tree trunk, captured in a forest beneath a clear blue sky.

This was the boat. It had to be.

"My old man's out here somewhere," I said, and I turned to Alpha. "Your mother might be, too. Harvest was part of this whole operation."

Alpha just looked at Crow and then looked back out at the water.

"What?" I said.

"She probably thinks you should give it a rest."

"Well, it ain't spring yet. And I ain't giving in now."

The chunks of ice got bigger and began to stick up real high. The boat wound between the frozen mounds, the jagged white peaks, and it crushed right through the small stuff.

We were wrapped tight in our plastic sheets and bundled together, watching the future drift into view. But the ice clustered up, thicker and thicker.

And at first we almost didn't see the island.

The island was wide and tall, and just past the brown shore were hills covered in snow. As we got nearer, a siren rose up off the boat and kept wailing so loud we had to plug up our ears.

"I'm too cold," mouthed Alpha, standing to shuffle back inside. The wind had picked up and the air was sleety. But I couldn't turn away from the island.

This was it, I reckoned. End of the line.

Got close and I could see that the island was floating. It had grown right out of a giant wad of trash. Plastic and metal and salvage, all wound up and mashed together in the water. A mile of scrap. A mountain of it. Bits of junk sticking up on the shoreline and jutting out of the snowy hills.

But on the beaches, you could see the trash had begun dissolving into earth again. So I reckoned that meant the island was ancient. Old enough to turn back into dirt.

Got closer still and I could see people on the ridgeline, climbing up toward us from the other side of the hills. They stood there, waiting on us. And as the boat drifted to the shore, I could see they were all dressed in purple, leaving no doubt as to whose island this was.

"Let's go in," Crow said, his voice as bitter as the rest of him. I hoisted him up with me, our teeth chattering.

We huddled inside the cargo hold with the rest of the prisoners, and it wasn't long before the boat let out a thud and slammed to a stop. People stumbled and fell, but I stayed on my feet, grabbing Alpha, and clutching Crow so he was held tight between us.

One by one the lights blinked out, until everything was black. Then the agents cranked open the doors to the deck and we began squeezing outside, all shoved together, one big wriggling mob.

I gripped Alpha's hand and I had Crow on my back. But we couldn't move all tied together like that — the crowd surged past and tore us apart. I lost Alpha between the bodies, and an agent swooped behind me, prying Crow's arms from my shoulders and dragging him away.

I tried to keep my head up, to suck in some air. And I peered around for Alpha but the shaved heads bobbing just all looked the same.

The agents had run a ramp off the deck and down onto the frozen shoreline, and I waited and pushed until it was my turn to skid down, my feet numb and slippery in the snow.

I landed in a pile on the plastic beach, amid crusty old bottles and boxes. Up on the hillside, the agents were staring down at us, wrapped in their purple fuzz, their faces buried inside huge hoods. They watched as we shivered and splashed in the puddles.

A rough path led up the hill, and it wasn't long before we were forced to climb it, spiked clubs prodding us forward, voices shouting for us to move. I remember staring up at the sky as the snow whirled, and I wanted to try not walking and see what happened. But my bare feet kept shuffling, staggering onward until I was at the top of the hill and staring down at a massive bio vat on the other side, steel walls rumbling as the innards worked corn into juice, sooty fumes greasing the sky.

"Banyan."

It was Alpha, calling from down the path behind me. I turned, tried to wait for her. But then another voice was calling my name.

I stared at the agents on the ridgeline, and one of them was running toward me — the same agent who was shouting for me, telling me to wait. And then the agent was pulling down her hood, and her face burst into the cold air like it might melt everything around her. Her breath steamed and her brown skin was flushed red.

I just stood there. Froze to the snow as the bodies rushed past. And as Alpha reached me, she took my hand, and stared like I stared as Zee ran across the hill toward us.

CHAPTER FORTY-FIVE

Chaos thawed out the whole freezing lot of us. Prisoners stumbled and fell as the agents tried to keep everything moving. But things weren't going to keep moving. The crowd ground to a standstill, just a pile of half-naked bodies stacked in the snow. The agents waved their rifles and swung their clubs, but woven through their commands, I could still hear Zee's voice, shouting and straining.

"Stop," she was calling. "Bring him to me. Bring him to me."

"Who is she?" Alpha whispered as she pushed in close, our plastic sheets clacking, sticky in the cold. But before I could answer, an agent had his hands on me and another was swiping the path clear with a club.

"Wait," I tried to tell them as they yanked me off the trail. "Stop."

I thrashed around, trying to find Alpha. I saw her come for me, but the agent swung his club and Alpha's blood burst bright and sprayed at the snow. I screamed for her, stretched my fingers out toward where she'd been. Then I saw her, still on her feet, trudging away with her head down and her arm bleeding. She was keeping on. Giving up. And I lost sight of her through the trampling mob.

"No," I kept whispering. But then I was off the trail, surrounded by agents, and Zee was kneeling above me as I curled up and shook.

I threw up then. Like something had popped. But it made things no clearer. It just made me more cold.

Zee took my head in her lap, and her hands were wrapped in the same fuzzy stuff as the rest of her. I seemed to sink inside her clothes.

I tried to speak, but I couldn't.

I wanted to tell her about Alpha. And Crow.

"Bring him inside," Zee said. She took her coat off and wrapped it around me. Then the agents lifted me up and they began carrying me, Zee telling them what to do, and them doing just as they were told.

I slept long and deep, but woke with a start. My plastic sheet was gone, replaced by a set of soft purple robes and even softer blankets that I'd twisted all around me. I unwound myself from the bed and pried my head off the pillow. Then I sat up and stared around the room.

No windows. Nothing to see. Just my bed with a chair beside it. A pair of fuzzy boots on the floor. I slid off the bed and slipped my feet inside the boots. I ran my fingers at my face and scratched at the stubble on my head. Then I stepped to the door and shoved it open.

The next room was a whole lot bigger and a whole lot brighter. Whole lot more busy, too. Desks and tables and gizmos and gadgets. Neon lamps. Cables in bunches. There were consoles flashing numbers, and tiny glass tubes hung like decorations across the walls. I blinked at the confusion, the mess. GenTech's logo was everywhere, but this hardly looked like their usual neatness. There was none of the cold precision that seemed to work for them so well.

"You look more like him," a voice said. "Now that you're awake."

It was a woman that spoke. And at first I thought it was Zee's voice. But it wasn't.

It was Hina's.

I steadied myself against a desk, knocking a rack of plastic vials to the floor, where they burst and splintered. Then it was silent again but for the soft hum of electricity that filled the room.

"I saw you die," I whispered.

She was hunched in a plastic chair, her face caught in the glow of a monitor screen. Her hair was long and silver, and her brown skin was creased and saggy.

But it was her, all right.

"So," she said, her gray eyes fixed on me. "How did I die?"

"You were eaten."

"Eaten?"

"Locusts."

"Sounds horrible."

"Yeah," I said. "It was."

"Well, we mustn't dwell on such things, Banyan." It caught me off guard, her using my name. And her voice was different. Strong sounding. More smart with her words.

"Come closer," she said.

"No," I said, just staring at her. "No. You go to hell."

"Be nice."

"Where's Zee?"

"She's where she always is."

I just shook my head like it might make her vanish. I glanced around the room for an exit.

"Come sit with me," the woman said. "Please."

"What is this place?"

"It's my laboratory."

"So which one was real? You or the other?"

"Real?"

"You're older, so I guess you were the first, right? The other was just a copy. That it? Like the Harvesters."

"You mustn't try to simplify things just to make it easier."

"Then why don't you tell me what the hell's going on?"

I started across the room but she was up out of her chair and bearing down on me. I was slow and she wrapped her arms around my waist, wrestling me against her. I was still weak. Too weak to fight.

"Where's Zee? I whispered, my face pressed in the woman's purple shirt.

"She'll be back."

"My head hurts."

"I'm sorry."

I turned to look at her. She was squeezing the daylights out of me.

"It's hard for me not to be angry," she said, her voice calm but her eyes wild. "You don't even know who I am."

"Sure I do," I said. "You're Hina."

"No."

"Her copy."

She shook her head.

"Her sister, then. Her mother."

There was a moment before the woman spoke again, when she just held on to me, and it was somehow as if I knew what she was going to say before she said it.

"I'm not Hina's mother," the woman whispered as she bent against me. "I'm yours."

CHAPTER FORTY-SIX

It wasn't true. That's what I told myself. Tried to tell her that, too. My mother was dead. Always had been. She'd starved to death. Starved. But I was having trouble focusing now. I couldn't think straight.

"Don't make it harder," the woman said. We were still wrapped together in the middle of the room.

I shrugged her arms off me. "You're full of shit."

"Why would I lie to you?"

"You can't know. How could you know?"

"I don't need to know," she said "The science knows for me."

"Science?"

"Your genes."

"My what?"

"They're a perfect match to my DNA," the woman said. "And your father's."

"My father?"

"Yes."

"Where is he?"

"He's here."

"He's what?" My fists were clenched. My heart had shot into my throat.

My old man. Here.

"I'll take you to him," the woman said. "When you're ready."

"I'm ready now." I started to shake.

"No, Banyan. You're not."

"Take me now," I screamed. I seized a glass monitor and rammed it at the wall, smashing it into shiny pieces on the floor.

The woman tried grabbing at me but I slipped past her, making for a door on the far side of the room. I had her beat, but when I reached the door it came swinging wide open and Zee was bustling toward me, all wrapped in purple, big grin on her face. She started to say something but I cut her off.

"What the hell?" I said. "Get me out of here. Get me out."

"I got you out," she whispered, her smile vanishing like a sun gone down. I tried to push past, but she was all rammed up against me and I was suddenly so damn tired and my legs wouldn't move.

"Take it easy," Zee said, then she stared into the room. "What did you tell him?"

I felt the woman loom up close. "That he's my son."

"And his father?"

"No. Not yet."

"You've seen him?" I said to Zee, but I was staggering now, slurring my words.

"Get him down," one of them said. And everything turned to sludge.

When my mind came back, I was back in the bed and all the lights had been cut. I tried moving my limbs and each one was sore. I felt something pressed against my thigh, pinning the sheets, and I squirmed my hands free to grab it.

Metal. Cold and jagged. I felt at the metal. The ridges and curves. I drew blood as my skin snagged on thorny steel.

"It's called a rose," Zee said from the corner of the room. I looked for her, but she was all shadowed and black.

"He made it," she said.

"Pop?"

"Yeah." Zee shuffled closer and lit a low orange globe on the floor beside me. "Our father."

"Ours?"

She nodded, but I looked away. My brain wouldn't go there.

I tugged the flower to the light and studied the craftsmanship — barbed wire that had rusted purple, woven into a long stem and bunched into a ball of leaves. My blood was smeared upon the petals.

"He gave this to you?" I said, and it made Zee smile the way you do at something sad.

"No," she said. "He made it for her. Your mother."

"My mother's dead. I don't know that woman."

"People here call her the Creator."

"I think crazy is what she is. Besides, she looks more like your momma than mine." I set the spiky flower on the bed and turned to Zee. She'd been dead enough to haunt my dreams, but now here she was, flesh and bones and GenTech purple.

"My mother was a replicant of yours," she said.

"A replicant?"

"A copy. A perfect copy."

"So how come I never heard nothing of it? How come we never knew?"

"Because our father wanted to keep you safe."

"Safe?" My mind groped at each word, at each new bit of information. But it was like everything was slipping past me and shattering on the ground. I wanted my father. I wanted to see him. But at the same time, everything felt wrong. And he'd never seemed so far.

"You'll see," Zee said. She nudged me over so she could sit beside me.

"So what? You're my sister?" My hands were trembling and I dug my fists at my side.

"I suppose," she said.

But I'd never had a sister. I never had anyone except Pop. I tried to make sense of it. I kept trying to start at the beginning, but then I'd just lose my way all over again.

"I should have looked for you longer," I told her. "On that slave ship. I got Hina out, though. But I couldn't save her. Not in the end."

Zee started to cry and it was enough to make me quit shaking. I tried to breathe proper, but I couldn't slow down.

"I couldn't do nothing," I said, the words tumbling out. "For Hina. Or Sal. And I think it might be my fault. Dragging them along."

"No," Zee said, and she tried saying something else, but her tears messed the words and then she just cried till she'd drained herself out. And when she'd got done crying, I could hear her wheezing through those crusted lungs of hers. That tight, shriveled sound.

"Hina remembered," I said. "In the end. Like she could see her whole life. And she was clean. Free of old Frost and clean of the crystal."

"What about Sal?"

"He saved me," I said, remembering him pulling me out of the mud pit. Remembering when I'd called him my friend.

"He used to try and hide me. When Frost got crazy." Zee started sobbing again. And I reckon Sal had been like a brother to her. No matter the shit that he'd said.

"They took you to Vega?" I said, thinking about that spinning wheel that had arced across the plains. "The Harvesters?"

"I don't know. I just woke up here."

"I didn't see one agent out there with a dust mask."

"The air's clean," she said. "All the time."

"So can it fix you up? Your lungs?"

"The Creator says they can't get better. But at least here they won't get worse."

"The Creator." I stood up off the bed, stuck my head in my hands. "Who the hell calls themself that?"

"It's her title. That's what everyone calls her."

"Kind of like you still got a mom, I guess."

"I told you," Zee said. "She's your mom. Not mine."

"It's impossible. My mom died. She starved herself so I could live."

"That's what our father told you?"

I rubbed at the back of my neck. I refused to believe that woman was my mother. The very idea sent a pain through my skull.

"Our dad came to build for the bigwigs," Zee said. "For GenTech. They wanted statues of the people who found this place."

"They're making him build?" For a moment I pictured my father and a thousand others all slaving over some GenTech shrine.

"That was when he first came to the island. Your mother said that's how they met." Zee scooped up the rose and placed it on the bed between us. "He made her this. But he never built the statues GenTech wanted. Soon as you were born, he took you and ran. Stayed hidden."

"Hidden?"

"Until last winter."

"Right," I said, and my body trembled as the very reason I'd come all this way carved through the confusion inside. "Last winter. When he got taken."

"No," Zee said, her voice soft. Her face like an apology. "He wasn't taken."

I went to speak, but I couldn't. I just seized up. Like an engine run dry.

"He traveled to Vega," Zee said. "He turned himself in."

"To GenTech?" The words crawled out my mouth and then crept down my spine.

"It was the only way he could get back here. Through the Rift. Across the water."

"To the trees," I whispered.

"Right." Zee almost smiled. "To the trees."

Don't know how long it lasted. Once I'd let it all sink in. Zee did her best to try and comfort me, but I didn't want Zee. All I wanted was my old man, and I shouted for him in the darkness and then I rammed my fists at the wall.

Eventually my voice gave out. I tried breathing but it felt exactly like drowning in that yellow river all those years before. Only this time there was no one to pull me back out. And that's what made it all hurt so damn much. Because Pop had been my only friend in the whole world. And he hadn't been taken at all. He'd just upped and left.

But why?

I started for the door but Zee grabbed me, pulled me back.

"You have to stay, Banyan. With me."

"No." I tried to force past her, but I was still too weak. "I gotta see him."

"You can't. The agents won't let you."

"You've seen him?"

"No one can."

"Why not?"

"Because they've got him locked up."

Locked up? I shouldn't give a damn, I told myself. So what if they'd tossed him in a cell and thrown away the key? Pop had left me. Ditched me. Made up some shit about hearing voices and he just snuck out the wagon and he probably never once looked back. Just ran through the dust storm. Headed for Vega. Headed for GenTech and this island of trash. Left me with nothing but things that were hollow. He'd lied to me. Always. And I'd believed in him.

Right from the start.

CHAPTER FORTY-SEVEN

I curled up in the corner with my guts like concrete. My skin was hot. But I was shivering. Silent. Trying not to let myself crack. Zee gave up talking after a bit. And once she'd slipped into a twitchy sleep, I peeled myself off the floor.

I shuffled back inside the laboratory and sat watching the lights and screens as they bubbled and flashed. It was almost like I was dreaming. Everything inside me was numb. I fell down in a chair and tried to be empty. But I kept seeing my old man's face. I kept looping over our life together, trying to figure out how he'd been able to walk away from me.

I tried to remember every little thing, searching for clues. But my father seemed a whole different person than the bag of memories I'd been carting around. He was like someone I'd never even known. A stranger.

I started turning over the steps it had taken to get to this place. I started to think about Alpha. And Crow. I worked myself up in a right state. And by the time the Creator came in, brushing snow off her shoulders, I felt I'd lost more than I ever knew I had.

"Why'd he do it?" I said, watching the woman shrug off her coat. I'd surprised her, but she tried to look relaxed about me sitting there. "Why'd he come back here? For you?"

The woman sank into a chair across from me and she made that same sad smile that Hina had used and Zee had perfected.

"He'd have never come for me," she said. "He came because of the experiments. Told me he'd waited till he'd raised you. He said you were free."

"What experiments?" I pictured Alpha, shorn and shriveled and covered in plastic. And I pictured Crow, his chopped-off body being carried away. "Where are the others?" I said, panic welling up inside me. "The others from the boat?"

"Don't worry," the woman said. "They're sleeping."

"Sleeping?"

"They're special, Banyan. And they're safe."

"Not like the ones you burned in Vega." I saw Sal's face like a ghost in my mind, remembered how the kid hadn't even screamed when he sizzled and smoked.

"Vega's nothing to do with me," the woman said. "That's the Executive Chief and the number crunchers. The bottom line. It's not something anyone enjoys. It's just something we have to tolerate."

I glared at her, trying to bend my mind around what was happening. This couldn't be my mother. I wouldn't let it be. My brain was getting spun up and caught on itself, but I needed answers and the need cut through like a knife.

"Tolerate for what?"

"Come closer," she said. "Please. I'll show you."

I stood behind her as she flicked her fingers at a control pad, bringing an empty black screen to life. Our faces were reflected in the monitor and I could see the woman had turned and was staring up at me, but then the screen turned purple and our faces disappeared. I watched as tiny white lines floated across the screen and met in the middle, small blocks getting bolted together, growing taller. Stitched like sections of scaffold.

"We're creating life," the woman said, her voice little more than a whisper. "And your father was very good at it."

"What is it?" My eyes were glued to the staircases growing in spiraled patterns on the screen.

"It's DNA. Nucleotide sequences. The building blocks behind every living thing."

"Science."

"It's nature. Your father was very bright, Banyan. He had a gift. He saw how things could fit together, the pieces that were missing." She shifted in her seat so she was closer to me, almost touching. Her whole body so near I could smell her. Sour and soapy. Cold and damp with snow. "For almost five years, I taught him, showed him my work. I trained him in DNA geometry, helical modeling. But eventually he could see through complexities that had blinded me. He never built the monument GenTech hired him for. He worked in the lab. Making trees. With me."

"Don't look like much of a tree," I said, and I felt her smile so hard beside me that her skinny shoulders bounced.

"Break something into small enough pieces," she said. "And you get a code."

"Like a map?"

"Exactly. A map you can change. Rebuild. We're building trees, Banyan. Replicating the trees we found on this island, altering them to bring them back to the mainland." I felt her hand on my arm. "We've been trying for decades. To modify the trees into something the locusts can't consume."

"Like the corn."

"But what worked for the corn wouldn't work for the trees. We've had to change their cellular structure into something more malleable. We've had to hybridize the tree DNA with that of another, more abundant species."

I stepped back from the woman. Turned from the screen. I pictured the old Rasta and that chunk of wood I'd knifed out of him. I pictured Alpha's skin, all plugged up with bark.

"Humans," I said, staggering backward. "You're using humans."

It made me sick the way she frowned, the lines on her face all scrunched up like there was poison on her tongue. I lost feeling and swayed, caught myself on the back of a chair. This was Project Zion. GenTech was taking folk and twisting them and god knows how many and this woman right here was at the heart of it all.

"Only the hybrid cells can be modified," she said. "And there's nothing else to use. The corn's too synthetic. We'd have used animals, but there's nothing left. Nothing but people."

"What do you do to them?" I whispered, as if the words had snuck out.

"We call it fusion."

"You kill them?"

"I don't kill anyone. It's a sacrifice, that's all."

"A sacrifice? For what?"

"So we can regrow the world, clean the air and the water. Wood and paper. Shelter. And fruit trees, Banyan. Real fruit trees."

"Right," I said, yelling now. "Regrow the world and stamp GenTech on every damn part of it."

She shot me a look like I'd punched her.

"And my dad helped do this?"

"He left when we realized what had to be done."

"Didn't want blood on his hands, that it?"

"He was afraid."

"Sure he was. Shit. Maybe he was afraid of you."

She stood and struck me, the back of her bony hand stinging my cheek. But somehow it was like I'd beaten her at something. Her eyes filled up and the breath shuddered out of her. And then she just turned her face to the machines.

"You still want to see him?" she said, like it was all she had left she could offer.

But I told myself it wasn't just Pop I'd come looking for. Hell, I reckoned I'd come looking for a thing that don't go leaving. And some damn thing that you can't leave behind.

"You can keep him," I said. "All I want to see is the trees."

CHAPTER FORTY-EIGHT

Zee wrapped me up in GenTech purple and tugged my head inside a bulky hood. I couldn't say anything to her. I just let her dress me, my thoughts spinning slow like wheels getting stuck.

"Come on," she whispered into the hood as she cinched up my jacket. "You'll feel better when you see them."

My head had drooped and I couldn't see Zee's face, but I figured she was smiling. And I tried to let the thought of that smile warm me, because all I felt now was lost and alone.

Don't go believing in fairy tales, Pop had told me. Don't go kidding yourself. No trees, he used to say. Nothing left.

But Pop had been lying to me. All of my life.

Zee led me down corridors and up steps, and finally we pushed outside, the freezing air trickling inside my coat.

I stared around at the patches of ice and the gray sky and the concrete buildings. Then Zee took my hand and guided me through the snow.

"She might've been a copy," I said as we began to scale one of the powdery slopes, "but I liked your momma a whole lot more than the real thing."

"Hina was real."

"Real enough, I guess."

"She was supposed to be a sign," Zee said. "I don't think I was even supposed to happen."

"A sign? A sign of what?"

"The Creator said that once they could produce people the same way the trees here reproduce themselves, she knew they'd be able to splice the two species together. So they sent Hina south. To find our father. To show him they'd done it."

"She went south, all right. Got herself to the South Wall."

"Our father had joined up with rebels. People that used to fight against GenTech."

"Yeah. I seen what was left of them," I said, and I remembered what Jawbone had told me about the pirates. I remembered their flag. The Army of the Fallen Sun.

"Hina was the breakthrough," Zee went on, sounding sort of proud about it. "Your mom thought our dad might come back and help, when he'd seen what was possible. When he'd seen they could make a perfect human copy. Your mom thought he might change his mind."

"You need to stop calling her that."

"The Creator, then. The Creator thought he'd come back."

"To do what? Make fake people?"

"Copying people was the first step. But only certain people's cells can be fused with the trees. The tattoo." Zee ran her hand across her belly. "It was coded with these numbers. Protein numbers. They'd figured out which combinations worked with the tree cells. So now they knew they had to find the people with the right DNA."

So the numbers weren't coordinates at all. Just more science. The science that determined whether you lived or died in that factory. The science that had killed Sal.

"Same kind of shit they pulled on the corn," I said. "Same shit. Just people this time."

"They're trying to fix things."

"Well, I reckon they should give it a damn rest."

"They grew my mom here," said Zee, her voice quiet.

"They just used her."

"I know."

"And this Creator woman, she's just using you, too."

"I don't care." Zee pointed at her chest as she breathed the cold clean air. She tugged at her fuzzy GenTech coat. "I've been used my whole life, I'll take this any day."

"Take what?"

"Being on the side that's winning."

"So you found Zion and you got what you wanted."

"I can breathe, can't I? And I don't have to be afraid anymore."

We were halfway up the slope and I was worn out from it. I stopped and stared back down at the compound. Just three buildings covered in snow – the one we'd emerged out of, a much larger bunker, and between the two of them was a small steel dome. There was not a single window on any one of the buildings. Agents were stationed at every door.

And according to Zee, my old man had once stolen me away from this place. So this was where I'd been born, then. This was where I was from.

I watched the smoking bio vat on the ridge across from me, pumping out juice like a giant metal heart. And here and there I could see bits of old junk poking out of the frozen landscape.

"Do you think he loved her?" Zee said.

"Who?"

"Hina."

"Sure," I said. "Least she weren't running around killing folk."

"But he still left her."

"He was good at ditching people. It's a skill, maybe."

"You want so bad to hate him. So should I hate him more? Hina always told me my real dad had no idea I existed. He must have left her before he even knew I was gonna be born."

I thought about the statue down in Old Orleans. And I wondered if it had really been built for Hina. Or had what Pop loved in the replicant been something he'd loved a whole lot longer?

And I must have been there, I realized. Back then. In Old Orleans. If everything Zee had said was true. I'd have been tiny. Just barely been born, perhaps. But I'd have been there. On my old man's back, buried in a blanket. Holding on as he built the statue that years later I came to finish. The statue he'd left with the face still missing.

"She was like a reflection," I said. "Your momma."

"I think in the end she reminded him of what he'd done. The experiments. This." She pointed down at the compound. "You were the only thing he didn't tie to this place. And when he gave you up, it was only so he could try and stop it all."

I pulled off my hood so I could stare at her, but Zee was all bundled and hidden away.

"What do you mean?" I said.

"The agents talk about it. Last winter. Everyone thought he'd come back to help finish the project. But he staged an uprising. Freed people, got them back to the mainland. People like that crazy old Rasta we found."

I thought about what the Creator had said. About Pop raising me and me being free.

Is that why he'd never told me?

Had he just waited till I was old enough so I could keep on with the building? And then he'd gone off to risk everything, to try to put all this right?

"Uprising," I whispered.

"Yeah. Until he got caught."

I pictured that photograph of Pop chained to the tree. And then I remembered the bootlegger we'd buried – the woman beat to death for giving out corn. She'd been our last client. Our last job together. Before Pop hightailed us on the road to Vega.

My heart got fast and the world got slow.

"And now they've got him locked up," I said.

"Right."

I remembered the old Rasta, a lifetime ago, shaking his staff at the sunrise.

"And they're gonna kill him," I said, my voice getting louder. "In the spring?"

"Sooner than that. Used to be that's when they'd do the experiments. But they've got it all figured out now. They're ready to bring a forest back to the mainland."

"They're gonna use 'em." I thought of Alpha. Crow. "The people from the boat?"

"Them and the rest they've gathered, the ones with the right DNA."

"But that woman said they're sleeping. Safe."

"They are. Until fusion kicks in." Zee pointed down at the main bunker. And somewhere down there, locked up, was my old man. Still bound in chains, perhaps. Still holding on. And Alpha was trapped down there, too. Was she sleeping? Was she dreaming her tree builder had drifted away?

"When does it start?" I said.

"Two more days."

I glanced up the slope, the way we were heading.

"And what do they call this place?"

"Promise Island."

I thought about that old Rasta again, his belly bubbled up with bark. I tried to remember the things he'd told me. And I thought about Pop as I slumped down hard on the snow.

Had he been protecting me?

He'd gone to fix something he had long kept secret, something he figured me too weak to know. But I'd made it here, anyway. Made it without him.

"Come on," Zee said, taking my hand and squeezing my fingers through our thick gloves. "We're almost there."

Top of the hill and I could see all the way down the other side. All the way down to the tops of the trees.

I stood there, staring down at the leafless branches that reached up at me. And I thought at once how pale and flimsy the trees appeared. Nothing I'd ever built resembled their fragility.

My legs made fast work scrambling downhill, and the movement felt like I was jump-starting myself. It began snowing again as I reached the bottom of the crunchy slope, and I stood for a moment, just ten feet from the spindled branches, watching as they danced in the wind and the white flakes fell.

I took a step forward. A few more steps. Then I was close enough to touch the thin trunks. The papery bark. I pulled off my gloves and shoved my sleeves to my elbows. Then I reached my hands to the trees and ran my fingers slow and cold upon them.

The bark felt powdery, but beneath it was slippery and smooth. Greenish white in color, with black knots like eyeballs. I pushed at a tree and it pushed right back.

I got closer, yanked off my hood, and stuck my face against the wood, breathing its smell and tasting it with my tongue, snow melting on my lips.

I stepped from one tree to another, moving my hands so as to never let them go.

I dug at the snow with my boot heel and studied where the trees plunged into the earth. I found leaves beneath the ice, some gold, some yellow, most of them black. They were soggy and mashed together, but I squeezed the leaves in my fingers and separated them out to dry. I bit into one and its veins were chewy. And then I just sank to my knees and I broke down and cried.

Zee sat on the edge of the forest, watching me, and when I got done crying, she shuffled through the slush and sticks and knelt beside me.

"You should keep your hood up," she said. "Or you'll freeze over."

My face was all snotty and wet and I wiped it with snow. "Don't look like nothing I ever pictured," I said.

"Me, neither."

"How long you been here?"

"A week or so."

"You used to it yet?"

"A little."

"I don't want to ever get used to it," I said. "Not ever."

"Imagine the spring, though. The leaves coming green. The seasons."

"Yeah," I said. The seasons. My specialty.

I stared into the forest, and there, in the middle of the stand, was an opening. A clearing. I stood and stumbled toward it.

"This is where they take them from," Zee said, coming up behind me. "In here was the one they really want."

"What is it?"

"Apples. An apple tree. It was right here."

I thrashed around in the opening, but the only trees I could see were the thin limbs, the dirty white bark like old pearl in moonlight.

"It's gone," Zee said. "They got it all worked up. Ready for the fusion."

"You seen one? An apple?"

"We're too far north. The Creator says the growing season's too short. They tried bringing a tree back to the mainland. Years ago. Grew it up in a glass building. But a swarm left their nest in the corn-fields and migrated over. They covered the glass and blocked out the sun, made a hole and squeezed inside." Zee shuddered. "But the locusts won't eat these new trees they're making. They can't even burrow inside them like they do in the corn."

"So GenTech's going to sell us apples now. And trees."

"And everyone will buy them, too." Zee shrugged. Then she saw the look on my face. "What? I don't want it to be this way. It's just the way it is."

"Why should you care? You're on the side that's winning."

"There were never any sides, Banyan. GenTech wasn't even searching for Zion. They were just fooling everyone with stories while they built what they need."

"Are there more trees on the island? Other things growing?"

Zee tugged the hood back onto my head, then pushed our hoods together, and I could feel her breath warm on my face as her lungs creaked and rattled.

"This is it," she said. "The last stand."

And this was it. One apple tree left, and they'd already gutted it. This was the GenTech Empire. This was where it got us. And I knew that the boat big enough was just big enough for all the bodies they needed. I knew this was cold blood killing on the most massive scale.

So my father hadn't been taken. But how many had been? How many mothers and sisters and husbands and wives? Didn't they all belong to someone? Didn't they deserve some protection?

I pulled away from Zee, put my hand on a tree branch and held myself steady. I stared up in the branches and then closed my eyes.

I pictured that half-eaten man on the forty, trying to drive his dead family home. I saw the lost faces on the Harvester transport. The bodies burning in Vega, and Sal being thrown to the flames.

I remembered Jawbone splattered lifeless on a plastic console. Hina consumed by the ravenous swarm. I felt death's fingers in the mud pit. And I felt the dead Rasta in my arms. Skin and bark, limp and knotted.

So much death.

So many hearts turned to stone and days that were stolen. The last things living and we were just ripping each other in pieces that could never again be put back whole.

It ends here, I swore to myself. It must end here. And I knew that Pop had been right to return, even if he thought it meant he had to leave me behind him. He'd been right to try and stop this hell he'd helped GenTech to start. Because being a builder can only get you so far, I reckon. Sometimes you got to be a fighter. Sometimes you got to fight.

"We have to get Crow out," I said.

"Crow?" Zee's voice pierced a hole in the air. "Crow's here?"

"Yeah. You might not recognize him. But he's here."

"Are there others? People you know?"

"No," I said. I didn't tell her about Alpha, though the thought of her tripped me – the fear of losing that girl had worked its way too deep to ever work its way loose.

But Alpha had believed in me. And I took that faith and it helped grow me stronger, and I had to be stronger now than I ever had been. Because I knew what I was going to do. I had to finish what Pop started. And that meant I was going to need Alpha on the inside.

For the uprising.

CHAPTER FORTY-NINE

Zee told me that before the Darkness, the white trees had grown all over the west and all across what was now the Rift. They were called Populus, back in the old world. Populus tremuloides. But they were also called Quaking Aspen, because back then there were enough trees around that people gave them two names apiece.

The apple tree, though, was of a kind rare even before the Darkness. It grew in mountains in far off places. Malus sieversii. A type of wild apple that had grown for a long time unaltered, before people knew how to mess with such things.

But here on Promise Island, here on this frozen lump of trash, the trees didn't need naming. They were just all that was left. And that night, after Zee had made the agents retrieve Crow and get him conscious, I carried what was left of the watcher to see what was left of the trees.

It was not a clear night, and it seemed somehow colder for the lack of moon, the absence of stars. I had Crow wrapped in blankets, and I'd tugged the blankets over my shoulder, then tied them around my waist. I was starting to get my strength back and made it up the hill slow but without stopping. Top of the ridge and it was too dark to see the branches below.

"Hold on," I said over my shoulder. "Not long now."

What had been snow was now ice and I slipped and skidded down the slope until we were all the way to the bottom. At the edge of the forest, I unwound the blankets and set Crow down, holding him upright and pulling off his hood.

Our breath steamed in the darkness.

"Closer," Crow mumbled, and I walked him nearer. "Lean me against it," he said, and I balanced him so he could hold himself tall with the trees in his hands.

"You want to go in deeper?" I asked him.

"Not yet."

I dug up some of the old leaves and showed them to him, but Crow just stayed staring at the bark between his fingers. It was so dark I could hardly tell, but I was pretty sure Crow was crying.

"I'm ready," he said finally, and I lifted him and carried him before me as I made my way slowly through the forest.

At the center clearing, I took a break and we sat there, surrounded by the empty hole in the trees.

"Thank you for bringing me here, Banyan," Crow said, and his voice had changed now so that it no longer sounded as if he was about to start laughing. More it sounded like he wasn't ever going to laugh again.

"What do you think of them?" I asked.

"I think they're Zion," he said. "I think they're worth living a life for. And I think if you hadn't dragged me out of that wagon, then I wouldn't be here now."

"I think we can save them" was all I said.

"No. They don't need us to save them."

"Yeah they do. The trees need us. And the people need us even more. Else GenTech's gonna kill a whole lot of people so they can own a whole lot of trees."

"They been killing people and owning everything since the Darkness. Probably a long time before that, too. Nothing going to change."

"There are more of us than them."

"Us? Didn't you say it's your own mother that's running this show?"

"She ain't my mother. She ain't nothing. We just have to bust the prisoners free. And we can take them." I pointed at the trees. "Not these. New ones they're building. We get our hands on those and we take the boat. Head down to the mainland."

"The mainland? You mean the Rift." Crow shook his head slowly. "I seen those lava fields from the south side."

"We got taken up here, must be a way back down."

"So we find a way through the lava and somehow get back there. What about the locusts? I always believed these trees would be different, but it's just that they're stuck out here, away from the swarms."

"These new ones they're making are different. GenTech's got them built so the locusts can't touch them, not for eating or nesting or nothing at all. Mixed up people and trees and scienced the hell out of them. That's why they've been rounding up so many prisoners. So they can build these new trees and send a whole crop back for planting."

"We may got the numbers," Crow said, when he was done being silent. "But they got those prisoners doped up and sleeping."

"Yeah. Dormancy's what Zee called it. Some sort of preparation they do. They're all right for about forty more hours. Then the splicing begins."

"So what do you want to do?" Crow said, his eyes staring through the night like they were digging for something.

"I want to wake everyone up."

Crow did laugh then. And his laugh sounded just the same as it used to. "Wake everyone up?"

"Just got to work the angles, that's all. Like you said, I'm connected here. That woman. The Creator. I can get her wrapped around my finger, I play my cards out right."

"And what about your father?"

"He's here," I said, trying to keep my voice steady. "Somewhere. We'll bust him out, too."

"You want it all."

"They're making apple trees, Crow."

"Apples?"

"Imagine bringing one of them back to Waterfall City."

"The Prodigal Son," Crow said quietly. "Returns to the Promised Land just to thieve it all away. Well, just like I always told you, Banyan. You're one crazy cool son of a bitch. Jah as my witness, you are crazy cool."

I'd gotten us back inside before we froze to death, and I set Crow up to rest in his room. Then I returned to the small room I'd first come awake in, making my way through the cluttered lab and the darkness, pushing inside the door, then clicking it shut behind me.

I lay on the bed, wrapped myself in the soft blankets. And it wasn't long before I was out cold and sleeping. But not much longer and the Creator was there, too.

Just as I'd figured.

She had her hand on my head, rubbing my stubbly scalp, and I let her think I was still sleeping, sort of snuggling my head at her fingers and making drowsy little sounds.

Eventually though, I cracked my eyes open and upon seeing her I stretched back, scooted over in the bed, and turned away as she sat down beside me.

"I've missed you so much," the woman whispered to the top of my head, her voice all scratched and skipping beats. I shook my head like I was keeping her words from touching me.

"You never came for me."

"I tried, Banyan. GenTech wouldn't let me. They didn't want me distracted." She lost her words for a moment. "And when I tried to stop working, to leave here, they told me you and your father had been killed."

"It don't sit right," I told her. "I don't remember nothing. I can't even remember you holding me."

Her body tensed beside me. And I knew I was in.

"That's because you were so small," she said. "When your father took you."

"So you never knew me."

"I used to imagine you here. I used to picture you growing up. I'd think of books we could have read together."

"Pop read to me all the time," I said.

"Really?" There was a hunger in her voice. I felt her bony arm try to wrap around me.

"Yeah. Lewis and Clark."

"He always loved to read about the explorers. Well, I should be glad you two had something to read. They haven't let me have books up here for five years. Kills productivity, they say."

"I still don't really get what it is you do."

She almost said something, but I cut back in.

"And you say you missed me. But you don't even know me." I sat up in the bed so I could stare at her.

"We could become acquainted," she said in a small sort of voice.

"And why would I do that?"

"Because I'm your mother." She tried to sound stern about it, but she was just straight begging.

I made her wait. I watched her silver hair fall ragged across her face.

"I could build for you," I said, surprising her. And that's the best sort of lie. I watched her eyes go wide and her lips tremble. "And you could show me your work. Help me decide if I'm hopping the next boat out of here or not."

"I could keep you here. If I wanted."

"But you won't. Not unless I want to stay. Zee probably thinks you're as much of a mother as she could hope to have left. But I ain't Zee. And you're gonna have to earn me wanting to stick around."

"So you want to build trees for me?"

"Sure," I said. "Soon as I've seen my old man."

"You can't see him. Not now." She stumbled on her words for a moment. "He's busy."

"Busy being locked up?"

"It's complicated."

"Sounds pretty simple to me. You had him locked up when he tried to stop your experiments."

"It's only because of me he's still alive at all."

I just shook my head, like I was weary as all hell just talking to her.

"Tomorrow night," she said. "I can take you to him then."

I didn't say anything for a bit. It was just one more day, and I had to work this just right. So what choice did I have?

"First thing in the morning, I'll start harvesting scrap," I said. "The island's full of metal. I can dig out the pieces I need."

"And where will you build?"

"Right in the middle of your forest."

"Where we've harvested?"

"Yeah. I'll fill the gap you made."

"And I can show you the progress we've been making."

"I just want to see Pop."

"You'll see him."

"There's something else, though. My friend. The one who's here resting. I need you to fix him for me."

She leaned in and kissed my forehead, and I faked a quick smile before jerking away.

"I'll try my best," the Creator said, getting up off the bed. And I tell you, that grin didn't look natural on her. Didn't look like it had seen much use.

"My whole life I've been trying to fix things," she said, heading for the door. "It's the only thing I really know how to do."

Then she left, and I lay wondering if through my memories or through my father, or through Hina or Zee, if somehow some part of me did know this woman. If some part of what she was and all that she knew was lodged inside me. But I thought about what Hina had told me when we'd been stuck on that transport, my gun leveled at the Harvester's head.

They can copy the body, she'd said. But not the mind.

And so it seemed to me that flesh and blood can give birth to another. But that's where the giving is ended. And that's where the debt stops as well.

When I finally slept, I fell into a dream about Alpha. Her skin felt real and her eyes blazed, and she was sweating as she raced across the plains to find me, her spiked hair silhouetted against a giant yellow moon.

You've forgotten, she kept telling me with her eyes. Because her lips weren't moving. A patch of pink bark had been sewn over her mouth, and I couldn't hear her beyond moaning, and I couldn't find her teeth or her tongue. So I just kissed her shoulders and legs and the back of her head and the bark on her belly and finally the place where her lips should have been. And it began snowing and I was caught outside and naked, dragging Alpha's body up over the hill to show her the trees.

Look, I kept saying, pointing at the white forest. Told you we'd make it.

But when I glanced back at Alpha, she was gone. And in her place stood a metal field of corn a hundred miles high, and inside the corn was the apple tree. And no one wanted the tree.

They just wanted the apples.

CHAPTER FIFTY

"What are you doing?" Zee asked when she found me in the middle of the forest, hacking away at the frozen ground.

"Mining," I said. "There's enough old tin and piping down here you could build trees a mile high."

"Build trees?" Zee tugged off her hood so I could see the expression on her face. "What would you do that for?" She pointed up at the forest. "We've got all the trees we need right there."

"Well, Zee. I reckon I'm a tree builder. Always will be. I reckon you either are something or you're not."

"That simple, huh?"

"Sure. Nice and easy."

"You want to show what you can do," she said, coming closer to where I'd been digging. "You want to show her, don't you?"

"Way I see it, I show her something, and she'll show me something."

"What do you want to see?"

"My father," I said. "Man I came here to find."

"And you're sure you want to see him?"

"Why? Can you take me to him?"

"Only the Creator can do that."

I studied Zee. That beautiful face. And it seemed like it was the third time the world had seen it. The original had grown old but the next one hadn't. And soon it'd be Zee's turn to sparkle and shine.

Long as her lungs kept working, anyway.

She was my family. My flesh and blood. But I didn't reckon I could trust her a damn bit. She was acting like she wanted us to have always been close. But back in the Tripnotyst's tent, she'd either been trying to save me or was just switching her allies around, and I never had figured out which. And regardless, she seemed pretty cozy with what was going on here on Promise Island. It made sense, I guess. I mean the lass had done well for herself on this pile of junk. I remembered that night when I'd found her asleep in Frost's house and her body had been bruised and battered, and how long had she had to live like that? How long had she suffered with Frost because our father had left Hina behind?

I'd take her with us. That's what I decided. But she couldn't know that. Not yet.

"Stick close, sister," I said, busting my shovel at the snowy dirt again. "You might learn something."

"Sister?" She gave me a funny kind of smile. "Well, if you're really gonna do this, how about I round us up some help?"

Zee brought me agents. Whole dozen of the suckers. They arrived all buried inside hoods and purple fuzz, but they sure shed some layers once I put them to working.

Outside of the uniform, the agents were just people. Just no one. Just anyone. Men and women. Old and young. They didn't share the same face, so why'd they all dress the same? Why'd they sell themselves short to be part of someone else's plan?

Because they were weak, that's what I reckoned. Most of them had hardly done a real day of work in their lives. Too used to marching folk around from behind the trigger of a gun. Not at all used to creating, to the hard slog of building, the strength it takes to transform one thing into something else.

Their smooth skin blistered on the fiberglass shovels, and they wanted to jackhammer the dirt, blast my scrap right out of there. I told them that'd just blow the salvage to bits. Told them they'd better do less talking and do more digging.

By evening, I had a stack of aluminum tubes and some hubcaps, a load of old bottles and cans, a reel of thick cable, plastic piping, a metal drum. And one good, big old rusty sheet of iron.

Perfect.

"I'll build tomorrow," I told Zee as we headed back through the forest.

"Are you gonna make it light up?"

"Sure, if you get me a generator. Some LEDs. But I'll need juice," I told her. "Lots of juice."

I got back to the compound just as it was getting dark, and the Creator was waiting on me outside Crow's room.

"Success," she said, her gray eyes tired but bright. "At least I think so. Usually we can repair someone with a small graft if they need it. But I've never tried to replace whole limbs before."

I wondered for a moment what it would take for this woman to be someone who just fixed folk with her science. I mean, this here patching up people proved useful. It had saved Alpha. And maybe it had saved that old Rasta once, before Pop had set the dude free.

"So it worked?" I said.

"It appears so. We'll know when your friend comes back around. I stimulated propagation, and the cells worked their magic. But whether or not his nervous system agrees with the plan, well, we'll find out when he wakes up again."

"How long?"

"He'll sleep until morning. But what about you, Banyan? How did it go today?"

"You'll see," I said. "Tomorrow. When I get done. But tonight I get to see my old man. Right?"

She smiled and put her hand on my shoulder, giving me an awkward sort of squeeze. "Come on," she said. "I'll show you some of my work."

The Creator led me across the snow, past the dome, and up to the large bunker. "This is our main staging area," she said, as we shuffled through the snow. "Where we conduct dormancy, and where we'll begin fusion."

She swiped a plastic tag that caused two sets of steel doors to peel open. Then she led me inside a giant chamber of bright lights and bodies.

Human bodies.

They were all stretched out together, head to toe and side by side. Their eyes were sealed shut, faces beyond sleeping. And all of them were naked. Limbs pale and floppy. Arms wired up with cables that ran to a giant purple vat that hung from the ceiling.

I scanned the bodies, far as I could see, looking for a face that could be Alpha's, knowing she was in there somewhere.

"I know what you're thinking," said the Creator, raising her voice above the drone of machinery. "But we're not killing anyone. We're transforming them. In fact, we're providing them with everlasting life."

"How do you reckon?" I said, buying for time while I kept checking for Alpha.

"We're going to make them magnificent, Banyan. They'll be the first of a whole new species. A locust-proof species. And they'll self-propagate, just as the white trees on this island have done for centuries. Reproducing asexually. New plants off the same shared root system. Once we start planting on the mainland, the organism will keep on growing. Don't you see? We're granting these single bodies the chance to multiply. To be eternal. Part of a forest without end."

I gazed across the field of human skin that'd soon be made of leaves and wood. I thought about the fire pit back in the factory, pictured Sal being cast into the flames because his DNA didn't match up with what GenTech needed. No eternal life for him, then. Not unless you could live inside ashes.

"Can't you just copy the bodies you want?"

"The gene pool needs diversity. We've had to match a core protein set, but the more variants we mix in now, the better off we'll be."

I kept scanning the faces. "So what keeps them sleeping?"

"Up there." She pointed to the purple vat on the ceiling. "It's a feeder. Keeps them under and gives them everything they need to get their bodies strong, get their cells ready. This time tomorrow, we'll add a solution that prepares them for fusion. Soon after that, they'll no longer be simply human."

I just stared at her, and she beamed with pride.

"The first crop of a brand new species. Trees made ready for the mainland. Regenerating like the white tree but growing fruit like our apple tree. And now," she said, taking my arm, "it's time I showed you the source."

CHAPTER FIFTY-ONE

She called the dome the Orchard, and it was smaller and much quieter than the bunker full of bodies. The Creator opened up the steel door with her plastic key. And once inside, I saw a glimpse of something from a broke-down dream.

I staggered and the Creator caught me. I would have pushed her away, pulled myself free. But I felt upside down, as dizzy as when I'd been sick back in the mud pit. All full of a fever that stretched out my mind.

I heard the Creator. She was speaking to me. Trying to explain what was going on. But she didn't refer to the man as my father. Or Pop. Or anything like that.

She just called him the Producer.

Locked up, Zee had said. My dad was somewhere on the island. Locked up. But no one had really told me anything. Because no one had said one damn thing about this.

Pop didn't need to be locked up.

He didn't need to be wrapped up in chains.

He'd left me out near the cornfields. Down in the dirt. But now, seeing him again, it was like he was leaving me all over. And it was like I was just watching, turning to stone as he floated away.

They had him inside a big old tank of water. A tank glowed up with golden lights. There ain't a way I can really tell what they'd done to him. There's not words built for what they had going on.

I swayed forward. Part of me wanted to run up and press my face at the glass. But I just waited, watching as the Creator strolled up to the tank and checked the gadgets that were wired against it.

I counted seven saplings.

Each one of them was fresh, bright green, budding in the liquid. Two of the saplings had grown out of Pop's legs, and one was growing on each of his hands. There was one on his head, one out the belly. And the smallest one curled out from his chest. Straight from his heart.

Pop's skin was green and knotted. Fibrous. The hair on his scalp had grown twiggy and black. His face was buried under a mess of green roots, and right where his mouth should have been was where a sapling wound upward in the golden lights.

I remember being grateful Pop's eyelids were sealed shut.

No faraway look in his faraway eyes.

Thought I might puke. Let it all spill out of me. But I just shuffled closer. My footsteps echoed as they scraped at the floor. I went ahead and got next to the glass, and I knelt down by the rubber wheels the tank had been placed upon.

No matter what you called the thing floating in there, it was still my father. What was left of him, anyway. And if what the woman said was true, he might somehow live on forever now. Just keep on going.

But not in the ways that mattered.

I closed my eyes and pictured that forest we'd talked of building. The metal trees and a house of our own. And I saw myself sitting amid the forest and every leaf and branch had turned rusty and broken and all the trees were nothing but holes. I had our old book in my hands, but I'd forgotten all the stories and I was ripping out the pages now, crumpling them and burning them along with Pop's corn husk sombrero. And I'd quit eating so I was just made of bones and even the locusts wouldn't touch me. And no one would touch me or see me or hear me as I began screaming for my father in the never ending night.

When I opened my eyes I was still screaming and the Creator had wrapped her arms around me and everything seemed to suffocate me. Heavy and loud. So I quit screaming. I just squatted there. Quiet. Still. The Creator crawled off me, sat on the concrete and watched me. And I knew I had to find a way to let go of this feeling. I had to find some way to keep in control. And I had to play things out right, in front of this woman. Everything depended on it.

So I told her what she'd done to my father was beautiful.

And you know what's messed up?

It was sort of beautiful. In its own horrible way. And I remembered what I'd said to Crow about heaven and hell and how they're maybe just the same thing anyway. Glory and hunger. Fear and love. All looped together so there's no place where one ends and the next one's beginning.

And then, as I stared into the tank, I thought maybe the world wasn't as dead as we'd thought it. Maybe it was just lying dormant. Waiting for seeds.

"The liquid preserves the microclimate," the Creator said, still watching me, her voice scuffed and loose. "Protects him from winter."

I swallowed. Almost spoke.

"He's safe," she whispered. "This is the one. Where every test went right." She stood, staring into the tank. "He's a hundred percent locust-proof. Free from harm. Forever."

I tried to see a way my dad was just sleeping inside what was growing in there. His mind still working, still thinking. Dreaming. Not dead, somehow. Not gone.

"What about his brain?" I whispered.

She shook her head. "He's more tree now than man."

The words stabbed at me. I felt them in my guts. My bones. Nothing makes the world seem hopeless like knowing it's empty. But I had to cut off those parts that the knowing infected. Those parts that can cause you nothing but pain.

"And what'll be left?" I said, clenching my fists as if I might squeeze out the hurt and let it drip from my fingers. "After you've used him."

"Just enough to regenerate for the next crop. His body became the perfect breeding ground. And we'll keep fusing these cells to human tissue until we've reached enough diversity."

"And then?"

"Then my work will be done." She put her hand on the wall of the tank, and it left a sticky smear on the glass. "His work, too."

Outside the Orchard, we stood huddled together as snow fell white against the darkness. I felt like I'd been punched flat and sucked dry. My head was pounding and parched.

"I am sorry," the Creator said, hunching her shoulders. "I'm sorry your father and I caused you so much pain."

The woman smiled at me and for the first time I felt bad for her, because I knew there was no part of her that could understand what I felt.

She'd stayed here, searching for a solution that cost hundreds of lives. Thousands, maybe. And no matter how she justified it, the way I saw it, everything the world now needed only GenTech was going to get. But how could she not see that? How could she choose to be so damn blind?

We crunched back through the snow with our hoods hiding our faces, making our way toward the building where Zee would be sleeping and Crow would hopefully be healing so as to be ready to fight. You got to be strong, that's what I told myself. For Alpha and all the other prisoners. For what was left of my father. For the taken. The burned. For the empty-bellied strugglers. On this island we could bust a hole in something wicked. And I'd die if I had to. Or I'd live. And bring home the trees.

There was an agent standing watch at the door to the building. He was bundled and wrapped as we were, buried inside a huge puffy coat.

"Good evening, Creator," the man said.

"Staying cold enough for you?" She swiped her electronic tag to unseal the door.

"Oh, don't worry about me, miss," the man said, and his voice wound my guts tight inside me. "I love to see the seasons. No matter how cold they get."

As the door began to slide back in place and lock us inside, I stared back at the bulky figure all covered in fuzz and GenTech logos. A gun on his back and a club in his hand. Just like all the agents. Except he had a voice I'd heard and would always remember. Because this agent wasn't just no one. Or anyone.

This agent was Frost.

CHAPTER FIFTY-TWO

I didn't sleep. I just waited at the side of Crow's bed, counting the seconds till he woke up again. The work they'd done on his legs had helped repair his skin as well, gave him a sort of sheen where before he'd been all scarred and blistered. The new limbs were something else, though. Strapping big legs, all scaly with bark. They were stuck outside the sheets, full of lumps and grooves, and they were bigger even than the originals had been. If Crow woke up able to use them, I reckoned those legs would have him standing about ten feet tall.

Crow's face was peaceful, looked like he was catching up on a whole lifetime of sleep. And I just sat there, restless, watching the watcher.

"Crow," I finally whispered.

"What?"

"You sleeping?"

"No. I be talking to you." He opened his eyes. "What you doing here staring at me?"

"Wanted to see how you're doing."

"Okay. We doing okay."

"The legs," I said.

"Yeah, man. I been trying to use them."

"How long?"

"Long enough, man. Long enough."

I stared down at his legs and they weren't even twitching. "Maybe it'll just take awhile," I said.

"Sure, Banyan. Maybe."

"I gotta tell you something."

"What?"

"Frost's here."

This got his attention and he turned his glare on full.

"Frost?"

"Yeah. I seen him."

"Old bastard must've volunteered himself."

"Why would he do that?"

"I don't know. Maybe he didn't have much choice. Or maybe he just paid his way up here. How in Jah's name would I know?"

"Listen," I said, not sure what I was going to say till the words were coming out. "I think we can use him."

"Frost? No, man. Frost can't be trusted."

"We don't need to trust him, just get him on our side for a bit."

"And then what?"

"Then we can get rid of him. Once and for all."

"You're cold, Banyan. Cold."

"Yeah? Well, you ain't got legs, pal. And I'm gonna need a little help here."

"Sell your soul to the devil, then. What do I care?"

"It's just an idea," I said, trying to calm him down.

"Just a bad idea."

"You partnered with him."

"And look where that got me."

"We only got till the end of the day. That's it. I got a plan, but I'm gonna need some help."

"You should talk to Zee. She'll help, man. She'll help."

"Okay. You rest up. Try to get those legs moving. I'll come back and check on you."

"You going to talk to Zee?"

"Yeah," I said, but I was lying.

I was going to talk to Frost.

I strode outside into the dead part of morning. Snow all over the ground and no sunrise. Frost was gone and a different, thinner agent stood guard at the entrance.

"The man here before you," I said. "You know where he went?"

The agent pointed and I took off the way he'd gestured, following Frost's footsteps all the way up the hill.

When I'd made it down the other side, I found Frost in the clearing, rooting around in the scrap I'd dug from the ground. He had his hood off and his fat face was pink and chapped by the cold. Dark roots had grown in behind his bleached white hair. I stood there watching him awhile from inside my jacket, concealed in the bulk and fuzz, and hidden by trees. Then I stepped forward and Frost jerked around at the sound of my footsteps.

"Oh, hey there," Frost said, taking me for just another agent. He went back to poking around at the salvage. "You know what the hell all this is for?"

"Yeah," I said, pulling down my hood. "It's for the tree I'm building."

Frost's eyes grew as fat as the rest of him.

"It's really you?"

I nodded, and Frost laughed.

"Crow was supposed to cut your damn throat."

"You can take that up with Crow, if you like. He's here, too."

"Is he, now? So we all made it, did we? You and me. The watcher." Frost made a slimy grin. "And the pretty little thing."

"How the hell'd you find this place?"

"Even agents can be bargained with."

"Coordinates didn't work so well, I guess."

"No matter. Keep digging and you find the dirt you need. Went and got myself employed." Frost spread his arms wide, showing off his purple threads.

"You should know your boy's dead."

"My boy?" Frost's grin broke down and his jaw clamped tight. "I left him behind. To keep him safe."

"You don't keep someone safe by ditching them," I said. "Sal came looking for you. And now he's dead."

Frost blinked at the snow. "Tell me you're lying."

"I ain't lying. They killed him."

Frost's hands were shaking, and he pulled his gloves off to scratch around at his knuckles and at the back of his arms. Been awhile since he'd had his fix, I reckoned. Not a whole lot of crystal on Promise Island.

"Your wife's dead, too," I told him, and Frost's hands stopped shaking.

"My wife?" His anger grew him taller, stretched his face into a grin you'd not call smiling. "She made you feel wrong just wanting her. And besides, there seems to be no shortage of that woman running around."

"Well, the one you were married to is dead."

Frost waved his hand in the air, like he was dismissing his grief. But I wondered if maybe he'd needed Hina like he needed the crystal, if maybe it's the needing that leaves you spiky and torn.

"Plenty more where that came from," Frost said. "Though she was an awfully lovely bit of ass."

Suddenly I got the feeling Crow was right. I couldn't deal with this guy. Glued to a vice that can ruin the best of them. And Frost weren't the best of them, not by a midnight mile.

But I needed him. And I let him talk.

"The Creator, now she's a real ballbuster, I'm thinking. But let's face it, she's getting a bit long in the tooth. Zee, on the other hand, now isn't she something? Why else you think I kept the little bitch around?"

"Got it all figured out, don't you, fat man?"

"Man's gotta have a plan, tree builder."

"So what the hell you doing out here?"

"Well, first of all." He pointed at the trees. "They're lovely, I'm sure you agree. And second, I aim to smuggle one back with me. To the mainland. I can't sell something to GenTech they already own, but you might remember you were supposed to be building me a forest. And I'm going to put one of these things right in the darn middle of it. Just see if I don't."

"That's it?"

"That's it. People will pay plenty to see themselves a real tree."

"The locusts, Frost. You got a plan for them as well?"

"Glass," he said, looking like I was the idiot. "I'm gonna cage it up in glass. Keep it safe."

"You're a fool," I said, and I strode right up to him. "You're a fat piece of grease and I could turn you over to them. Right now."

"But you're not going to, are you? You followed me out here, I figure you got something to say."

"You're thinking too small," I said. "That's your problem. One of these trees ain't gonna get you nowhere at all."

"Go on."

"What you really need is something the locusts can't go eating. What you really want is the thing that makes GenTech different from the rest of us."

"You mean that thing in the Orchard."

"That's exactly what I mean."

"Nice little pipe dream you got there, Mister B. But maybe you didn't spot the troop of heavily armed agents. Or see the doors that open according to only one key."

"There's a whole army I guarantee would be happy to start fighting. Just gotta wake them up, that's all."

Frost stared at the hill. He chewed his lip.

"They'd need weapons," he said finally.

"You're an agent, aren't you? Can't you track down some guns?"

Frost gazed back and forth between me and the trees.

"Who's in on this?" he said.

"You and me. And Crow."

"What about Zee?"

"Yeah. She's coming with us."

"Then you can have my help. But I get her. I get Zee when we're finished."

"Okay," I said, and a switch got flipped inside me. Frost could not leave the island, that's what I was telling myself. He just could not leave this place.

The fat man reached out his hand with the missing finger. And I shook it. Maybe I shouldn't have.

But I did.

CHAPTER FIFTY-THREE

One hour past sunset and everything would change. By my best guess, that was when the medicine would start turning the prisoners into something that weren't human. That's when we'd lose our army. And that's when I'd lose Alpha.

But that wasn't going to happen, I told myself.

I wouldn't let it.

The sun set around three, and there'd be an hour of darkness for Frost to smuggle the weapons into the bunker and shut down the system so as to wake up the prisoners. My job was to create a diversion. But I also had to find a way to get the key to the Orchard. I figured the first job was pretty easy. The second task, not so much.

Frost was a gamble. I knew that. Any way you looked at it, he was nothing but risk. But what else could I do but try and use him? Way things had unfolded, Zee couldn't be trusted to keep her mouth shut. And Crow couldn't even walk.

I kept asking Zee to check on him, and she'd wade off through the snow then shuffle back to the forest, but the news was always the same.

No news.

The morning passed too quick, and I got sloppy with my work. I built a single tree in the middle of the clearing. Just one damn tree. But without my normal tools, and maybe because of the way I was feeling, nothing seemed to go quite right with it.

I was tired. Running on fumes. But I bent the rusty iron into a twelve-foot funnel, and that's what I buried in the ground. Then I broke up the tubes and used the metal for branches that I set to turn on the hubcaps, rigging cans and broken glass where the leaves should have spun.

Told you. Kind of a rush job.

The important part was what I did with the cable. And with that big metal drum. I patched up the drum so it'd hold without leaking, and then I built it into the crown of the tree. I strung the cable out of the drum and ran it all the way around the forest. Took me ages. I had to set it just right, connecting all the treetops into one giant wire canopy.

One other thing — before I ran that cable out, I'd soaked it in a big old barrel. A barrel full of the same stuff I'd poured inside the metal drum that I'd tied high in the tree.

Juice.

My secret ingredient.

Remember, when you build it's all about the details. Well, this was a detail that was going to make this forest come alive, all right. It'd be illuminated brighter than all the LEDs you could harness.

And then it would burn.

Right down to the ground.

• • •

Zee got back from checking on Crow just as I finished rigging up the cables. The cold air was pretty ripe on account of all the juice, and Zee scrunched her nose as she stared at the tree.

"What do you think?" I asked her.

"I've seen better, I'm not gonna lie."

"Guess that's what you get for rushing greatness."

"That's some stinky kind of greatness. Looks better than it smells, I'll give you that."

"Generator's leaking."

"So you can't get the lights going?"

"We'll see," I said, needing to change the subject. "How's Crow?"

"Same as he was two hours ago. And two hours before that. But he says he wants to come and see your tree."

"No," I said. "He can't come over here. You gotta make sure he stays where he is."

"Why?"

I wanted to tell her that I needed her and Crow safe and out of the way, but I couldn't tell her why. Not yet.

"Just do me a favor and keep Crow where he is. Out of sight."

"But he wants to see your tree."

"Why?" I snapped. "It's just a piece of junk. Tell him to keep where he's at." I should have already told Crow my plan and now I was panicked. There wasn't any time.

The sun was getting low in the sky and I'd told the Creator to be here at first sign of dark, told her I'd show her my work. My lousy fake tree.

Zee coughed on her crappy lungs. She stood staring at me.

"Listen," I told her. "You run along back to the base and keep

Crow company. You tell him Banyan said to just sit tight. Can you do that?"

She didn't say anything.

"I'll be right along," I said. "Just sit tight and wait for me."

"Okay," she said, then she turned and ran through the forest, and I just stood there watching her, waiting until I could see her high up on the slope beyond the trees.

I poached a nail gun out of the toolbox they'd given me. I shoved the gun deep in the pocket of my big coat. And then I sat in the snow and I waited for sundown.

CHAPTER FIFTY-FOUR

The Creator appeared on the hillside as the sun disappeared behind it. She was right on time. And she was alone. Just as I'd told her.

I'd started to get pretty damn cold, so I was pacing around the clearing and flapping my arms about, stomping my feet. It got dark real quick. Too dark to see. And I heard the woman get close before I spotted her again.

"Banyan," she called, snapping through the branches. I watched her fire up a flashlight and wave it around the clearing. "Where are you?"

"Right here," I said. "Right here."

She found me with her torch beam and I watched her tug down her hood, and her face was smiling like I'd not yet seen.

"Turn off the light," I said. "It's supposed to be a surprise."

"But I can already see how beautiful you made it." She was up close to the tree now, messing her hands in the glass-bottle leaves.

"It's not quite finished, though," I said, and I was suddenly impatient. "You gotta stand back here to see it right."

"Oh, but it's lovely, Banyan. Such craftsmanship."

I pictured Frost waiting with his guns in the dark. I pictured Alpha and all those empty faces that needed me. And how much time was left? How much longer before it would all be too late?

"Come on over," I said, trying to sound all cheery about it. "Come stand with me."

She trudged through the snow, taking her own sweet time. But then she was close beside me, staring up at the new addition to her forest. And that was when I pulled the nail gun out and pointed it at her chest.

"I'm gonna need that key to the Orchard," I said, my voice shaking as much as my damn hand. "The tag that gets you in there, I'm gonna need it."

But she just stared at me through the darkness, and her face was suddenly as old as the earth and as bitter as the cold wind off the water.

"The key," I said. Kept saying it, too.

"What are you going to do?" she whispered.

"I'm taking him. Pop. What's left of him, anyway. Taking the trees back to the mainland. Setting them free."

"No," she said. "I mean, what are you going to do to me?"

I tried to steady my hand. "Just give me the key, woman."

"I'm your mother, Banyan."

"Like hell you are," I said, suddenly shouting at her. "I don't even know you."

"Because he stole you from me. Because he stole you and now I deserve this?"

"You don't deserve shit, lady. And there's a hundred bodies waiting to die in that bunker to prove what you are."

"What?" she screamed back at me. "What is it you think I am?"

"You're a killer," I said, and I pushed the nail gun toward her. "And a thief. And I'm gonna take that key."

But I couldn't do it.

Just couldn't.

Everything had gone wrong and now she was crying and I began to hate myself for it. I wanted to stop her from crying and just let her go. Forgive her, I guess. That's what I wanted.

But there was no time for that now.

"Come on," I said as she crumpled and wailed. She was sinking in the snow and I tried to grab at her, feel in her pockets, find the tab that I needed so I could just start my diversion and get the hell out of there.

Then I suddenly felt like too much time was wasting, like I needed to get this show on the road. So I left the woman where she was and took aim at the tree, pointing the nail gun right up at the drum full of juice. I began squeezing the trigger.

But something stopped me.

I heard footsteps in the snow behind me but before I could turn, I felt a club smash my head. One of those spiky bastards. GenTech issue. Driving right into my skull and turning the whole world white.

I hit the snow all splayed out and bleeding. I blinked until my eyes could see again, and then I spun my face to the sky. The nail gun was gone. Long gone.

And there she was. That face that was going to just keep haunting me. Zee. Standing above me with the club in her hand and her body all breathless and her face covered in snot and tears.

She was saying something but I couldn't hear her. And it wasn't because of my head being busted or the ringing in my ears. It was because in the distance, over the ridge, there were gunshots. And all I could think was that Frost was in trouble. And that my whole plan had already failed.

CHAPTER FIFTY-FIVE

I sat up and swiped my hand at the blood gushing out the back of my head. I felt dizzy. Sick as hell. My mother was still folded on the snow and weeping and I wondered why it had hurt her so bad. Hadn't she done the same thing a thousand times over? Doing something wrong so you could put something right?

Guns fired in the distance again. Like tiny claps of thunder.

"What's happening over there?" Zee said.

"I don't know."

"Yes you do. Sit tight, you said." She shook her head. "Trying to get rid of me."

"I wanted to keep you safe. I wanted to bring you with me."

"And what about her?"

"Don't worry about me," said my mother, standing tall and wiping the snow from her clothes.

There was a moment. Just a moment. A handful of seconds where the two of them stared at each other as if trying to make up their minds about me. I stretched my fingers deep in the snow and groped around for something I could use.

"Your father would have been shot," my mother said, turning to glare down at me through the dark. "When the agents caught him, they chained him to these trees and they raised their clubs and cheered."

But I was done listening. My fingers had found something solid. The plastic piping I'd scavenged for my tree but found no place to put. I grabbed that chunk of tubing now and I swung it around my head, forcing the two of them back.

Zee raised her club, brought it down, but I blocked her and pushed her away from me. Then I cast aside the tubing and plunged back into the snow. I dug and thrashed and then my hands were upon it. The nail gun. Clamped in my fist.

Zee was bearing down on me again, but I had that gun in my hand and I lofted it toward the crown of the fake tree and I let the nails fly.

Metal on metal. Sparks on fire. And boom. Just like that, the drum blew wild and flaming, and it filled the clearing with light. I watched the fire zip over the cables, searing the night sky as if welding it shut.

Everything glowed, then exploded. I buried my face in the snow and listened as the world snapped and crackled. And when I could see again, the canopy was a fiery web above me and the whole forest was burning.

Every last tree.

I'd never seen anything burn like that. The trees caught alight like that's what they'd been put on this earth to do, just to spark up the night and flame on and on. No smoke. Not yet, anyway. Just balls of red and gold that swelled and spiraled and breathed heat down billowy upon us.

Flames streamed down the trunks of the trees, and soon we were surrounded by fire. I was sweating inside the thick coat, and I yanked down the zipper and crawled out of the purple fuzz as I scrambled to my feet. I shoved the nail gun down inside the back of my pants and pushed forward through the melting snow.

Zee and my mother had charged to the edge of the clearing, but they'd stalled there. Nowhere to go but straight forward. Into the fire.

"Come on," I screamed, but they couldn't hear me above the roar of the inferno. So I grabbed their hands and pulled them along with me, deep inside the tangle of flames.

We plunged through the burning forest, and as bright as it was, it was impossible to see. I lost my grip on Zee's hand and got behind her, pushed her before me, the three of us stumbling single file toward the cold blackness that waited at the edge of the trees.

As we ran and tripped and breathed in the ashes, my chest wound up and my eyes got blurred. And I panicked. Because I'd killed them. Each one of them. Each one of those beautiful trees. Except for one, I kept reminding myself. Except for the one locked in the Orchard, on the far side of the hill.

Zee's coat caught fire and I had to yank it off her, unpeeling the bulk from her skinny body, then throwing the coat in front of us, trying to beat back the blaze.

I lost track of them both for a second. I called out. Screamed Zee's name. Then a tree crashed down and knocked me backward, igniting the shirt on my back.

I rolled in the snow and I steamed and fizzled. Then I saw Zee. Out in the clearing. I staggered blind. Lurched forward.

And finally I broke free.

"What have you done?" she kept screaming, beating me with her bare hands as I crawled onto my knees.

"Stop," I called, trying to breathe again. I glanced back into the forest, and the only thing that wasn't burning was that crappy metal tree in the center. The tree I'd built too fast.

"You burned them, Banyan. Killed them. All of them. After everything we've done."

"No," I said. "There's more. There's more." I stood, grabbing her hands and pinning them beside her. "In the Orchard. We have to get to the Orchard. And then I'm getting us out of here. All of us."

She got a hand loose and swung her fist but I blocked it. She tried to say something but then started coughing, her lungs shredded and smoky. And when she finally stopped choking she just stared at me, her lips trembling and her eyes wide.

"We can't let them have it, Zee. We can't let them do this. They do just what they like. With all of us. You get in their way and you're nothing. And as long as they control what grows and what doesn't, people can't ever be free."

"There'd be trees, though. Blue skies and clear water. Fruit growing everywhere. Air I could breathe."

"Trees won't grow everywhere if only GenTech can grow them."

"But how do we do it without them? You don't know what you're doing. You can't grow these trees with a hammer and nails."

"We'll try," I said. "We try so no more people get killed for some experiment. So no more people have to suffer."

Zee fell to the ground and put her hand on her chest, her throat twitching. "My lungs," she croaked, tears in her eyes. "I can't do it. I can't go back."

"I'll keep you safe," I said. "And we'll get trees around you. I promise."

"Why?"

"Because you're my sister. And I won't leave you behind. Not if you'll come with me."

She grabbed my wrist and stood beside me and I held her then, her hair soft on my face as she sobbed and shuddered.

"But I need that key," I said, staring back into the flames. "I need the Creator."

"She's there." Zee pointed and I spun around.

And there she was. Halfway up the damn hill.

CHAPTER FIFTY-SIX

I scrambled up the slope as fast as my legs would carry me. I didn't pull the nail gun out. It was no use. I couldn't pull the trigger. Not on her. Not now.

She was moving pretty quick. But I was so much quicker. I was gaining on her, a few steps closer each time she glanced back to check. I lunged at her. Wrapped my arms around her waist to tackle her. She pulled the electric tag from around her neck and went to hurl it at the snow.

We fell bundled together, my hand locked on her wrist as I pushed her beneath me. She threw the key as best she could and then rolled on my back, beating me as I dug my hands through the snow, searching.

I found the plastic tag and shoved it down the side of my boot, ignoring the woman slapping and screaming at me, her face all wet and stretchy.

"You need to come with me," I told her as I staggered to my feet. "I'll get you out of here, I swear it."

"To do what?" she shrieked, her voice wretched. "To burn like everything else?"

"No," I said, and I leaned into her, taking her shaky, wrinkled hands in mine. "To regrow the world. That's what you want, isn't it? But not just for GenTech. Not like this." I jutted my chin in the direction of the compound. "Those bodies in there are people. They're somebody's sister or father. They're somebody's son."

She stared at me and I had no idea if she was buying it. But it was too late now. My diversion had done its trick. And up on the ridgeline, the agents were lined up and panicked, pointing their gloved hands and their stupid hoods down at the fire that was rolling below them.

Zee scampered up beside us and we hunkered down in the snow, watching the agents above. I heard gunshots on the other side of the hill and felt my insides crawl. What was Frost doing? What had happened down in the bunker? Was Alpha free yet? Or was it too late? Would I always be too damn late?

"What now?" Zee said.

"I'm getting over that ridge." I pulled out the nail gun and balanced it on the snow, aiming up at the agents. "You with me?"

"I'll come with you. But you can't shoot your way through them. Let me talk to them."

"No," my mother said. "I'll talk to them."

I stared at her.

"Your father was right," she said. "You're more free than he ever imagined. But if you want to break him out of here, then you're going to need my help."

"You'll betray GenTech?"

"I don't care about GenTech," she said as she started up the hillside. "All I ever cared about was the trees."

I shoved the gun back in my belt and we staggered to the ridgeline, where my mother yelled at the agents and commanded them to move.

"Get down there," she told them. "Salvage anything that's not yet burned. Any stick or twig or leaf. I'll need it. All of it."

"But there's been a breach," said one of the men. He pointed down the hill, where gunshots were bouncing at the walls of the bunker, cracking open the night. A lone gun was firing out from between the steel doors. Just one gun. Just Frost.

"We'll make do with what troops are down there," my mother told the agents. "Besides, we can always harvest more people. We won't get more trees."

The agents began down the one slope and we set off down the other. I was leaping and sliding and forgetting to breathe. At the bottom, I gave Zee the key and the nail gun and told her I'd meet her in the Orchard.

"We'll get the Producer ready," my mother said. "Make the tank mobile. Ready to move."

"Be quick," I told them. And then I was running again, heading straight for the bunker full of bodies. My mind was stuck in one zone and it wasn't ever going to shift. Because the trees mattered. More than anything.

Except for one thing.

I sprinted right through the line of agents with my hands in the air and my jacket gone and my clothes ripped and smoking.

"Don't shoot," I kept yelling, running straight at the rifle that was stuck out of the bunker's doors. If it was Frost, he'd see me, recognize me. And it had to be Frost. Had to be.

"Frost," I shouted, feeling bullets hit the frozen ground near my feet. But the bullets were coming from behind me. From the agents.

I hit the snow and slid into the bunker, feet first, my hands still in the air and my face staring up at the barrel of a gun.

"Where the hell have you been?" Frost said, grabbing me by the scruff of my neck and pulling me inside.

"What's happened?"

"Nothing's happened. What use is an army you can't wake up?"

I stood. Stared past him. All the bodies were still stretched out, limp and cold.

"What time is it?" I said.

"Past four, you idiot. Closer to five. What took you so damn long?"

"Didn't you switch it off?" I pointed at the vat of poison that hung from the ceiling.

"Switch it off? How the hell do you switch it off, genius?"

"I don't know. You're the one's supposed to be a freaking employee."

I ran straight into that field of bodies, staring up at the big purple vat and the cables that ran out of it and plugged into every arm in sight.

Then I just started yanking at the cables. I grabbed as many as I could in one hand and began tugging them free.

The cables popped loose and I tripped, fell facedown in flesh. I stumbled up, began running again, pulling the cables from out of their sockets, searching the faces for the one face I knew.

"Banyan." It was Frost. "They're storming the building. I can't hold 'em, kid. I can't hold 'em."

I ran through the bodies, kicking at them, shaking the cables out and knocking them loose.

"Wake up," I screamed, needing help, now more than ever. Knowing I couldn't ever do this alone. "Wake up."

I tore out cables and kept on moving. I was halfway through the field. And I'd not found Alpha.

Not a soul had stirred.

Gunshots cracked at the doors. Frost was swearing and shouting.

And then I did find my girl. But every part of me screamed that I'd arrived too late.

CHAPTER FIFTY-SEVEN

"Alpha," I whispered, tugging the cables out of her and scooping her body all floppy in my arms. "Come back," I said, rocking her against me. I was crying and trembling and the world broke as the loss of her snapped into place.

I'd waited too long. Tried to do too much. And I reckoned saving her was all that ever should have mattered.

"Come on," I kept saying. "Come back." I pinched her eyelids up and I kissed her. But nothing. I felt for her pulse. Weak and slow. But still beating. Still there.

Her skin was a pale shade of green, and I felt the bark on her belly where they'd stitched her together, and that wood was throbbing like it was surging full of life. I took my hand and I pushed there, kneading my fist in her stomach like I might loosen up the juice inside her. And when she still wasn't moving, I just put my head on her belly and I held her and wept.

I heard the gunshots outside getting louder, the voices of the agents. Close. Real close. But then there was a new sound. An odd drone that howled louder as it turned human and broke into words.

Voices. All around me. Moaning out in confusion. A chaos of babbles and bluster. The sound you make coming back from the dead.

They were with me. They were with me.

A hundred voices, and one more was all I needed to hear.

"I love you," I said, squeezing Alpha tight.

"I know, bud," she whispered, but it sounded just like she was singing. One of her old world songs, maybe. Or a new song, all of its own.

Must have been a hell of a way to wake up. Come around to the sound of gunfire and people screaming, a fat man and a skinny kid trying to shove a rifle in your hand.

It was Alpha that led the charge, of course. You should've seen her. Raising up her gun with a battle cry that turned the whole bunker silent and put the whole world to shame.

"We gotta outgun them," I told her. "Push them back. Then make for the boat. The lake's just over the ridge behind us."

"What about you?"

"I'm gonna get what we came here for. But I'll meet you there. At the boat."

"No," she said.

"I'll be there. I promise. But you gotta get these people free."

She kissed me then. Just for a second. And I gripped against her like she was metal and I was all full of lightning, charged up and jagged and of that moment alone.

"I'll meet you there," I told her.

"Okay, bud. Just make sure that you do."

I shoved a gun at someone whose hands were empty. Then I made for the doors, where a bunch of naked bodies were working their weapons and forcing the agents to find cover, forcing them back through the night.

Squatting behind my front line, I studied the twenty yards or so to the Orchard, gearing myself up to make a run for it.

But then Frost's fist was clamped tight on my arm.

"Where you heading?" he said.

"Heading for the tree."

"Not without me, you ain't."

So we waited there together, watching the agents being driven back, biding our time till a break in the shooting. Then, staying low, we hustled out into the night.

We bent in at the wall of the bunker as we scurried through the darkness, just moving one foot after the other, till we were almost there.

A bullet hit the snow with a thud. Then another. Closer.

Frost raised his rifle as he jiggled along, ripping off a quick round in the direction of the agents. I sprinted straight for the steel dome and bounced against the door, pounding my fist till the door slid open.

I leapt forward, Frost barging in behind me, and we fell in a pile on the concrete as the door sealed tight behind us.

The overhead lights had been shut off and the gold lamps of the tank lit the room like an electric sun. My mother had shed her thick layers and was busy moving the tank with a control pad, punching at keys that made the wheels beneath the tank start to twitch and turn. Zee was stood by the door. Frozen. Staring at Frost.

"Hello, Zee," the old bastard said, his face dripping with a grin. He stood up, and she shrank away from him.

"We gotta hurry," I said. "Is it ready to go?"

"Almost," my mother said. She flicked a switch on the wall and a hollow black box began to come down off the ceiling, dropping toward the tank like a metal cloak.

"Banyan," Zee said, her voice shaking. "What the hell is he doing here?"

"I'm taking you home," said Frost. "You and the tree."

I got up to the tank and started pushing it so it would be in line with the descending black shell. But in the glass I could see Frost reflected behind me. And before I'd spun around, I knew what had happened.

Son of a bitch had his gun on me.

"It's over, Mister B," he said. "It ends now for you."

"No," I whispered. But it was too late.

Last thing I saw was his pudgy finger squeezing down on that trigger. Then a flash of light made me blind for a second. And when I could see again, there was blood in the air.

The bullet had hit.

But not me.

She'd leapt in front of me at the last possible moment. And it was the last thing my mother would ever do.

I held her in my arms as we sank to the floor, me still breathing but all the life seeping out of her.

"What have you done?" I whispered, my voice like someone else speaking.

"Keep him safe" was all she said, every bit of her fading, her voice all in pieces. She started croaking and wheezing and she jabbed a finger at the glass tank behind me, and its golden light glowed and flickered in the wide blackness of her eyes. She wanted to say something more but I could tell circuits had been ripped loose inside her, and her mouth twitched and gurgled and I started to cry. And too late, I started to tell her I was sorry. But she was gone. Her thin shoulders cold already. Her skin stiff to my touch.

I stared at Zee crouched in the corner. Then I watched Frost lift his rifle back up, and he'd never dropped his smile.

"Now, tree builder," Frost said, pointing the gun at me again, "it's your turn to die."

But before Frost could pull the trigger, Zee unloaded the nail gun into the side of his head, one nail right after the other, striding closer to her target as he crumbled and fell. And all of a sudden it was over. Frost was dead. Punched full of holes.

Except I knew it wasn't over. Not quite.

Not yet.

CHAPTER FIFTY-EIGHT

Whatever kind of metal they'd made that fancy box out of, I was still scared a bullet could get through and smash the whole tank to hell.

That would end Pop's trip back to the mainland real quick.

So we had to catch a break in the shooting before we took the tank out of there and made for the last hill, before we followed the trail that led up and over, before we could drop down and board the boat on the water below.

But the shooting was still raging. Back and forth. Neither side making much of a difference.

I sank back inside the Orchard but left the door open, the tank cloaked in the black metal and wheeled up against the wall behind me, out of the line of any shooter out there blowing up the dark.

Zee had pulled a jacket over my mother's body, and the purple GenTech logo practically sparkled in the gloom.

"They're cornered," Zee said, glancing outside with me. "Trapped in the bunker."

"Yeah. And they're gonna run out of bullets before the agents do."

"We need to do something."

"I'm working on it."

"We need to get Crow."

"No, we don't," I said.

Because there he was.

The watcher was hobbling along on one leg and dragging the other behind him. He'd busted out of the other building and was cutting right toward the bunker, a sub gun in each hand and his head held high in the air.

He towered ten feet tall and his two guns drew the enemy's fire, forcing the agents to scatter, and allowing the prisoners a moment to advance.

In that moment, the doors to the bunker burst open and a hundred naked bodies flooded into the night. Those who'd been sleeping now charged forward, fearless, surging like a wave of bones and skin.

The agents didn't know which way to shoot – the giant tree man with wooden legs, or the shaved bodies with arms full of holes. And pretty soon, the agents were backed up against the far slope in their puffy suits. And we were winning.

For now.

I turned to Zee. "This is our chance," I said. "We gotta get to the boat before they get reinforcements. There's a lot more agents still at the burn."

"What about all them?" Zee pointed at the uprising.

"Don't worry," I said. "They're coming with us." I grabbed the rifle out of Frost's dead hands and I charged out into the battle.

I called for Alpha and I called for Crow, but all I could see was bodies and bullets in the night.

“Fall back,” I yelled. “Make for the boat. The boat.”

Some of the prisoners heard me and I pointed back at the trail that led to the water. “Get to the boat,” I told them. “Run.”

“Leaving so soon, little man?”

I twisted around and stared up at Crow. His damn legs were as tall as I was. “How you feeling?” I said.

“Oh, I been better. But I sure as hell been worse. Where’s Zee?”

“She’s over there. In the dome.” We took cover behind a crate of cargo as bullets drilled the ice around us.

“And Frost?” Crow said.

“He’s dead. Zee killed him.”

“Did she, now? Good for her.”

“We gotta get everyone back, though, to the lake. There’ll be more agents coming.”

“Then you better tell boss lady, if you wanting folk to move.”

Crow pointed and I spotted her immediately, and I wondered if planting trees and settling down was something that girl was ever meant to do. Because she was sure in her element, out here among the blood and fury.

Alpha had ripped up one of the GenTech cloaks and wound the purple fuzz around her. She had blood on her arm, a gash on the side of her leg, and she was kneeling down in the snow, hands reloading her weapon while her eyes scanned the hill.

“We gotta fall back,” I yelled at her through the sound of the gunshots. “Alpha. Fall back. Now.”

She stood and hollered and I pointed behind me at the hillside, toward where the bio vat rumbled and steamed. And then we were running that way. All of us. Fast as we could move.

At the Orchard, I told Crow to keep moving – he was pretty slow and all, slipping along on his new pair of legs.

"We'll be right behind you," I told him. "Meet you at the boat."

"Aye," Crow said. "Be quick about it." I watched him head up the hill with the others. Then me and Alpha ducked inside the dome.

"Who's this?" Zee said, staring at Alpha.

"I'm his girl." Alpha grabbed the control pad. "Who the hell are you?"

"She's my sister," I said, and then I had Alpha help me pry open a panel on the metal box, and I pointed inside the tank where the saplings were springing out of the green remains of my father. "And this is my dad."

"Got yourself one weird family, don't you, bud?" said Alpha, swinging the panel shut. And I guess she was right. But you got to take what you can get, I reckon.

You take what you can get.

CHAPTER FIFTY-NINE

We busted out of the Orchard with the tank cloaked black and wired up, and Alpha sat above it with her hands working the controller and the wheels spinning in the snow.

"Come on," Alpha called, and she dragged Zee on top of the tank with her. But I paused a moment, then told them to go on.

I ran back into the Orchard. My mother's body was still lying there, and I pulled the coat off her face. I watched her for a second with no part of me thinking.

It was like I'd seen her die two times over. Because she'd caught that bullet the same way Hina had stopped the locusts in the cornfields. They'd both given themselves up. Made their own ending. For me.

I thought of taking her body but decided against it. This was where she should lie, I reckoned. On this island she'd chosen. In this steel tomb. She deserved more of a burial, though. And I figured I should say something. But as I pulled the jacket back over her face, I could find no words that would do. All that came to mind was the song me and Pop used to sing, the song forever stuck inside the dash of our old wagon. The song about dead flowers and the guy leaving roses on a dead girl's grave.

I didn't feel like singing, though. So I just got up and bolted out of the Orchard, dodging bullets as I raced up the hill.

The tank was rolling ahead of me and I could see Zee was driving now, her hands on the control pad. And Alpha was standing tall, working her gun and keeping the trail clear behind me. I caught up to them and jumped for the top of the tank, and I knew beneath the black metal those green saplings were swimming in the golden light.

Alpha helped me up and we squeezed together, and it wasn't long before we'd crested the hill and were about to sink down the other side. We waited until we'd almost lost sight of that big old bio vat. And then Alpha shot the thing clear full of holes.

I could feel white light heat as the explosion soared and cut the agents off on the other side of the ridge. And I could see Crow on the deck of the boat below, waving and calling our names as everything became lit in fiery colors and the lake showed the flames back to the sky.

"So what kind of trees are they?" Alpha shouted, after a third boom had echoed and flared.

"Apple trees," Zee said. "A whole new kind."

"Well," said Alpha, wrapping her free arm around me but still clutching her gun. "Where to now, bud?"

"I don't care," I said as the tank bounced onto the beach. "Just so long as we all go together."

And so we left Promise Island to the sound of gunshots fading. The agents could only watch from their smoking ridgeline as our boat disappeared from their shore.

Alpha said all we needed were stars, and the sky was chock-full of them. A map of cold white light overhead, guiding us south until sunrise. And deep black water beneath us, carrying us back toward home.

Home?

Is that what it was? That big old chunk of dirt?

I reckoned it was. Or I reckoned it could be.

We got the survivors dressed and fed in the cargo hold, and we got Pop's tank stowed deep in the hull. And then I left the others in the cockpit with the charts and gadgets, Crow trying to figure our position on a GPS.

I sat by myself on the deck of the boat and stared south, the freezing wind sticking to my skin and turning me numb as I thought about my father.

We weren't ever going to build that house in the treetops. And I reckoned I'd miss him every day of my life. But I wondered if we might build one more forest together. If I might plant up those saplings and watch them grow tall.

And I dared to think about a world where there were trees again growing. And if the trees had made it, then what other things might be out there, somewhere, still hanging on? The wild things that make the world worth believing in. That's why folk had started tree building, after all. To have something to believe in. To prove you can take one thing and make one thing into another.

I imagined what I'd do in a world where trees spread their roots through the soil and made all the air worth breathing. But as I stretched out on that cold steel and felt my head sore and heavy and I ached all over, I realized everything that could still go wrong ahead of us. I wondered who'd come looking for this boat across the water. Or who might be waiting when the boat docked dry. And then I tried to picture what sort of hell was hidden amid the lava and steam. The wastelands of the Rift.

Had to be a route through, though. GenTech had found a way. And you got to think positive. That's what Pop always said.

So I quit thinking about what might come and I stared up at the constellations, picturing the faces I reckoned I would always keep close. The ones who had passed and the ones still breathing.

And I thought about the statue down in Old Orleans, the woman my father had built and the face I had finished with the thousand shiny pieces, reflecting the world back at you, no matter how many times you looked.

END OF BOOK ONE

ACKNOWLEDGMENTS

Writing ROOTLESS was an adventure, and I'm grateful to the family, friends and teachers who helped me out along the way. I'd also like to acknowledge all the artists who inspired me; people I've never met but who lifted me up whenever I sat down to write. I'd like to thank all the wonderful people at Scholastic, the Andrea Brown Literary Agency, and the Henry Miller Memorial Library in Big Sur, CA. I'd like to thank each and every reader. And I'd like to extend special thanks to the three people who helped me turn this story into a book: My agent, Laura Rennert. My editor, Mallory Kass. And my inspiration, Allison Benner.

ABOUT THE AUTHOR

Before he wrote stories, Chris Howard wrote songs, studied natural resources management, and led wilderness adventure trips for teenagers. He currently lives in Colorado, and *Rootless* is his first novel. Visit him online at www.chrishowardbooks.com.